KILLING TIME IN CHARLESTON

A NICK JANZEK CHARLESTON MYSTERY
(BOOK 1)

TOM TURNER

TRIBECA PRESS

JOIN TOM'S AUTHOR NEWSLETTER

Get the latest news on Tom's upcoming novels when you sign up for his free author newsletter at **tomturnerbooks.com/news**.

ONE

A YEAR AFTER WHAT HAPPENED IN BOSTON, JANZEK FLEW DOWN to Charleston, South Carolina, for his college roommate's wedding. It took him about five minutes to fall in love with the place. Beautiful old houses, five-star restaurants on every block, streets crawling with killer women and, best of all, no snow in the forecast. What was not to love?

He had wandered off from his friend's wedding reception with Cameron, the twenty-eight-year-old sister of the bride. Together they discovered the culinary gusto of an out-of-the-way spot called Trattoria Lucca, then followed it up with some jamming music at a quasi-dive he figured he'd never be able to find again. Last thing he remembered was teetering down a cobblestone street, arm around Cameron's shoulder, looking for a place that had either Lion or Tiger in its name. That Cameron, what a handful she turned out to be.

The day after the wedding he canceled his return flight to Logan Airport, then on Monday morning walked into the Charleston Police Department on Lockwood Street. The résumé he had knocked out in his hotel room that morning had a typo or two in it, but that didn't seem to bother the chief of detectives who hired him on the spot.

Now, three months later, he was coming down the home stretch: Interstate 26, just north of Charleston. The first half of the trip down had been a little dicey, since the day he had picked for the move had turned out to be especially cold and windy. He was driving a U-Haul, his car on a hitch behind it, and had been wrestling the steering wheel of the orange-and-white cube the whole way down. A few miles before Wilmington, Delaware, a gusty blast blew him into the path of a rampaging sixteen-wheeler, which roared up on his bumper like an Amtrak car that had jumped the tracks. It was a close call, but things quieted down after he hit the Maryland border.

He had the window down now and was taking in the warm salt air, which reminded him of the Cape when he was a kid and life was easy. He was looking forward to the slow, Southern pace of Charleston. Kicking back with a plate full of shrimp and grits, barbeque and collards, or whatever the hell it was they were so famous for, then washing it all down with a couple of Blood Hounds, a bare-knuckled rum drink bad girl Cameron had introduced him to.

He was thinking about how he might get his lame golf game out of mothballs, psyched about being able to play year-round. One thing he'd miss would be opening day at Fenway, but he'd heard about Charleston's minor league baseball team and figured it would be good for a few grins. One thing he'd never miss would be staring down at stiffs on the mean streets of Beantown.

The ring of his cell phone broke the reverie. He picked it up, looked at the number, and didn't recognize it.

"Hello."

"Nick, it's Ernie Brindle. Where y'at?" Brindle was the Charleston chief of detectives, the man who had hired him.

"Matter of fact, Ernie, I'm just pulling into Charleston. A few miles north. Why, what's up?"

Brindle sighed. "Looks like it's gonna be trial by fire for you, bro. I'm looking down at a dead body on Broad Street... it's the mayor. The ex-mayor, guess that would be. How fast can you get here?"

Janzek had figured he'd at least get a chance to unload his stuff from the U-Haul before his first-day punch-in.

"Thing is, Ernie, I'm driving this big old U-Haul with all my junk in it. Can't I just drop it—"

"No, I need you right now. Corner of Broad and Church."

Janzek stifled a groan. "Is Church before or after King Street?"

"Two blocks east. Just look for a guy under a sheet and every squad car in the city. Not every day the mayor gets smoked."

"Okay, I'm getting off I-26. I see a sign for King Street."

"You're just five minutes away," Brindle said. "Welcome to the Holy City."

"Thanks," Janzek said. "Kinda wish it were under different circumstances."

Janzek rumbled down Meeting Street, breathing in the fragrant scent of tea olive trees. He got stuck behind a garbage truck and his first instinct was to lay on the horn, but something told him you didn't do that in Charleston. Up ahead, he saw a horse-drawn carriage jammed with gawkers. The garbage truck and the carriage were side by side—like blockers—creeping along at ten miles an hour. The smell of horse manure wafted through his open windows and replaced the sweet tea olive smell.

Janzek finally saw an opening, hit the accelerator, and slipped between the truck and the carriage. Broad Street was just ahead. He had never seen so many squad cars except at an Irish captain's funeral up in Southie. Ernie Brindle was keeping an eye out for him, and when he saw the U-Haul pull up, he directed Janzek past the long line of black-and-whites to a spot in front of a fire hydrant. Janzek got out and walked over.

Brindle, a short, intense guy with hair he didn't spend much time on, eyeballed Janzek's mode of transportation. "Jesus, Nick, not just a U-Haul but dragging a sorry-ass Honda behind it?" Brindle shook his head. "Thought you were s'posed to be a big-time homicide cop."

Janzek glanced back at the car that had served him long and loyally. "I'm not much of a car guy, Ernie."

Janzek looked down at the body sprawled half on and half off the sidewalk. Brindle pulled the sheet back. The late mayor was dressed in an expensive-looking blue suit, which was shredded and splattered with blood. A crushed gold watch dangled loosely from his wrist.

"So, what exactly happened?" Janzek asked, looking around at the cluster of cops, crime scene techs, and a man he assumed was the ME.

"According to a witness," Brindle said, "he was crossing the street when a black Mercedes 500, goin' like a bat out of hell, launched him twenty feet in the air."

"So... intentional then?" Janzek said.

"Yeah, for sure. Guy said he saw the driver aiming a gun."

"In case he couldn't take him out with the car?"

Brindle nodded. "I guess."

"Pointing it out the window?"

"Uh-huh," Brindle said.

"So, he was a lefty," Janzek said. "Guy say whether he fired it or not?"

"He didn't think so. Didn't hear anything, anyway."

"How'd he know it was a 500?"

"He's a car salesman," Brindle said. "On his way to the bank."

Janzek knelt down next to the body to get a closer look. It was clear the mayor had landed on his face. His nose was shoved off to one side, and his forehead and cheeks looked like a sheet of salmon.

The guy he figured for the ME, who'd been talking to two men nearby, came up and eyeballed him with a *who-the-hell-are-you?* look.

"Jack," Brindle said to the man, "this is Nick Janzek, new homicide guy." Then to Janzek, "Jack Martin is our esteemed, pain-in-the-ass ME."

"Good one," Martin said, crouching down next to the body, then looking up at Janzek. "So, how come you caught this one, Nick?"

Janzek didn't know the answer.

"'Cause I liked his sheet," Brindle said.

"Who you got him with?" Martin asked Brindle.

"Delvin."

Martin shook his head and glanced over at Janzek. "Urkel? Good fuckin' luck." Then he noticed the blue parka Janzek was wearing. "You plannin' on goin' skiing or something, Nick?"

Janzek glanced down at his coat. "Just drove down from Boston. Weather was a little different up there."

Martin nodded and kept looking Janzek over.

"Hey, Jack," Brindle said, "how 'bout examining the mayor 'stead of Janzek?"

Martin ignored him. "Boston, huh?"

"Yeah," Janzek said. "Massachusetts."

"Yeah, I've heard of it," Martin said, looking over Janzek's shoulder at the U-Haul. He shook his head, shot Brindle a look, and muttered, "Just what we need down here."

"What's that?" asked Brindle.

"Another frickin' wiseass Yankee."

TWO

Picture Twelve Oaks in *Gone with the Wind*, a two-story Greek Revival-style house with enough piazza and balcony space for a small platoon of soldiers to do marching drills. Leading up to it was a long, perfect allée of live oak trees and, in between, a smooth tabby driveway. A black butler in a dark suit, white shirt, and a tie with the logo and coat of arms of Pinckney Hall on it watched from the porch as Ned Carlino pulled up in his Tesla Roadster.

Carlino got out, stretched, and looked around as Jeter, the butler, walked down the last few steps to greet him.

"Hey, Mr. Carlino," Jeter said, his bushy white eyebrows arching, "welcome back to Pinckney."

"Thanks, Jeter. Good to be back."

Ned Carlino, fifty-four years old and a stocky five eight, was not a man you'd ever mistake for Rhett Butler. Born in a socially unacceptable suburb of Philadelphia, he had gotten a scholarship to Villanova, then another one to Harvard Law, and quickly became one of the best ambulance chasers around. Back then, his card read *Personal Impairment Attorney*, but everyone knew.

His first big case came at age twenty-six when Hector Nunez, the hotheaded, power-hitting, Philadelphia Phillies right fielder, lost it after a called third strike in the fifth game of the playoffs and flung his bat in disgust. It clanged off the metal railing in the boxes to the left of the Phillies dugout, then bounced off the head of an out-of-work cleaning lady from across the river in Camden.

Turned out to be the best thing that ever happened to her.

Carlino, who was watching the game in a bar because he hadn't paid his cable bill, beat it over to Thomas Jefferson Hospital—where he figured they'd take her—in just twenty minutes. Practically beat the ambulance. He crept up to a woman at the nurse's station in the ER and told her he was a cousin of the woman who had been hit by the bat, even though she was sixty and Hispanic. The nurse looked at him funny, but Ned was not about to be deterred.

Long story short, the former cleaning lady, Ned's new client, got four million dollars when his expert witness convinced the jury that she would have constant migraines and possibly life-altering seizures for the rest of her life. The expert witness was convincing, and Ned, even more so. Half of the four million went to the woman and the other half to Carlino's firm, Suozzi and Scarpetta—or Sleazy and Sleazier as one TV news reporter dubbed it. Carlino managed to wangle nearly a million for himself. He immediately paid off his cable bill, bought a BMW, and moved to the Main Line. After five years of following his sensitive nose to massive settlements—including one where he represented the widow of a three-pack-a-day smoker and wangled twenty million dollars out of National Tobacco Company—he decided to seek legal respectability and become a trial lawyer.

That was thirty years ago, and, surprisingly, a few of the big Philadelphia white-shoe, establishment firms pursued him despite his low-born Italian heritage and somewhat unsavory reputation. Because—unsavory or not—Ned Carlino was a winner. Along the way, in the great tradition of most American success stories, Carlino decided he needed to burnish his image and erase all hints of his past. He first became a prodigious collector of modern art, outbidding a

Connecticut hedge fund owner on a Jim Dine and several Jasper Johns. Then, in addition to his townhouse in Rittenhouse Square and his Nantucket beach house, he bought a third house on the Intracoastal in Palm Beach and a fourth on Sullivan's Island outside of Charleston. Three years after that, he sprang for the five-thousand-acre Pinckney Hall plantation, forty minutes south of Charleston. Lastly, he became a philanthropist and sat on the boards of a hospital and a library in Philadelphia, to which he had just donated nine million dollars for a twenty-thousand-square-foot wing. *The Edward G. Carlino Research Library* was etched elegantly into the building's limestone facade.

"Jeter, grab my bag in the trunk and take it upstairs," Carlino said. "I'm going over to the guest house."

Jeter smiled wide, and his teeth looked like a freshly painted picket fence. "William is waitin' on you there, sir."

Carlino walked across the driveway, then down the antique-brick path to the guest house where he pushed open the massive mahogany door, which he'd had shipped over from a tumbledown manor house in England. He walked into the vast living room, painstakingly decorated piece by piece by Madeline Littleworth Mortimer herself. He waved at William across the room and gestured that he needed a drink. William nodded eagerly and reached for the Myers's rum bottle.

The first girl he saw was Ashley. Twenty-three, give or take, she was wearing black-and-silver spandex tights, a gypsy top, and red jellies—teen dream, circa 1994. She was shoving quarters into an antique slot machine, which was lined up next to a collector's item Gottlieb pinball machine on the far wall. She looked up and gave him a Marilyn Monroe pop of the lips and a fluttery smile.

Justine was sitting in a pudgy, leather couch facing a huge fireplace with a mantelpiece from a Normandy castle. She was wearing a miniskirt with pin-striped tights, a white silk top, and Tory Burch flats. Under the tights was one of the best pairs of legs in South

Carolina. The look was girl-who'll-do-practically-anything-to-get-ahead, circa 2018.

"Hey, Mr. C," she said, her hoop earrings jiggling beneath her Jennifer Aniston haircut. She came up to him and gave him a prodigious kiss on the lips. "So glad you're back, lover boy... I missed you *desperately*." She knew exactly what he wanted to hear.

He kissed her back, then reached down and cupped her remarkably perfect breasts. She smiled up at him and pretended to like getting pawed.

"Missed you too, honey," he said, marveling at how tight her stomach was, "but I told you, lose the Mr. C, it makes me feel old."

"Sorry... Ned," Justine said with a wink. "I got the sheets all turned down."

"Hold on, girl, I haven't even had my first drink yet."

Martha was sitting on a barstool as Carlino approached. She turned to face him. William, behind her, was adding a lime wedge to his drink. Martha, twenty-five and runway-model striking, was dressed in a short tartan skirt. Her legs were spread, a few inches beyond discreet, revealing a black thong and light coffee-colored thighs. Bad girl cheerleader, circa... hard to tell.

"Welcome home," she purred.

Carlino walked over and kissed her on the lips.

"Oh, *baby,* can't wait to rip your clothes off," she whispered and winked at William, who pretended not to be listening, "and do all those naughty things you like so much." She was the one who talked dirty, but in such a refined way.

William was a six-eight, former basketball player from Clemson who blushed easily. He set a drink down in front of Carlino. "Good to see you again, sir," William said. "Hope you enjoy the drink."

Carlino took a long sip and wiped his lips. "I always do, William." Looking back at Martha, he said, "You know something? I'm thinking about changing your name. You're way too hot for Martha."

"What's wrong with Martha?" she asked, ratcheting up the smile.

"It's just not sexy. I mean, Martha Washington, Martha Stewart... Martha Wiggins."

"Who's Martha Wiggins?"

Carlino chuckled. "My old neighbor growing up. Two hundred pounds, three chins, five-day growth. I'm thinking—I don't know—Willow or Miranda, or maybe Vruska."

Martha laughed. "What? I'm Russian now?"

He nodded.

"Of course," she said. "Whatever you want me to be."

Ned's cell phone rang. He punched the green button. "Hello, Rutledge," he said, smiling at Martha. "Yeah, I'm looking forward to seeing you and Henry down here tonight. Got a couple of girls just dying to meet you."

He looked away from Martha and listened. "Yeah, I know, terrible thing that was." He chuckled. "People just gotta be more careful how they drive in Charleston. But, hey, the good news is I got the perfect guy lined up to fill the mayor's shoes."

THREE

A MAN IN BLUE JEANS AND A FLANNEL SHIRT WAS SITTING ON the front steps of 163 Queen Street, waiting. Janzek pulled into the driveway with the U-Haul, took a parking space and a half, and left his Honda hanging out six feet, blocking the driveway a little. He got out, saw there was enough room for cars to get by, and walked around to the front of the house.

Janzek, a solid one hundred seventy-five pounds, had catlike emerald-green eyes and dark hair he wore on the long side. A two-inch scar ran down the left side of his face and stopped at a sturdy chin that had taken a few shots over the years. He used to be six feet tall, but at his last physical, to his great distress, the nurse measured him at five eleven. He couldn't accept it and asked her to remeasure: five eleven again. He just sighed. He'd always thought the shrinking process started later than age forty.

The man in blue jeans was on his feet now.

"Judd?" Janzek asked, and the man cracked a wide smile.

"That's me," Judd said, giving Janzek a firm five. "Landlord, plumber, electrician, you name it. But hopefully, everything'll work fine, and you'll never need me at all."

"I hope so," Janzek said. "Sorry I'm late. I had a little unexpected business to attend to."

"No problem," Judd said, getting out his keys and sliding one into the front door. "Welcome to one sixty-three Queen Street. You Yankees would call your apartment a third-story walk-up... me, I call it the penthouse suite."

"I like that better," Janzek said as he followed Judd up the carpeted steps. "And, just for the record, I'm not a Yankee, I'm a Red Sox."

Judd laughed, put the key into the door on the third floor, and pushed it open, stepping right into a tiny kitchen with appliances from the eighties or nineties. Janzek followed Judd in, stooping a little.

"It's very handy," Judd said, "the kitchen being the first thing you come to. Means you don't have to hump your groceries any farther."

Janzek pointed a finger at him and smiled. "You're quite the salesman, huh, Judd?"

"Thanks. I guess that's a compliment," Judd said as they walked into the living room, roughly the size of the U-Haul with windows."Cozy, don't you think?" Judd said, pointing to a fireplace.

Janzek looked out the window at the street below. "Looked a little bigger in the pictures."

"Trick photography," Judd said, gesturing toward a door. "But check out the master."

Janzek followed him in. The apartment was actually very nice, although the pitch of the hardwood floors made him feel like he was on a small ship in a big storm.

"These floors are like a damn ski slope," Janzek said.

Judd was prepared. "Yeah, a typical Charleston single house. Whole city is built on a swamp, you know. The houses settled over the years."

Janzek looked at him and smiled. "Sure you don't mean *sank*?"

Judd laughed and walked through the bedroom. "Hey, check this out," he said, opening a door on the other side of the bedroom. Janzek followed him out onto the balcony.

"Best view in town: the Charleston roofline," Judd said with a sweeping gesture.

Janzek put a hand over his eyes and did a quick 180 of the view. "A hell of a lot of churches in this town."

Judd nodded and smiled again. "They don't call it the Holy City for nothing. Actually, that magazine, *Travel and Leisure*, called it the best city in the country."

"Oh yeah?" Janzek figured he'd be hearing that again.

Judd's head bobbed with hometown pride.

Janzek's cell phone rang. He looked down and saw the Charleston area code. The only people he knew in Charleston were his college roommate, Cameron, Judd, and Ernie Brindle, and it wasn't any of their numbers.

"'Scuse me a sec," he said to Judd. "Hello?"

"Detective Janzek?" said a woman's voice.

"Yes?"

"This is Linda, Charleston Police dispatch. Chief Brindle said to call you. There's been a rape. A college girl. Chief wants you to interview her soon as you can. She's in room five-oh-four, Roper Hospital. Name is Chelsea Watson."

Click.

Janzek fished his sunglasses out of his vest pocket. "So, tell me, Judd, how do I get to Roper Hospital?"

Judd eyed him with concern. "You not feeling well, Nick?"

As Janzek quickly learned, everything was close in Charleston. And then he found out that Roper Hospital was as nice as most Boston hospitals. He walked in, and it actually smelled good. Not all disinfectant and medicine but flowery and with a hint of something—coffee maybe—thrown in. He took the elevator up to the fifth floor and made his way down to room 504. He walked into the room and saw a pretty girl lying in bed with a black eye and dark, purple bruises on her face. Her eyes were open, and she was staring at the ceiling as if she were searching for something.

"Chelsea?"

The girl glanced over and nodded slowly.

"How you doing? I'm Detective Janzek, Charleston Police."

It sounded so weird. First time he had said it.

"I'm all right," she said in a somber tone.

Janzek noticed one of her teeth was chipped.

He smiled at her. "Are you okay answering a few questions?"

The little nod again, but her eyes had an ocean of pain in them. Janzek had an urge to pat her on the shoulder, tell her she was safe now.

"I'm sorry about what happened to you," he said instead, looking around for a nurse. "Can I get you something? Orange juice, maybe? Or a ginger ale?"

She just shook her head and smiled through the anguish. Then a few tears ran down her cheeks.

"I know how painful it is to talk about it," Janzek said.

But for the next twenty minutes, Chelsea Watson did. She described what a boy named Quatro, and three other boys whose names she didn't know, did to her the night before. She and Quatro had gone to a Mexican restaurant on King Street called Carmelita Bernstein's, and Quatro immediately began knocking back shots of Cuervo Gold. He urged her to keep up, but she stopped after one. She said she counted seven shots for Quatro, but she may have missed one when she went to the ladies' room. He made a little joke about "Cuervo for Quatro."

Then he had ordered burritos and tacos, a large portion of which had ended up on his button-down J. Crew shirt. An hour after they got there, he staggered out with her behind him. She said this was her first date with him and had already decided it was also her last. The clincher was when he'd waited for her to come up with half the money for the check, ninety percent of which was his tequila shots. She'd thought he was a gentleman, she said, but knew better after the nonsense with the bill. This was confirmed when he opened the restaurant door and barged out first, almost cross-body blocking her out of the way.

She told him she wanted to go home, but he ignored her and said there was going to be a trivia game back at his fraternity house. They walked into the fraternity house and went down to the basement, a dank-smelling room with a lot of ripped and stained Naugahyde couches. There were no windows in the room and no trivia game. He told her it was probably just starting a little late.

He went and got two Pabst Blue Ribbons out of an old refrigerator. Someone had Magic Markered *the mood enhancer* in big black letters to the left of the refrigerator's door handle. Chelsea said no thanks to the PBR. Quatro insisted. She faked like she was taking a sip. He put his arm around her and pulled her close. She stiffened and resisted. He started tearing at her clothes. She screamed. He put his hand over her mouth and raped her on one of the black couches.

Then two other boys who had apparently heard her screams came down to the basement. She told Janzek that, one by one, they had raped her, too. One even used an empty beer bottle on her.

Janzek's first instinct was to go straight to the frat house and beat the hell out of them until he extracted confessions. Instead, he leaned down and patted her shoulder softly.

"I promise you, we'll get these guys," he said and immediately regretted it. There was no way he should be making a promise like that. How did he know if he could deliver? He was in a place he didn't know the first thing about.

She looked up at him, forced a deeply pained smile, and mouthed, "Thank you."

FOUR

IT HAD NOT BEEN THE SLIGHTEST BIT SUBTLE: A GUY WITH AN AK-47 squeezing off twelve shots from a fire escape into Janzek's bedroom at three fifteen in the morning a year and a half ago. Janzek's wife of five years, Caroline, was killed instantly as her side of the bed was nearest the window. Janzek was lucky. A bullet ripped into his face just below his left eye but at an angle, so it broke his cheekbone and exited two inches below. He ended up with a scar that went straight down from just below his left eye.

Janzek figured the perp could have been any number of hard cases whom he had put away over the years. And the hit could have been ordered from a jail cell. Or been done by a family member who had been talked into it. Could have been a lot of people.

Later, on the day it happened, Janzek was at his desk at the District 4 police station on Harrison Street, patched up and shaky. It was better to be active, he figured, than sit around mourning. He was devastated but absolutely determined he was going to track the killer down by nightfall. It didn't quite work out that way. Four months later, his boss, an ill-tempered tyrant named Declan O'Brien, told him it was time to "lose his obsession."

Janzek asked him what he was talking about.

"You're like Harry Bosch...spending half his life tryin' to track down his hooker mother's killer."

"Who's Harry Bosch?"

O'Brien shook his head in disbelief. "Jesus, Janzek, you know what TV is?" he'd said. "*Bosch*. It's a big show on Amazon. From those Michael Connelly books."

"Never read 'em," Janzek said. "I stick to Shakespeare."

A good line wasted. O'Brien had absolutely no sense of humor. "Whatever," O'Brien said. "You just need to spend more time on your other cases."

Janzek sighed and counted to fifteen. An extra five, so he wouldn't totally fly off the handle. "I spend as much time on 'em as I always do."

"Bullshit. Your clearance has slipped a little. You're not closing 'em like you used to."

It was true that he had hit a snag on his last one, and the one before that had looked like an open-and-shut case until the prime witness vanished. Then, a few months after Caroline's murder, came Janzek's depression. He didn't know if it was because of the guilt he felt over her dying instead of him. Or if it had something to do with the fact that he was drinking more. And doing drugs. Or that he was so damn lonely. All three probably and maybe a few others, he guessed.

What he was sure of was he missed her terribly. Her laugh. Her sense of humor. Holding hands with her. Kissing her. Watching her putter around in her tiny garden in front of their house. Getting crushed by her every night at *Jeopardy*. They were just getting serious about having kids, too. Something that would never happen now. God, he missed her.

His lead suspect in her death was the first man he had ever put behind bars back when he started out fifteen years ago. A man named Jarvon Carson who had killed his girlfriend in a drunken rage and afterward showed zero remorse. But Carson had money and hired a good lawyer who pled down the murder charge to manslaughter. The reason he suspected Carson as being the killer was that in court, after Janzek stepped down from the witness stand, Carson caught his eye and made an unmistakable gesture of slitting his throat.

Janzek found out that Carson had gotten out of Walpole State Prison five weeks before Caroline's murder, and he'd tracked him down at his brother's place in Malden. They had a tense conversation on the porch of the brother's house.

"What the hell do you want?" a grizzled Carson said after his brother went and got him. He had gained a sizable paunch, lost a lot of hair, and had big bags under his eyes.

"Answers," Janzek said. "For starters, Monday night, last May thirteenth, where were you?"

Carson scratched the three-day growth on his chin. "How the fuck would I know? That was six months ago."

"You have a blue Ford Explorer, don't you?"

"What if I do?"

"'Cause on that night a blue Explorer was caught on a camera in the alley behind my house."

"Lots of blue Explorers in the Bay State, my friend," Carson said. "You got nothin' on me, Janzek, and if you did, I'da heard about it by now. By the way, real shame about the little woman."

Janzek reached out and grabbed Carson by the shirt. "Shut the fuck up, goddamn lowlife."

Carson tried to pull back. "Get your hands off—"

But Janzek tightened his grip. "One more time. Monday night, last May thirteenth, where were you?"

Carson had sneered. "I'm sure I could come up with an alibi if I really needed one."

Janzek shoved him back. "You'll be hearing from me, scumbag."

"Call my lawyer. You remember him? The guy who ran circles around you."

Janzek turned and walked away, but Carson didn't move from the porch.

Janzek opened his car door, got in, and pulled away. He looked back through his rearview mirror and saw Carson run his finger across his throat.

CARLINO HAD HAD THREE OF WILLIAM'S STIFF, RUM DRINKS and wasn't exactly sure whose arms he had woken up in. He looked across the king-sized bed.

Oh yeah, Ashley.

He got out of bed, went over to his ample walk-in, and put on one of the brand new, white, fluffy bathrobes. He went into the bathroom, looked in the mirror, and admired the crisp, blue letters that spelled out *Pinckney* on the breast pocket. Above it were his initials in the tight, little circle that Madeline Littleworth Mortimer had painstakingly designed. He had rejected her first three designs. She told him he was a very exacting man. He had no quarrel with that.

Looking down at his watch, he realized he had scheduled dinner with Rutledge Middleton and Henry Neble in the main house at eight o'clock. That was a half hour from now.

He pulled out his cell phone and dialed.

One ring.

"Yes, Mr. Carlino," the woman's voice said. "How can I be of service?"

"Jessie, I want to have dinner in the guest house instead of up there in the main house," Carlino said. "You can just bring it down. Reheat it or whatever."

Jessie was used to her boss's quixotic ways.

"No problem, Mr. Carlino," she said. "Still at eight?"

"Make it eight-fifteen," he said. "And I don't want to serve the Chateau de Saint Cosme. That Davis Bynum pinot noir will be just fine."

"Yes, sir."

Why waste the good stuff on guys who wouldn't know the difference?

"Are my guests here, Jessie?"

"Yes, sir," Jessie said. "Mr. Middleton got here about an hour ago. Mr. Neble early in the afternoon. He went out hunting."

Carlino got dressed and walked out into the living room. Henry Neble was talking to Martha, and Rutledge Middleton was watching the Golf Channel on the giant, retractable flat screen next to Justine who was trying not to look bored.

The two men and two women turned and greeted him. Justine gave him her 1000-watt smile, which was her way of implying that if he wanted companionship for the night, she was available. He knew her eagerness to please was motivated solely by the fact that he always gave the girls ten crisp hundred-dollar bills in the morning if they got the nod for overnight duty.

Henry Neble came scurrying over and thrust out his hand.

"Hey, Ned, how's it going?" he said. "Think I bagged the limit out there."

Carlino didn't particularly like shooting. Not that he had anything against killing things, he just didn't like loud noises and drinking bourbon first thing in the morning.

"That's great, Henry," he said, stifling a yawn.

"Next thing I'm gonna do is bag the limit in here," Neble said, giving Carlino a wink.

It drove him crazy, men who winked plus had shitty senses of humor.

"Go for it, Henry," Carlino said. "That's what the ladies are here for."

He looked over at Martha who was listening in.

"Right, Vruska?"

"Whatever you say, Mr. Carlino."

His standing rule was they could call him by his first name when they were alone together or in the throes of passion—which was usually the same thing.

He turned back to Neble.

"We're going to eat down here, Henry, instead of up at the main house," Carlino said. "A nice, thick steak."

That was another thing. Carlino hated the taste of duck, quail, or anything that flew. For one thing, he wasn't big on picking buckshot out of his mouth. For another, he was a carnivore through and through.

Carlino looked at his watch again.

"We're eating at eight-fifteen," he said, walking away from Neble over to Rutledge Middleton.

Middleton had his arm around Justine's shoulder, inching his way down.

"Hey, Rut," he said, "dinner in fifteen minutes."

Middleton cringed at being called Rut. If it was anyone other than Carlino, he would have straightened them out. "Rut" sounded so undignified when you had the name and social pedigree of being born Rutledge Ashley Middleton III.

"Sounds good to me, Ned," Middleton said.

Carlino walked away. He wanted to check his e-mail and pulled out his cell phone. Sixty-one e-mails in the time it took him to get his rocks off. He didn't look up when he heard the door open and his staff bring the dinner down from the big kitchen up in the main house. He just kept scrolling down his e-mails, half of which he'd never respond to.

Ten minutes later, all three men were carving their steaks.

The women never joined Carlino and his guests for dinner. Carlino was of the old Italian school which believed women didn't have much to contribute on the subject of business, politics, the state of the world, or sports. So, Justine, Ashley, and Martha were in their respective bedrooms doing their nails or in the gym out back, tuning up their abs.

Carlino watched William pour the wine. "So, bring me up to speed, Rut."

Middleton finished chewing. "Well, I got a contract on the

twenty acres owned by the Shane Brothers," he said, proudly. "I had the broker use an LLC so they'll never know it's us."

Carlino frowned. "Us?" he said. "I think you mean *me*."

Middleton looked like a kid caught shoplifting.

"Yes, exactly," he said. "I meant you, Ned."

"And what about the ten-acre piece?"

"We're getting closer," Middleton said. "The sticking point is not price. The eight million is fine. It's getting them to agree to make it subject to the zoning change."

Carlino had no patience for small-town guys who couldn't see the obvious.

"So, offer 'em another two million and make it contingent on the change. Come on, man. Besides, we *are* going to get it. It's in the goddamn bag. Why do you think we're getting the new mayor?"

Middleton nodded. "I'm on it, Ned."

Middleton and Neble had been working behind the scenes to buy land for the construction of a two-hundred-room luxury hotel and casino on landfill off to one side of the Ravenel Bridge, the graceful, state-of-the-art bridge supported by two elongated diamond-shaped piers. They were one parcel short of what they would need for the project. Carlino was a major stockholder in Monarch Hospitality, which had casino hotels in Las Vegas, Atlantic City, and Nassau.

"And Monarch's fully committed, right?" Neble asked.

Carlino glared at him.

"What do you think this whole exercise is about, for Chrissakes? Of course, they're fully committed. This is going to be their first boutique casino."

Neble took a pull on his wine like it was a beer. "What exactly is a boutique casino again, Ned?"

"A casino about a third the size of ones in Vegas but catering to upscale gamblers. The opposite of the slot machine crowd. Monarch likes the Charleston demographic. Not the cheap locals who don't have two nickels to rub together, but northern guys who have houses down here. Makes sense, 'cause now those guys have to go to Atlantic City, goddamn armpit city of the armpit state."

Carlino snuck a glance at Middleton. He could see Middleton quietly seething about his reference to "cheap locals" not having two nickels to rub together. Carlino knew that hit him right square in the groin.

Carlino had noticed how Middleton had absolutely no ability to hide what he was thinking. Like there was a ticker tape running across his forehead, every thought flashing by in big, neon letters.

Probably a really shitty poker player, Carlino guessed.

Still, he needed him, if for no other reason than Middleton was on the city council: the body of very ordinary people with very average intellects who were going to make the call on his very, very important, billion-dollar project.

After dinner, it took Neble no more than three minutes to get busy with Ashley. Little did he know that his every awkward love-making move was being recorded by a camera inside the bedroom's smoke detector.

Carlino got another drink from William and a Havana cigar, a box of which he kept behind the bar. He didn't want to keep them out in the open so they'd be wasted on the likes of Neble and Middleton.

He came over and sat down next to Middleton, who was telling Justine about an electrifying violin concerto at the Hibernian Society he had attended the night before.

"Justine, if you would, give Mr. Middleton and me a minute alone, please."

"Of course," Justine said, standing. "By the way, I'm just crazy about violin concertos," she said, blowing a kiss to Middleton.

Carlino put his hand on Middleton's shoulder.

"I need to go over a certain math problem with you, Rut. One I'm counting on you to help me with."

"Math problem?"

"Yes," Carlino said. "Right now, we've got something that adds up to three that needs to add up to six. And we've only got five weeks to make it happen."

Middleton nodded.

"You're with me, right, Rut?" Carlino asked.

Middleton nodded again. "Yeah, sure am. Six votes is what we need to get the casino passed and three is all we got."

"Correct," Carlino said. "The late mayor had a lock on eight votes against, meaning out of the eleven council members, all we got, at this point, are you and the two others."

"Yeah, Barnhill and Roberson."

"Exactly," Carlino said. "So that's our little math problem, Rut. And I'm counting on you to do something about it."

Middleton smiled confidently. "Your confidence is not misplaced, Ned."

"Good. So, tell me all about the needs and desires of the other people on the council. Like, maybe one of them needs money 'cause he's behind on his mortgage, or another one's got big medical bills..."

Middleton was nodding like a bobble-head doll.

"And in return for their votes," Middleton said, "we might be able to solve their financial problems. Bail them out of their respective jams, right?"

"You got it," Carlino said. "Or maybe you find out one of the councilmen has a thing for—I don't know—teenage girls, let's say."

"And, it turns out, a few pictures of them—say, in compromising positions—just happen to fall into our laps?"

Carlino slapped him on the back.

"You know, Rut, all of a sudden I have a very good feeling about our little math problem. In fact, I don't think it's gonna be a problem at all."

Middleton was nodding again.

"Yeah, Ned, no need to sweat it," he said. "And by the way, I think I might already have our first candidate all lined up. Our fourth vote, that is."

"Good man," Carlino said, taking a long drag on his cigar. "Tell me all about him."

"Actually, it's a *her*," Middleton said. "And a very hot-blooded one she is."

FIVE

Through the U-Haul office in Boston, Janzek had lined up a guy who worked part-time at the U-Haul in Charleston to help him with his move. But Janzek had to call and cancel him when he was pulled in on the mayor's murder. As a result, he had no one to help him move his stuff— including heavier, more unwieldy things like his mattress and box springs—up the three flights to the penthouse suite. So, he ended up sleeping on the floor that first night, a blanket and sheet between him and the heart-of-pine floor.

Then, at three in the morning, a dog in the apartment below started barking like it had chased a herd of cats up a tree. It kept barking for half an hour. Janzek wanted to stuff a pair of tube socks in its mouth and wondered why its owner wasn't doing something about it. Between thinking about the murder and rape and listening to the dog bark, he ended up getting two hours of sleep. Then he hit rush-hour traffic on the short drive to the police station on Lockwood Drive. How could there be rush-hour traffic, he wondered, in a town one-fiftieth the size of Boston?

He walked into the station, trying not to look like a zonked-out guy with two hours of sleep desperate for a mug of Joe.

"Hi, I'm Nick Janzek," he said to the woman at the glassed-in window. "New guy in Violent Crimes. I'm looking for Delvin Rhett, my partner."

"Oh yes, Detective, we've been expecting you. Welcome aboard," she said; nice smile, Chiclet teeth. "I'm Janice. I gotta photograph you, get your ID and everything. But first, I'll get Delvin."

Janzek nodded as she dialed three numbers.

"Delvin," she said, "get your ass out here. Your new partner."

"Thanks," Janzek said.

A few minutes, later a wiry black man—five ten or so with a wispy Fu Manchu—walked up to Janzek. He remembered what the ME had said, referring to Rhett as Urkel. Fact was, take away the facial growth, the guy was a dead ringer for the guy on that old TV show. *Family Matters,* he thought the name was.

Just by the way he walked, kind of a glide, Janzek could tell Rhett was a gregarious man. A talker was his guess.

When it came to partners, Janzek was more a fan of strong, silent types.

Rhett walked up to Janzek and stopped a few inches inside of his comfort zone. Janzek wanted to back up a step but stayed put. Rhett's face was a little too close. Janzek could see one lone follicle of hair on the upper part of Rhett's cheek, like it was just out of his shaving zone.

"I'm Delvin," Rhett said, thrusting out a skinny, long-fingered hand. "Welcome, man."

Rhett's handshake was almost too firm, like he was overcompensating.

"Thanks," Janzek said. "Nick Janzek."

Rhett nodded. "Trial by fire, huh, Nick?"

"Jesus," Janzek said. "No kidding. Is it always this busy?"

"Nah, this is more than normal," Rhett said, then gestured. "Come on back, I'll show you your office."

His office had two long, skinny windows with an old, wooden desk and a lot of metal file cabinets behind it. The desk looked old enough to have a bottle of Four Roses stashed in the bottom drawer. On top of it, though, was a Samsung laptop that looked brand new.

There was an old black-and-white picture of the Empire State Building on one wall, which seemed totally out of place. He guessed maybe the guy before him had a New York connection. The place was fine for his purposes. He was not into fancy offices or cars.

"So, where's your office, Delvin?" Janzek asked.

Rhett pointed. "That cubicle over there," he said, chuckling. "You know, being a black guy in the south and all."

Janzek laughed.

"Just kiddin,'" Rhett said. "Fact is, I only got on homicide two years ago."

"As opposed to an old lifer like me," Janzek said.

Rhett laughed.

"Yeah, right, you're only forty, man," Rhett said. "Hey, I'm looking forward to hangin' onto your coattails. Takin' down the mutts and miscreants of Chucktown."

"We'll see about that. So, tell me about the mayor," Janzek said, walking around his desk and sitting in the musty leather chair behind it. "I didn't get too much out of Ernie."

Rhett sat down and put his hands together.

"Okay, well, first thing, Jim McCann was a guy who got things done, a real good mayor," Rhett said. "Ruffled some feathers along the way, though."

Janzek noticed Rhett's interlaced fingers tighten.

"Second thing is," Rhett said, lowering his voice, "the man was a major-league poon hound. Booty Man was one of his nicknames. That ruffled some feathers, too, as you can imagine."

Janzek nodded slowly. "You mean 'cause some of the women mighta been married to other men?"

"You catch on quick, Nick," Rhett said, nodding.

Janzek smiled and looked out his window. A crane was lifting a huge steel I-beam a few blocks away.

"Okay, so we got the jealous-husband motive," Janzek said, turning back to Rhett, "what else?"

"Another possible is," Rhett said, "someone didn't like his politics."

"Which could mean a lot of things."

"Sure could."

"How 'bout we come back to that later," Janzek said. "So, was McCann married?"

Rhett nodded. "Yeah, for like thirty years."

"So, why don't I talk to the wife?"

Rhett beamed. "And I talk to the girlfriends?"

"How 'bout we split 'em up. I do half, you do half," Janzek said, looking back out at the crane and the I-beam.

"So you can meet some women?"

Janzek smiled. "Sure, why not?" he said. "Hey, I got a question for you."

"Shoot."

"How come Ernie dumped both the mayor's murder and the rape on us? I mean, I'm the new guy and you're—"

"—the jive black dude just graduated from traffic cop?"

Rhett got up, closed the door, and sat back down.

"Thing is, we been on a bad streak here. A string of unsolved homicides. Five in the last six months, to be exact. Brindle's taken a shitload of heat and my guess is when you and your big-time rep came along, he grabbed you, figuring you were his guy."

"Who are his usual go-tos?"

"Two guys with the best clearances are Gregg Dillard and Jimmie Driggers, but they been runnin' cold lately. Dillard's distracted with a wife who's got cancer and a son with a meth jones. Driggers...I don't know what his deal is. Guy's not in my top ten anyway. He's like Ernie's second cousin."

"Yeah, Ernie mentioned him," Janzek said. "Said he was going to put him on the mayor, too. Backup to us, was how he described it."

"Yeah, that's 'cause Driggers pissed and moaned about not

catching it," Rhett said. "So, where's your place, Nick, where you living at?"

"Down on Queen Street. How about you?"

"Three doors down from where I grew up. Up on Carolina."

"So, if you're from here, how come you got no accent?"

"You mean southern or...*negro*?"

"I was thinking southern, but okay, either one."

Rhett slouched down a little.

"'Cause my old man's a professor at the Citadel. Didn't want any of his kids drawling like crackers or speakin' Ebonics," Rhett said as a big smile spread across his face. "For that matter, didn't want any of us growing up to be cops, either."

SIX

Janzek's quick read on Sally McCann was that she didn't miss the mayor as much as she missed being the mayor's wife. He was doing his usual first steps: interviewing the vic's spouse, which would be followed by going to the vic's funeral. Things he always did, but things that hardly ever cracked cases.

Sally McCann told him she had grown up in some backwater fifty miles to the north of Charleston—she mentioned the name of the place, like Janzek was supposed to have heard of it. It was clear that she had been in a big hurry to put the place in the rear view.

Socially ambitious was a phrase that quickly came to mind. She talked more about the Preservation Society and being on the board of the Gibbes Museum than she did about her recently deceased husband. As to why he was recently deceased, she had so far proffered no theories. She did say that he was a fine husband and father. Then, in the next breath, she mentioned how she and the late mayor were benefactors of the Spoleto Festival and the big antique show put on by the Historical Society.

Janzek nodded. That was nice.

He didn't quite know how to play the infidelity thing, so he came right out with it. Asked her, in a polite way, using just about every euphemism he knew. She got where he was going, then acted outraged by the question. Like Jim McCann was a marital saint.

So, he decided to take a new tack—picking up on what Rhett had just told him—and threw out a question about whether McCann had any political enemies. Anybody who would want him out of the picture because he either got in their way or was opposed to something they wanted. That got her more chatty. A fair amount of people seemed to fit that bill, she said. There was a group that was pretty worked up about the mayor being an advocate of the cruise ships, she said. Cruise ships? Janzek asked. She looked at him funny, like, *Come on, where you been, Detective?* At that point, he told her he was pretty new to Charleston but didn't tell her less than forty-eight hours.

She explained that a lot of people— particularly the snappy south of Broad Street crowd— hated having the big Carnival cruise ships steaming into town and dumping the great unwashed, photo-snapping, ass-packers onto the streets of Charleston. How they never bought anything but ice cream cones and T-shirts and made the downtown look so horribly tacky. And how they slowed down traffic on East Bay Street to a turtle crawl. Then she careened off on another subject: how there was a faction who wanted to bring casino gambling to Charleston, which her husband was dead set against. Apparently, their plan was to fill in and develop some unused swampland somewhere. Make some mixed-use "catastrophe"—her word—that would create a million ugly condos and apartments in the shadow of the hotel casino. Then she launched into something she clearly didn't have much of a handle on—the continuation of a highway that there was apparently a lot of opposition to. She ran out of gas trying to explain it.

Finally, she allowed that she felt it unlikely that someone would actually murder "his honor" —her phrase—just because he was against their project. That seemed a tad extreme, she volunteered.

Janzek nodded, though he had seen people killed for a whole lot less.

So, it seemed he was back to jealous husbands as the most logical suspects.

He decided to take another cut at the subject with Sally McCann and rephrased the question.

"Going back to something before, could there have been someone who thought your husband might be paying undue attention to—ah—a loved one of theirs?"

She reacted just as vociferously as before.

"Detective, my husband was a very loyal, loving man," she huffed.

Loving, for sure, thought Janzek.

Janzek snuck a look at his watch. Realizing he had hit the wall, he was eager to wrap it up. He had an appointment with the rape suspect, Quatro, in a half hour and was ready to work up a good rage and fury on his way to question him at the station.

As he started to thank her, Sally McCann glanced at her watch and shot to her feet.

"Oh my God," she said, "I've got my bridge game in ten minutes."

Strange, Janzek thought, it seemed like it was just another day in the life of Sally McCann. The day after her husband caught a bumper to the knees.

SEVEN

JANZEK WAS IN HIS CAR THINKING ABOUT THE GIRL, CHELSEA Watson.

He flashed back to what he had been like twenty years ago in college.

In a word, a fuck-up.

Procrastinated everything. Particularly homework.

Drank like a fish.

His dorm room looked like a bomb had gone off at the local Salvation Army.

Okay, he did play hockey, so at least he was in some kind of shape.

And he went to classes. Most of them, anyway.

A dream date... he was not. Horny... habitually.

But the idea of raping a girl—no matter how much he had to drink or what the circumstances were—that had just never crossed his mind. Totally foreign. Nowhere near his radar screen.

If a girl said no to his quasi-pathetic advances, he'd cajole and wheedle, for sure, but if he couldn't convince her of the undeniable logic of sleeping with him, then he'd just move on. Hope maybe she'd call back a few days later and say, "You know, Nick, I've been think-ing... and, well, maybe I missed out on a big opportunity the other night."

Yeah, right. Like that ever happened.

He was eyeballing the twenty-one-year-old kid in the soft room at the station. The little punk wasn't even coming close to making eye contact with him. Quatro's eyes had cruised across the dirty beige ceiling, then over the top of the beat-up conference table between them, then hovered on the plastic flowers on the coffee table in the far corner. In short, everywhere but Janzek's eyes.

"So... Rutledge Ashley Middleton the fourth, aka Quatro," Janzek said, "being drunk is a real shitty alibi. That 'dog don't hunt,' as you people would say. You think you can just drink a bunch of tequila and get a pass for your actions—"

"Wait, hold on, I—"

Janzek's hand slashed the air.

"Shut the fuck up. So, your story is she said yes? Is that what you're telling me, Quatro?"

Janzek spat out the nickname like it was a rancid piece of meat.

Quatro nodded gingerly. Like he was afraid Janzek might back-hand him across the room.

"And you're telling me she was just dying for you and your posse of drunken mutts to—"

He couldn't say it. He just shook his head and glared at the kid.

He had been at it for two hours and couldn't break him. The kid just kept saying that Chelsea Watson consented, and then after he and she did it, he passed out and didn't know what happened next.

Unfortunately, Janzek had seen the drunk defense work in the past. Or saying the woman wanted it.

Quatro claimed he couldn't remember much of anything except her saying yes. She definitely said yes, he kept repeating. And Janzek couldn't trip him up.

"So, let me get this straight, you actually asked her to sleep with you?"

Quatro thought for a second.

Finally, he nodded and said yes.

"I got news for you, frat boy, the way it usually works is a guy and a girl are just going along and it happens. There's no asking, no Q and A."

"Well, this time there was." Quatro said. "I asked her, she said yes."

Mutt with a bone, Janzek thought, standing up.

Rhett had come in fifteen minutes before, whispered to him that the kid's father had posted bail and was waiting outside.

Janzek circled Quatro like a shark.

"Okay, Quatro, daddy's here." Janzek lashed him with sarcasm. "I don't suppose that would be Rutledge Ashley Middleton the third, by any chance?"

Quatro nodded sullenly, his eyes again looking everywhere except into Janzek's.

Janzek opened the door of the soft room. Quatro skittered through it like a cockroach. As if he expected Janzek to boot him in the ass.

A stony, buttoned-down man in his fifties was in the reception area.

Quatro ran up to him and hugged him.

The man's reaction was subdued. As if he had bailed out his reprobate kid before and wasn't thrilled about doing it again.

Janzek walked up to the man.

"If I could interrupt this little reunion, Mr. Middleton," Janzek said, "I'll be needing to interview your son again."

Middleton gave him the top to bottom.

"Who are you?"

"My name is Janzek, Violent Crimes." He started to say, *your son's worst nightmare*, but bit his tongue.

"What are you charging him with?" Middleton asked.

"First-degree rape."

"Forget it, it won't stick," Middleton said, shrugging his shoulders as if the charge was beyond absurd.

"Well, I guess that's why we have juries, Mr. Middleton," Janzek said. "Maybe you should talk to your son. Ask him what happened. I'd be curious to know whether you believe him or not."

Middleton's expression hadn't changed.

"I know my son, Detective...." Middleton shot Janzek a hostile look. "What did you say your name was again?"

"Janzek."

Middleton put his hand up to his chin.

"Never heard of you," he said. "Is that like a...Polish name or something?"

Janzek took two steps closer to him. "Yeah, it's exactly like a Polish name."

Middleton pursed his prissy lips and smiled. "You look like a guy from New York, or somewhere up there."

"Boston, actually."

"Same thing," Middleton said. "Got that Yankee arrogance going for you."

Janzek just smiled. "Sorry you feel that way, Mr. Middleton. Just doing my job."

Middleton didn't hesitate. "Well, why don't you go back up there and do it?"

EIGHT

Mona Tregalas, known to a lucky few in college as "Moaner," owned a shoe store at the corner of Wentworth and King. Mona was forty-five and married to a sixty-five-year-old man who had lots of money and didn't trust Mona as far as he could throw her. And since he was a wizened hundred and twenty pounds and she was a toned, hard body, that wasn't very far.

They had been married for a little over two years, and Mona had thus far respected her marital vows, though it hadn't been easy. Well, actually, she had one little slipup, but only her best friend knew about it. Mona had a queen-size libido and a wandering eye but didn't want to jeopardize the big allowance that her husband, Gus, provided her with. The shoe store was basically a hobby and lost a few thousand a month, but it didn't matter because it gave Mona purpose. Mona's other purpose was serving on the city council. She was an outspoken and opinionated woman, and people liked her spunk and public-spiritedness. Mona could always be counted on to oppose things. She found opposing a lot more exciting than going along with.

Mona was in the vanguard of opposition to casino gambling in

Charleston. Her father, a man who had worked in the garment business in New York City, was an inveterate gambler who was exposed to gambling in a major way when casinos first came to Atlantic City in 1978. His game was roulette, where the odds favored the house more than most other games, and by the fall of 1982 he had lost all his money and was forced to declare personal bankruptcy. A familiar pattern followed: He began to drink heavily, his wife of twenty-nine years divorced him, and soon he was living in his Pontiac, at the mercy of a local soup kitchen.

Mona, who loved and idolized her father as a child, ended up hating him for what he did to her mother, three brothers, and herself. On February 4, 1984, Mona's birthday, her father was found frozen to death in an abandoned Newark warehouse.

Mona was one of the biggest supporters of Mayor Jim McCann and had helped him field eight strongly committed votes, including their two, against the proposed Charleston casino. People on the council called it the "Mc-Mona bloc," and the two of them were working hard on the remaining seven members, their goal being to turn it into a unanimous vote against the casino.

But then, as it happened, the mayor was hit by a car. So much for the Mc-Mona bloc.

<hr />

TRAJAN VOLMER, BLUE-EYED, BROAD-SHOULDERED, AND sporting a crisp British accent, walked into Mona's shoe store on Tuesday morning. Trajan's mother, figuring her sons were destined for greatness, had named them after Roman emperors. His brothers were named Tiberius and Caligula, but Caligula shortened it to Cal. Women found Trajan irresistible; told him he had a young Hugh Grant thing going for him.

As he walked into the store, Mona looked up at him, smiled, and said, "Hi there, welcome."

He gave her his thousand-watt smile and said, "Thank you, *dahling.*"

Mona was a woman who loved good-looking men with big muscles, and Trajan had pecs, abs, delts, and what appeared to be a bulge in his tight blue jeans. He was wearing a faded black T-shirt, which he had bought one size too small. She was helping a customer but stared at him so long and intently that the woman Mona was waiting on turned around and looked at him, too.

"Lovely store," he said, then to Mona, "Got any tassel loafers in size thirteen, by any chance?"

Mona's store clearly sold nothing but women's shoes. She started to answer—

He flashed a smile. "Just kidding, love."

He went over to a rack and picked up the first shoe he saw, studying the heel intently.

Then he put it down and picked up the shoe next to it and did the same.

A few minutes later, he heard the door close and the customer was gone.

It was just him and Mona.

"Can I help you find something," she said, "besides a size thirteen tassel loafer?"

She had a nice laugh, a taut body, and red, luscious lips. She was way hotter than Trajan expected. In fact, he wasn't expecting hot at all.

The job was not going to be unpleasant the way some, unfortunately, were.

"I'm just—" He hadn't really come up with a story yet but was a natural at winging it. "I'm just looking for something for my sister. She's got a birthday coming up."

He wasn't entirely sure the woman bought it, but it didn't matter.

"Oh yeah?" Mona said. "How old is she?"

Trajan laughed his bold, confident laugh. "Good question, twenty-seven, twenty-eight. I have to do the math... born in 1991."

"Yeah, twenty-seven or twenty-eight," Mona said. "What are you thinking? Casual? Formal?"

Trajan put his hand on his cleft chin. "That's another good question."

"Are you here visiting?"

He could see her amping up her inner sex kitten.

"No, actually, down here for work," Trajan said. "I live up in Philadelphia... well, England originally, as I'm sure you could tell."

"What do you do?"

He handed her a card.

"I'm opening up another office," he said. "Got ones in L.A. and Philly."

"A model agency, huh?" Mona said, reading his card. "Why are you picking a small place like Charleston? I mean, it's not exactly L.A. or Philadelphia."

"I don't know," he said. "We were thinking about Atlanta or Charlotte, but I just liked the vibe here. Lots of great-looking women, for one thing."

He knew he could dust up his rap a little, get a little better answer to the Charleston question.

"So... are you interested?" he asked.

She laughed and pointed at herself.

"Yeah, right, I'm about twenty years too old to be a model. Too short, too."

"Oh, I don't know, we got plenty of other thirty-five-year-olds working for us."

"I'm a little older—" but then she stopped and smiled. "I love flatterers."

"I'm Trajan, by the way."

"I know, I saw it on your card," she said. "I'm Mona."

His baby blues drilled into hers.

"So, what are you doing tonight, Mona?"

"I'm married."

"Okay, then what are you doing tomorrow night?"

NINE

Janzek was still not fully moved in yet at Queen Street.

Rhett had volunteered to help him. Janzek thanked him but said he could hire somebody from the temporary workforce place he had heard about up on King Street. But Rhett insisted, so Janzek said okay. It probably wouldn't take them more than an hour, max, since he didn't possess much in the way of worldly goods. A bed, a bureau, a sofa, a few paintings, and a bunch of pots and pans, to be exact. Looking at his stuff had kicked off a whole, soul-searching thought process for Janzek: Just where did he stand in life compared to his friends from high school and college?

Like Tony, his old roommate. The guy who had gotten married down here three months ago and was indirectly responsible for him moving to Charleston.

Tony had more damn things. Like a house on the water in Sullivan's Island, which was filled with expensive-looking furniture and paintings that looked as if they were actually worth something, as opposed to Janzek's lame collection of Hopper prints that he had bought at the Gardner Museum with Caroline five years before. Tony also had a Porsche, a boat, a surfboard, and a high-paying job at some new Internet company. Janzek had a Honda with dents and a hundred thousand miles on it, no boat, no surfboard, and a job that paid ten thousand less than what he was making up in Boston.

Then there was another college roommate, Sam, the investment banker in New York. And Landon in L.A. Landon wrote screenplays, two of which had been made into movies. And then there was him... a lowly cop—a guy who an asshole with three last names, beady little eyes, and a worthless, rapist son said, "never heard of you" to.

He and Rhett were wrestling his box springs up the narrow stairway to his penthouse suite.

"You don't have much stuff," Rhett said.

Rub it in, Janzek thought. Like what Rhett was really saying was that at age forty he should have more shit. Four decades on the damn planet and this was all he had to show for it?

"Just sayin'," Rhett mumbled.

"I travel light," Janzek said, defensively.

"You plan on buying shit here?" Rhett asked as they angled the box spring through the kitchen.

"Like what?" Janzek asked, slightly out of breath.

That was another thing: He was actually out of breath going up the steps. What had happened to Nick Janzek, the great athlete, the guy who'd gotten four letters from Boston College? How could he be out of breath, going up a measly fifty steps? Maybe he was going to have a massive coronary any minute, keel over in the kitchen? Nobody'd ever find him until he started to smell like the local fish market.

"Just makin' observations," Rhett said, pointing at Janzek's Sanyo TV. "For one thing, you gotta get yourself a big flat screen instead of that little piece o' shit. I mean, come on, a Sanyo? And you need a Barcalounger with dual cup holders... you know, guy stuff? How the hell do you watch football on that thing?"

They set the box springs down on the metal framework on the floor. "So, is that it?" Rhett asked, looking around Janzek's apartment.

"Yeah," Janzek said. "Hey, thanks for your help, appreciate it."

Rhett nodded. "No problem, man," he said. "Then after the Barcalounger, you gotta get a girlfriend. This place could use the female touch."

"All right, all right, I get it," Janzek said.

"Jeez, don't get all sensitive on me now," Rhett said, picking up a thick, blue patch sitting on top of some framed pictures on the fireplace mantel. It said *Boston Police,* then below it, *AD 1630.*

"What the hell's this?" he asked, holding up the patch.

"Oh, nothing, just something they give you."

"For helping little old ladies cross the street?"

"Yeah, something like that."

Rhett put the patch back down on the mantel and picked up a picture of Janzek in a BC hockey uniform. "Your glory days, huh, Nick? All-American I read, right?"

Janzek nodded. "Yeah, but second team."

"Yeah, yeah, lose the modesty," Rhett said, putting the picture down and picking up another one of three unsmiling men. "Who are these hard cases?"

Janzek sighed. "My old man's the one on the right," he said. "Mighta seen the guy in the middle on wanted posters."

Rhett pulled it closer. "Looks familiar. Who is he?"

"Whitey Bulger," Janzek said. "My old man's boss."

Rhett's eyes got bigger and his mouth formed a perfect O. "No shit," was all he said.

Nick shook his head. "No shit—" he paused. "My old man's dead. Whitey got killed in prison a while back. No further questions."

"But you can't—"

"No further questions, I said. We're done with that subject."

Rhett put up his hands. "Whatever you say, Nick," he said. "But can I ask you a question on another subject?"

"Depends on what it is."

Rhett grabbed his chin. "That three-day growth thing. How do you get it so perfect? I mean, it's just the right length. Nice and macho."

Janzek laughed. "Glad you think it's macho, Delvin."

Rhett set the picture of Janzek's father down and started walking toward the door. "Okay. Tell you what, why don't I show you 'round the town."

"That oughta take about five minutes," Janzek said.

"Don't give me that Boston superiority bullshit," Rhett said, shaking his head.

They walked down from the penthouse, then got into Rhett's car, which was much nicer than Janzek's Honda.

"Okay, just to make sure you don't get lost," Rhett said, starting the car up, "we're gonna drive around a little, brush up on the local geography."

"Okay, how tough can that be?"

Rhett pulled out onto Queen Street. "You'd be surprised," he said, pointing at a street sign that said Legare Street, just north of Broad.

"Okay, so this is a quiz," Rhett said pointing at the street sign. "How do you pronounce that one?"

Janzek looked at it and raised his arms. "*Le-gare*. I mean, what else could it be?"

"That's what you'd think," Rhett said, taking a right onto Coming Street. "Actually, it's *LeGree*... as in that Simon dude."

"Well, that's pretty fucked up," Janzek said as they drove past the College of Charleston campus. "How'd they come up with that?"

Rhett shrugged. "Beats the shit out of me."

They went north a few more blocks.

"Okay," Rhett said, pointing to a sign that said Vanderhorst Street. "How about that one?"

Janzek shrugged. "*Van-der-horst*? I don't know..."

"Like it looks, right?" Rhett said. "You're way off. It's pronounced *Van-dross*."

"*Van-dross*? What the—"

Rhett shrugged. "Who knows?"

"Okay," Janzek said pointing at a sign a block away that said Smith Street. "And I suppose that's pronounced Smythe?"

"No, Smith is Smith," Rhett said. "There's actually a street up in North Charleston called Rhett Avenue."

"Oh yeah. Named after you?"

Delvin chuckled. "Nah, named after my great grandfather"— he paused— "a notorious white slave master, so they tell me."

TEN

It was Sunday.

Janzek had made his bed, hung his stuff in the closet and was, essentially, moved in. It had taken a total of an hour and a half. Next stop was to return the truck to the U-Haul on King Street, which was open on Sunday. He was beginning to get the sense that everything in Charleston was on King Street. He walked downstairs, out the front door, and right in front of him was a beautiful woman and her dog.

The dog saw him and started to bark. He recognized the bark. It was the same little bastard that had woken him up two nights before.

He smiled at the woman but not the dog.

She smiled back. The dog kept barking. She shushed him.

"Sorry about Otto," she said. "You must be the new guy—in apartment C?"

"Yeah, the penthouse suite," he said. "I'm Nick Janzek."

"Becky Hall. Nice to meet you, Nick."

"You too."

"I'm in apartment B," she said. "I guess you'd call it the sub-penthouse suite."

He laughed, squatted down, and patted the dog he had wanted to use for target practice.

"Cute little guy," he said, hoping he sounded sincere, then stood up.

"Well, I gotta go return that U-Haul out back," he said, "the one that's taking up half the parking lot."

She cocked her head to the side. "I've got a few friends coming over tonight," she said. "If you're not doing anything, why not come by?"

"I'd love to. What time?"

"Say, six."

"I gotta work 'til seven or so. Is that too late?"

"No, we'll still be knockin' 'em back," she said. "You're working on Sunday?"

"Yeah, you know, new guy on the job. Gotta impress the boss."

"I gotcha," she said. "Well, so see you then."

He figured what the hell, it would be nice to meet a woman or two.

Then he flashed to Cameron, the hottie from his friend's daughter's wedding three months ago. How it had somehow slipped her mind back then that she was engaged and scheduled to be married within the month. Maybe it was the three Blood Hounds she had put away at the reception.

Cameron had put her finger on the top of his scar and had run it down the length of it.

"How'd you get that?" she had asked.

"Sleepwalking."

"Yeah, right. How'd you really get it?"

"That's my story and I'm stick—"

"There are cool scars and ugly scars," she went on, raising the Blood Hound to her lips. "That's definitely a cool one."

But Janzek couldn't stand to look at it. It was a constant reminder of Caroline. How she had been raked with three bullets meant for him. When he shaved, he put his left hand over it so he wouldn't see it.

He dropped off the U-Haul, unhitched his Honda, and drove to the station. Rhett was there too. They talked over the McCann case for a half hour. The problem was there wasn't that much to talk over. Because the fact was—so far, anyway—they had absolutely no hard evidence. No car, no driver, no motive. They had done all the standard stuff. Put out calls to virtually every body shop within a hundred-mile radius of Charleston, asking if any of them had done any repair work on the bumper or grille of a late-model Mercedes Five Hundred. None of the body shops had—or at least weren't admitting to it. They both knew there was always the possibility that whoever the driver was had slipped a mechanic a few bucks to keep quiet. Or that the Mercedes was on a cargo ship halfway to South America. Or in a swamp nearby, sinking fast.

They had also interviewed all the witnesses they could round up and had gone door-to-door on Broad Street and all the surrounding streets to see if anyone had gotten a look at the driver. No one had. Including the guy who had been walking to his bank as he watched the mayor get cut down.

At two o'clock, Janzek told Rhett he was going to go to the Charleston library. To go through old newspapers and read up on the mayor, get some history on local issues. That was his standard operating procedure in Boston, and it had helped him on a number of cases.

It didn't take much digging to confirm what McCann's wife had told him: McCann was for the cruise ships and completely opposed to the casino that both South Carolina senators were vigorously backing. McCann was quoted as saying that the cruise ship issue was "basic economics," that the disgorging ships brought in a lot of business to the "little guys," and "just because the elitists south of Broad don't want—what they call— 'riffraff' on their streets, I'd like to point out, they don't own those streets."

On the subject of the proposed casino, McCann was quoted in the *Post and Courier*: "Let's call a spade a spade. Casinos bring in an element incompatible to Charleston. And that's why I'm adamantly opposed to it."

After two hours of back issues of *Post and Couriers*, Janzek felt he was becoming something of a Jim McCann expert.

Three hours later, at 7:15, Janzek knocked on Becky Hall's door. He was wearing a blue blazer and khakis, as safe an outfit as you could get when you had no idea what the dress code was.

She opened the door. There were four women and two other men there. The two men were wearing identical blue jeans—tight, dark blue Levi's—and long-sleeved shirts. Becky was dressed in a short, black skirt, which didn't cover much of her very shapely, toned legs that had somehow escaped Janzek's attention earlier in the day.

Crosby—who was a guy—did a double take when he asked Janzek what he did for a living. Crosby was a banker and the other man, Bob, was a commercial real estate broker. Patterson—a woman who made it clear she was not to be called Pat—was an architect who seemed to take herself pretty seriously. Dena was an antiques dealer, and Becky — Janzek found out after a while—was a lawyer. Janzek never got around to talking to the fourth woman.

Becky was in the kitchen refilling her Pinot Grigio when Janzek went in to get another beer.

"Having fun?" Her eyes were large and metallic blue. "Sorry about Patterson," then she dropped her voice, "girl could use a sense of humor."

"I'm having a great time," he said. "Thanks for having me."

IT WAS NINE O'CLOCK NOW AND JANZEK AND BECKY WERE ALONE,

sitting out on the porch off of her apartment. He was on his third Fat Tire beer and, he guessed, she was on about her third glass of Pinot Grigio. She told him she was from Charleston originally, had gone to the University of North Carolina, then University of South Carolina law school.

He started to think, as he listened to her talk about the law firm where she worked, what a mistake it would be to get anything going with her. But it was time. He had mourned Caroline's death for almost a year and a half. The voice of a little man on his shoulder was whispering in his ear that if he went out with her—or worse, slept with her—and it didn't work out, what a complete disaster it would be. He imagined them bumping into each other in the hallway. Or when they were taking out the trash. Or when he brought home another woman. Or she a guy.

But then, while she was talking about somebody in her office, he imagined having sex with her. The idea had obvious appeal and back before he was married he would have just gone for it. He hadn't had sex since Caroline's death. Oh wait... how could he have forgotten Cameron? Then he had a pang of guilt about that, but it wasn't like she'd ever said anything about being engaged.

Then another little voice piped up, 'Come on, dude, go for it. What are you waiting for? What's wrong with a little commitment-free sport fucking?' Not that he had any idea she was even remotely interested. Problem was, he still had a couple hundred pounds of baggage he was lugging around in his mind. Plus, nowadays he felt he actually needed to feel something as opposed to just jumping in the sack. That wasn't the way he used to be back in his pre-Caroline days.

While all this was clanking around in his head, Becky came over and sat down next to him. Then, without warning, she leaned over and kissed him.

"Whoa," he said, "where'd that come from?"

"Oh, I don't know," she said with a mischievous smile.

She smelled fantastic; her perfume, even the Pinot Grigio on her breath; something earthy but sweet at the same time. Her hair smelled good too.

They kissed again.

Then she pulled back.

"You know, this is a really bad idea," she said, running a hand through her hair. "What if we slept together, then you dumped me? Can you imagine—running into each other all the time? The word *awkward* comes to mind."

He put his hand on her smooth cheek. She kissed his hand.

He stood up.

"Where are you going?"

He smiled down at her. "What you just said."

"I know," she said, with a shrug, "but, hey, I do awkward things all the time."

He laughed, leaned down, and kissed her on the forehead.

"Good night," he said. "I know where you live."

He drove back to the station house and got in another few hours of work.

ELEVEN

Janzek and Rhett were in Ernie Brindle's office the next morning. Brindle wasn't at all like Janzek's chief in Boston. The guy up there, Declan O'Brien, was a man who rode his guys like a relentless taskmaster to get cases solved. He didn't care about their personal lives or give a damn if they ever saw their wives, girlfriends, or kids. Just get the fucker behind bars was all he cared about. Janzek missed a lot of the guys on the job up there but definitely not O'Brien.

Brindle seemed a lot more easygoing. His style was more like, *Okay, we got a job to do, a guy to catch, but let's do it carefully, methodically, not rush into it and mess it up.* He wasn't one of those "first forty-eight hours" guys either who figured if you didn't get your guy by then, you never would.

Janzek and Rhett had spent the day before going down a list of owners of late-model black Mercedes 500s, and so far, all of them had solid alibis. And none of them seemed spooked when he and Rhett started peppering them with questions.

The other part of the day had been spent studying tapes on every surveillance camera on Broad Street. The problem was most of the cameras were not facing the street itself but instead were trained on shops or the sidewalk. They finally found one that recorded the Mercedes flash by, but it was from the passenger side and the driver was just a dark silhouette. They also checked cameras on East Bay Street where an eyewitness said the Mercedes turned onto after hitting the mayor. Nothing there either.

Then Janzek got Brindle to authorize a reward for information leading to the capture of the driver and had the shot of the car blown up. Two uniforms distributed copies of it to every house and shop on Broad Street and the surrounding areas. But not one call had resulted.

They had been in Brindle's office for fifteen minutes. Rhett had advanced the cuckolded-husband theory again. Brindle was going with the one that the killer didn't like the mayor's politics and, at the moment, Janzek was on the fence.

"But the dude was really flagrant," Rhett said, referring to the mayor. "Like the time he got caught with his pecker out, paying his respects to Senator Dawson's wife."

Brindle just shook his head. "That's very colorful, Delvin," he said, "but I ain't buying it. I think he pissed off someone big-time. About something he did or was about to do."

"Like what?" Janzek asked.

Brindle shrugged. "I have no idea," he said. "Maybe going against the 526 connector."

"What's that?" Janzek asked.

"An extension of Route 526. Bunch of real estate developers stood to make a lot of money if it went through, but McCann got it voted down and made a ton of enemies."

"You really think someone would kill him over something like that?" Janzek asked, realizing that Sally McCann had referred to the 526 connector.

"I'm saying it's a possibility," Brindle replied. "I mean, we don't have a whole lot of other scenarios at the moment."

"I still think it was 'cause he was bangin' the strange," Rhett said.

Brindle shook his head. "What the fuck, Rhett? You tryin' out for the Eddie Murphy role here or something?" Brindle said, referring to the old movie *48 Hrs.*

Janzek laughed. "You're dating yourself, Ernie."

"Yeah, dude's even older than you," Rhett said.

Brindle rolled his eyes and shook his head.

"All right," Rhett said, "so we got it narrowed down to business or personal."

"Well, no shit, what else could it be?" Brindle asked.

"On the personal side," Janzek said, "we went through the list of 'women friends.' Nothing there so far."

"But there's one I still haven't checked out yet," Rhett said. "Broad's put me off a couple of times."

Brindle perked up. "Who's that, Delvin?"

"Owner of that bookstore up on King," Rhett said.

"Want me to try her?" Janzek asked.

"Sure, I'll email you her name and number."

Janzek nodded and looked over at Brindle. "This may be a stupid question, Ernie, but what do you know about the new mayor?"

"Pollack? Smart guy. On the city council," Brindle said. "What are you really asking, Nick?"

"I don't know," Janzek said. "Just following your thought that maybe the killer didn't like McCann's politics. But maybe he *does* like Pollack's."

"Could be," Brindle said, nodding. "Maybe something there."

"What about Pollack himself as a suspect?" Rhett asked.

Brindle scratched his head. "So he'd get the mayor's job? Doesn't exactly strike me as a job you'd kill for."

TWELVE

Mona had actually dialed the first three numbers on Trajan's business card with the intention of canceling their date. But then she thought, why should she? If they played it right, Gus would never get a whiff of it. What was one glorious night—because she had a feeling it would indeed be that—with the handsome young Brit who had sent her a huge bouquet of flowers that now festooned the rack right next to her Aldo Rendisi shoe display.

She had gone on nights out with the girls in the past, and though Gus didn't love it, he put up with it. The first time he had protested, saying, "So what do you girls do— drink too much and flirt with young guys?" Well, yeah, that was the general idea, but she had just looked at him with a withering stare like, *Come on, Gus, you know me better than that*, and pretended to be offended.

"We go out," she explained, "sure, have a few drinks, but just talk, gossip, and laugh. Why would you *even think* to put strange men in the equation? I mean, for God's sakes, Gus."

That had pretty much shut him up. And the fact was that the three times she had gone out before, it actually had just been talking, gossiping, and laughing. Although the last time she and her girlfriends were actually on serious prowl but didn't come across any prey except three drunk, overweight salesmen from Charlotte. A little drunk would have been okay, but these clowns could barely walk.

Then she remembered the fourth time. Oh well, we all have a slip-up or two in life.

Trajan struck her as a man sensitive to her desire for total discretion. As someone who would make sure that they didn't come within a hundred miles of anyone she or Gus knew. He told her on the phone that a friend had loaned him his house on Sullivan's Island and had added that you couldn't even see the neighbors' houses. He was going to pick up a couple of lobsters and said how it was a perfect night to be outdoors. Mona told him the best thing would be to pick her up at her gym at seven. She was going to take along a change of clothes to the shop, then go from there to the gym. Get toned up in a Pilates class. Do a few extra sets of crunches.

On second thought, she said, just to be safe, why not meet him a few doors down from her gym in front of the stores that closed earlier? He said sure, he'd be in a black Lexus.

At 7:05, he reached across and opened the passenger-side door for her.

She slid in and gave him a smile. She didn't feel guilty, she just felt naughty.

They drove across the bridge, through Mt. Pleasant, chatting away about—of all things— whether Trump had any girlfriends stowed away in the White House.

"And I'm a Republican too," Mona added with a smile.

They pulled into the circular driveway of the big oceanfront house on Sullivan's Island.

"Wow," Mona said, taking in the house, "who's your friend?"

"Just another guy from Philadelphia," Trajan said. "He's pretty generous about letting friends use the place when he's not around."

They went inside and Mona was impressed.

"This place is beautiful," she said.

"Yeah, told me he had a really good decorator," Trajan said.

He got them both drinks, and then they went outside and walked down to the pool. They sat in two chaise lounges in front of the pool house.

They talked about Trajan's model agency and how much time he was going to spend in Charleston. He explained that he was there really just to get it set up and operating smoothly, that he was in the process of finding someone qualified to run it once he got it off the ground. Mona asked him some questions, and he fielded them pretty well, considering everything he knew about the modeling business he had gotten from Google. It was easy to wing it, though, since the business model was so simple.

There was a fully stocked bar in the pool house too, so after a while, Trajan made them another round. She followed him into the pool house. He had found that, with all its couches and the best sound system he had ever heard, it was just what the doctor ordered for a seduction.

"Who do you like to listen to, love?" he asked, walking over to the Moon Audio system.

She was leafing through a big coffee-table book about houses in Mustique.

"What?" She looked up and smiled.

"Who would you like to listen to?"

"Umm... I don't know, got any Dire Straits?"

"At the push of a button," and that's what he did.

Money for Nothing came on.

"Dance?" he asked.

"Love to."

And he took her in his arms, and they did a slow one to the song that wasn't exactly danceable.

Halfway through it, she pushed into him and looked up into his handsomely deceitful eyes. At the end of the song, he kissed her and walked her over to one of the couches. They slid down into it and, kissing her, he started unbuttoning her top button. He reached in and unsnapped her bra with his right hand, then, with his left, started caressing her breasts.

She started to breathe in short bursts, and reached for his polo shirt, pulling it over his head.

"Oh my God," she said, "you are so gorgeous."

"That's supposed to be my line."

"Well, then, say it," She said.

"You are *sooo* gorgeous."

He ran his hand over her taut nipples.

She was feverish now, unbuckling his belt, unzipping his zipper, and sliding his pants off.

"Hang on one second, love," he said, standing up.

"Where're you going?"

"Just getting the light."

He walked over in his boxers to the rheostat switch, dimmed the lights, then flipped the switch for the two infrared cameras built into the ceiling.

THIRTEEN

CARLINO WAS TALKING TO HIS BROTHER, RICH, ON HIS CELL.

"The pedal got greedy," Rich said.

"What do you mean?"

"The driver of the Mercedes wants another twenty grand."

Carlino didn't even hesitate.

"Tell Martone to pay him a visit. He's good at curing greed."

Rich laughed. "That's what I thought you'd say. Consider it done."

Ned Carlino had no tolerance for someone who made a deal, then reneged on it. In this case, Jefferson Davis. Davis was a twenty-five-year-old Iraqi army vet who Rutledge Middleton had recruited, and Rich had hired for the job based on his being an experienced sharpshooter. Supposedly, Davis had forty-five confirmed kills in Iraq. It turned out, though, that his sharpshooter skills weren't necessary. Because Ned Carlino had changed his mind and told his brother to try to make it look like an accident. Rich Carlino and Davis then spent two weeks together tracking the mayor and found out that —like most people—his days were pretty much a routine. The mayor got to his office somewhere between 8:15 and 8:30, and at 9:30 on the dot every day, he walked three blocks from his office on Broad Street to get a coffee and blueberry muffin at the Bake Shop on East Bay. Then at 5:00 his day was basically done, but his social life was just beginning. Once in a while he'd go straight home, but usually he went to a duplex he owned in an LLC up on Grove Street. It was his love shack, and Rich had been impressed with the quality of women he ran through the place. One in particular, Rich told his brother: little miss smoking-hot in a red mini dress.

Rich told Ned about the mayor's daily habits, and Ned came up with the plan.

Jefferson Davis could clearly take the mayor out with one shot whenever he wanted, but a Lee Harvey Oswald–style assassination would attract more than just local law enforcement attention. It could get the FBI and God-knows-who involved, Carlino warned Rich. But if they made it look like a hit-and-run, it would draw far less notice. As it turned out, the local cops quickly determined it was an intentional homicide. Still—Carlino was certain—it got far fewer eyes on it than if Davis had done it with a sniper rifle from the roof of a building.

And besides, it didn't really matter because Carlino was supremely confident he'd get away with it. The way he always did.

Whatever method they used, Rich had reassured his brother beforehand, Jefferson Davis was the right guy for the job. Rich described him as a street-smart, war-hardened, black dude who wouldn't screw up.

"Wait," Ned had said to his brother. "Black dude?"

"Yeah," said Rich. "Why?"

"'Cause of his name," Carlino said, "that's why. Last time I checked, Jefferson Davis was head of the Confederacy in the Civil War."

"Really?" said Rich. "I didn't know that." Rich was not a student of history. Or much of anything.

JEFFERSON DAVIS WAS UP AT THE CITADEL, CHECKING OUT THE college again.

He wanted to be like his brother and go to a military college, but his grades weren't anywhere near as good as Marcus's, and there was no way in hell he was going to get into the Naval Academy like Marcus had. But forget about his grades—there was also the fact that he had a record. The armed robbery charge was not something the guys at Annapolis were going to look too favorably on. He knew he could forget about West Point too.

The Citadel, though, he had started to think a while back— maybe he just might have a shot there. If, somehow, he could just bury the armed robbery charge. Maybe the lawyer could make it go away. And, sure enough, the lawyer told him he'd do everything he could to make that happen. But, as far as getting a meaningful amount of scholarship money, forget it. And, he was pretty certain, the tuition cost was way more than the paltry amount he had banked on the mayor's hit.

So, bottom line, he had no other choice: He had to call Rich Carlino and tell him he needed more money. To at least cover his first year at the Citadel. Hell, that wasn't too much to ask.

He was walking around the campus checking out all the metal carcasses again. There was a World War II fighter jet in front of a three-story building and a big, gray Sherman tank near a parking lot, someone's not-so-subtle reminder how the Citadel taught their students to fight and kill.

He had read all about how the Citadel had good programs in engineering and economics too. He had also checked out the College of Charleston and actually was interested in a couple things they had there. Like a major called cybersecurity. He could see getting into something like that, but still, the Citadel was definitely more his speed.

Davis was sitting in his Mitsubishi, looking out onto the big, green grass quadrangle surrounded by buildings in the architectural style of a fort, when he spotted a cute girl— maybe eighteen or nineteen—in his side-view mirror, strutting down the sidewalk at a good clip. She was walking about as fast as he'd ever seen anyone walk. Then, suddenly, she did a sharp 45-degree-angle turn. It was like it had been choreographed. Even in a starchy uniform, he could see she had some dangerous curves on her. He hopped out of the car, ran after her, and caught up. She was humping along like a storm trooper on speed.

"What you doin', girl?" he asked. "Walking like that? That some military walk they make you do?"

Not turning her head or moving her lips hardly at all, she said, "Yeah, hundred twenty steps a minute."

His legs were churning to keep up.

Barely decelerating, she did a hard left, 90-degree turn and almost knocked him over.

"Jesus, girl, easy."

She ignored him and powered up again. He had to scramble to stay up with her.

"Why you have to walk like that?"

"All us knobs do."

"That's what they call freshmen, huh?"

She gave him a curt nod.

"So, a hundred twenty steps a minute, then those 90-degree corners?"

"Uh-huh."

"Looks like fun," Davis said, starting to huff a little.

"What do you want?" she asked. "Why you hangin' around here anyway?"

"Oh, just killin' time, waitin' for a guy," he said. "Hey, how 'bout a phone number?"

Her eyes zigged over, but her head didn't move.

"Who are you?"

"Sergeant Jefferson Davis, Army Ranger, fifth platoon," he snapped off with authority, knowing it was like a white dude telling a chick in a bar he was a big honcho at some Wall Street investment bank.

"Fo' real?" she said.

"Which one you mean? Ranger or sergeant?" he asked, breathing heavy now.

"No, Jefferson Davis," she said.

That slowed him down, but only briefly.

"I mention my Silver Star?" he said, smiling what one old girl-friend called his *can I see your titties* smile.

"Six-four-zero-three-eight-three-eight," she said

"I'll call you," he said, "once I have a chance to catch my breath."

FOURTEEN

GENEVA CRANE, THE OWNER OF RED TRUCK BOOKS ON UPPER King and one of the women who former mayor McCann had on his secret list, was the one Delvin Rhett hadn't spoken to yet. Janzek called her from his office, and she picked up after the first ring.

"Red Truck Books, this is Geneva."

"Ms. Crane?"

"Yes."

"My name is Detective Janzek, Charleston Police. I'm investigating the murder of Mayor McCann and wanted to talk to you about it."

"Oh, yes, that other guy called before," she said. "Why do you want to talk to me?"

Janzek looked up at the picture of the Empire State Building on his wall.

"I'm interviewing everyone who the mayor came in contact with the last two weeks before his death."

"So, I'm a suspect?" she said, in a tone like, had he spotted any extraterrestrials lately?

"No, ma'am, it's just part of standard investigation procedure. Do you have any time this afternoon?"

"Ah..." she hesitated, "okay, let's get this over with. How about you come by here at, say, three?"

"Sure, that's good. Where's *here*?"

"Four-eleven King. Red Truck Books."

"Thanks. See you then."

He was ten minutes late.

He walked into the bookstore and up to the girl at the desk.

"Hi, I'm here to see Ms. Crane?"

The girl looked like maybe she was a part-timer from the college.

"She's back in her office. Can I tell her—"

"Detective Janzek."

The girl gave him a quick, perfunctory smile and walked around the counter.

"I'll go tell her you're here, sir."

A few moments later, the girl and a woman came walking toward him from the back of the store.

He had been expecting his version of a librarian—skinny, stern, no shoulders, hair in a bun—but Geneva Crane was flat-out beautiful.

She was five-ten or so with medium-length jet-black hair and stunning blue eyes.

She had the most sharply defined cheekbones he had ever seen. Angular and honed, like they could cut you almost; draw a little blood even.

"Hello, Detective," Geneva said to Janzek, holding out her hand. "Want to come back to my office?"

"Thank you," he said, shaking her hand. "This won't take long."

"Follow me," she said.

He followed her back to her office, which was small but tidy and smelled of fresh flowers. It lacked the musty odor of what he expected a bookstore office to smell like.

"Have a seat, Detective. I was thinking... you're the first detective I ever met. A few policemen here and there. A motorcycle cop named Dennis is one of my good customers. But you're my first detective."

Janzek sat down opposite her, trying to come up with a bookish response.

"Well, I'll try to acquit my profession well."

It was so unlike him. Like he was trying to create a good impression.

"I need to ask you, Ms. Crane, what was your relationship with Mayor McCann?"

She frowned. "So far, you're *not* acquitting yourself too well, Detective," she said, "since I had absolutely no relationship with Mayor McCann except as taxpayer to public servant."

"According to my records provided by his office, you met with him three times in the two weeks prior to his death, twice at his office and once at an apartment he rented up on Grove Street."

Her big blue eyes flickered.

"Are you trying to imply something? Because if you are, you're way off base. I called McCann a day after the second meeting in his office and requested to meet with him again. He asked if I didn't mind coming to his home office instead of the one on Broad. I said sure."

She grabbed a pen and started tapping it.

"Ms. Crane, that wasn't where he lived, that was a place where he—"

"Seduced women?" she said, her tone ratcheting up. "Well, how the hell was I supposed to know that? Or the fact that the man was a total lecher."

"So, what was it that you were meeting with the mayor about?" Janzek asked, trying to make the question sound casual.

Geneva tapped the pen faster. Then she lowered her voice. "I was trying to get his support for something."

Janzek nodded.

"I'm trying to get funding for a... project."

"You mind telling me what it is?"

She leaned back in her chair.

"What difference does it make?" she said, then: "Okay, long story short, I'm trying to get funding for a facility for families of wounded veterans. Where the wives, parents, whoever, can stay while the vet gets treated at the VA hospital."

Janzek nodded. "Sounds like a noble cause."

Geneva just rocked in the big leather chair and didn't say anything.

"So, can you tell me what happened when you went to see the mayor on Grove Street?" Janzek asked. "And what time it was, if you remember?"

"Just past five. He offered me something to drink. I thought that was okay, seeing how the unofficial Charleston drinking hour is five sharp." She smiled. "Well, noon in certain parts of town."

Janzek smiled. "So, then what happened, Ms. Crane?"

"So, then he gave me a glass of white wine, and he filled a big highball practically to the rim for himself. I basically gave him the exact same pitch I gave him the first two times we met. In fact, I didn't really see the point of meeting the third time since I'd already given him the pitch. Everything including the projected costs, an architect's rendering of what it would look like—the works."

"So, you went over all of that again with him?"

She nodded.

"Then what?"

She went back to pen tapping.

"I think you can guess, Detective."

"He tried to seduce you?"

"It wasn't nearly as pretty as that," Geneva said. "He refilled my drink and right after that, tried to kiss me. I was *so* out of there. I didn't want to lose my shot at getting funding, but I wasn't about to—"

Janzek stood up. "Thank you, Ms. Crane, I appreciate you seeing me. I hope you get your funding. It sounds like a very worthwhile project."

"It is," she said, standing up. "After kind of a shaky start, you acquitted your profession quite well, Detective."

He smiled and nodded a thank you.

Geneva walked out of her office, toward the front door, and he followed her. She got to the door, turned to him, and put out her hand.

"Nice to meet you, Detective."

"Me, too, and thank you again," he said. "By the way, how's your supply of historical fiction here?"

She pointed to a section on the back wall.

"Pretty good. Anyone in particular?"

"I like the English writer Bernard Cornwell," Janzek said. "He lives here, supposedly."

"Yes, he sure does, down on Tradd. I think I have three or four of his books. He's really good."

Janzek noticed her full lips and aquiline nose.

"Maybe I'll get him to sign one," he said, putting his hand on the front doorknob. "Well, they don't pay me to hang around and talk about books. Like I have a clue what I'm talking about."

"I'm sure you can hold your own," she said. "Maybe stop back in when you're not... 'on the job.' That's the expression, right?"

He nodded.

FIFTEEN

Chris Martone's flight got in from Philly at eleven that morning. First, he thought about boosting a car from the Charleston Airport but thought better of it. He figured even the Charleston cops, who probably weren't rocket scientists, could make a connection that he was a flown-in hitter if someone ever ID'ed his car after he popped Jefferson Davis.

Last time he was in Charleston he noticed how close the Boeing plant was to the airport. So, he walked out of the airport terminal and just kept going until he hit the plant about a half-mile away. He walked around the parking lot there and finally found an azure blue Chevy Cobalt with a window open. Some bonehead had actually left the key in the ignition too. Maybe figured, who'd ever steal this piece of shit?

Martone dialed Davis on his cell as he pulled onto Highway 26. Told him that he was about to become his new best friend since he had a bagful of hundreds for him. Two hundred one-hundred-dollar bills, to be exact. Davis said he'd be waiting for him at the Citadel in a black Mitsubishi.

"What's the Citadel?" Martone asked, figuring it was a bar.

"It's the military college in Charleston," Davis answered.

Martone got directions, figuring it was a strange place for a drop, but what the hell, what difference did it make? His first thought, after Rich Carlino called him, was to find out where Davis lived and crawl under his car and plant a bomb in the middle of the night. That was so much more creative than just popping a guy. Plus, he was really good at making bombs. Small but powerful ones. But then there was always the possibility a wife or a girlfriend could borrow the car that day, so he nixed the idea.

Twenty minutes later, Martone drove down Moultrie Street through the gates of the Citadel, took a right when he saw the big lush grass quadrangle in the middle of a lot of gray, fort-like buildings. He noticed an old tank and a fighter jet on display, apparently there to remind students what their missions were. He saw the black Mitsubishi up ahead parked in a lot facing the quadrangle. He got a little closer and saw a black guy at the wheel. He drove past him, stopped, and backed into a spot next to him. Davis glanced over. Martone had to manually roll down the window because the Cobalt beater didn't have push buttons.

"Jefferson Davis?" Martone asked.

"That's me," the black guy said. "Nice wheels there, dude."

Martone wasn't much for banter when he was on a job. But he had to know. "What are you doin' at this place, man?" he asked, looking out at a few people in uniform walking real fast on the other side of the quadrangle.

"Watchin' my new woman strut her stuff," the black guy said.

Martone wondered if the guy had been smoking something.

He reached down for the gym bag with the Nike swoosh on it.

"Got something here for you," Martone said.

"I was hoping so."

Martone put the bag on the passenger seat and pulled out the silenced Glock so Davis couldn't see it. Then he looked around. No one was anywhere near them.

"It's not what you were expecting," Martone said, raising the

Glock.

Davis didn't even have a chance to change his expression.

Martone fired once. He saw blood splatter on the passenger-side window. Davis, as if in slo-mo, eased forward, gently almost, onto the wheel of the Mitsubishi. The horn didn't honk.

Martone backed up the Cobalt and drove around the quadrangle. It was a nice-looking campus. Neat and orderly. He thought maybe his son, Anthony, should check the place out. Maybe even apply. He could probably get in. He had 1400s on his SATs, after all. APs in English and Philosophy. Vice president of the Honor Society. Probably a slam dunk for the kid. He thought about going to the admissions office. Getting a catalogue and an application but thought he probably better get a move on. Someone would notice the guy before too long, then the cops would be showing up.

His flight back to Newark was at ten the next morning, which left him plenty of time just in case there was some screw-up. It was only one thirty in the afternoon. He thought about calling up and trying to get an earlier flight out. Then he thought, "What's the rush?" Last time he was here, Charleston struck him as a pretty cool place. He had read about it in some magazine in his dentist's office too. *Travel and Pleasure* or something. He took a right, not knowing where he was going. It was a one-way street called Rutledge. He drove a little further to another street called Calhoun and hung a left. It looked like he was right in the middle of another college. "Jesus, colleges all over the place," he thought. He saw a sign that said *College of Charleston*. A bunch of kids all walking around. Skateboards, fancy bikes, skimpy tops, backpacks or knapsacks, whatever they called them these days. Expensive-looking casual clothes. Looked like a rich kids' school. He took a right on King Street. More good-looking, spiffed-out, preppy kids. He couldn't see Anthony here. Besides, it looked like a party school and didn't want his kid getting shitfaced every night.

He drove past a horse-drawn carriage with a fat guy wearing one of those funny, gray Confederate caps, holding the reins. The guy was turned around, talking to a bunch of tourists in the back of the carriage, giving them the spiel, telling them the historical significance of some old beater of a building. It looked like the horse had the route memorized. Like it was on automatic pilot.

But as Martone drove past the carriage, he realized it was a mule, not a horse. He went past a J. Crew, then slowed down next to another carriage. This one was being drawn by a horse. Looked like the poor old dude had a lot of miles on him. Martone rolled down the Cobalt's window and listened in for a few seconds. The man was telling his passengers about how some cannonball had gone through the roof of a house he was pointing at.

Martone waved his hand to catch the driver's attention and shouted up at him. "Yo," he said. "Got room in that buggy for one more?"

The man looked down at him and squinted.

"Sorry," he said. "You can't get on in the middle of a ride. Just go over to Anson Street. They run every ten minutes or so."

The driver went back to his spiel.

Martone had no idea where Anson Street was and gunned the Cobalt past the carriage. A car was pulling out of a spot up ahead. He almost rammed it, pulling into the space it was vacating. He parked and turned off the ignition.

Martone got out and caught up to the horse-drawn cart that had just lumbered past him. He grabbed the back of a seat and pulled himself up into the cart. The driver looked at him like he was a Somali pirate boarding a tanker.

"Whoa, whoa, mister," he said. "You can't do that, I told you—"

Martone shoved a fifty-dollar bill into his hand.

The man turned back to the other passengers who were all looking at Martone funny.

"That wall over there," the driver said, not missing a beat, "took a direct hit from a Fort Sumter cannon—" then he did a little well-rehearsed snicker—"you know, during that little dustup between the states."

SIXTEEN

Rutledge Middleton had to speak to his son, Quatro.

He had him trained so that no matter what his son was doing—or wasn't doing, as was usually the case—that when his father's number popped up on his phone, Quatro damn well better answer quick. No letting it go to voicemail, and in fact, it was best if he picked it up right after the first ring.

"Hey, Dad, what's up?" Quatro said, out of breath.

"What are you doing?"

"I'm in the gym, on the treadmill."

"Well, get off the goddamn thing, and give me your full, undivided attention."

"Yes, sir," Quatro said. A beep, then the humming background noise ceased. "Okay, Dad, I'm all yours."

'Yeah,' Middleton thought, 'exactly the problem.'

"That girl, the thing that happened at your frat house, I want you to make it go away. Last thing I need is to see your name in the paper. You got me?"

Nothing. Just Quatro breathing heavy. Finally: "Got any ideas, Dad? Like, what I should do? Like, I mean—"

Middleton usually had to draw his son a map.

"Do whatever you have to," he said impatiently. "If you have to sell your car and give her the money to make it go away, then that's what you gotta do."

"But, Dad, not my Mustang?"

Middleton heard the click of another call. He looked down at the number and didn't recognize it.

"I gotta go. Like I said, sell that goddamn Mustang if you have to."

"But, Dad—"

Middleton clicked over to the incoming call.

"Hello," Middleton said.

"Mr. Middleton," the voice said. "It's Jimmie Driggers."

"Oh, hey," Middleton said. "What's going on?"

"Might be a problem," Driggers said. "This detective might have found a connection between the driver and Jim McCann."

"The driver? Who the hell's the driver?"

"Jefferson Davis. The guy who got whacked up at the Citadel."

"Oh yeah," Middleton said. "What do you mean, 'a connection'?"

"Well, this guy— Janzek's his name— was investigating the crime scene up there—"

"Christ," Middleton said. "I met that guy. Hard-ass from off, right?" *Off* was Charleston-ese which meant anywhere but Charleston.

"Yeah, Boston, I think," Driggers said. "S'posed to be goddamn Sherlock Holmes. So anyway, Jefferson Davis had McCann's address on him. But worse, had a key to the Mercedes in his pocket."

Middleton thought for a second. "But nothing connecting Davis to me, right?"

"No, nothing."

"That's good," Middleton said. "So, how they gonna know that key was to the Mercedes that took out the mayor? Far as they know, it could be to any goddamn Mercedes. No way that puts Davis behind the wheel."

"Well, no, it doesn't exactly, but—"

"Davis got rid of the car, right?" Middleton asked.

"Yeah, least he told me he did. I just figured I'd let you know. What I've heard about this Janzek guy scares me."

"All right, I'll get back to you," Middleton said. "Gotta talk to my people."

"His people" —meaning Ned Carlino.

He hung up and punched in Carlino's number. To Middleton's relief, Carlino was not the least bit worried about what Driggers said. In fact, it seemed as if he'd almost anticipated the news. It was time to move on to the next step of his plan. Time to set up their scapegoat, Carlino said.

Jimmie Driggers was a longtime detective on the Charleston police force and a second cousin to Ernie Brindle. He didn't spend much time at the station on Lockwood Drive because he was usually out in the field or his favorite gin mill and, in fact, hadn't even met Janzek yet.

Janzek had heard about Driggers from Rhett. Rhett told him Driggers had a reputation for clearing a lot of cases, but he was not Driggers's biggest fan. Said it was all about clearance rate to Driggers, that it didn't much seem to matter whether he got the right guy or not. But then, Rhett admitted, he didn't really have any solid proof of that. "But you know how it is," he had said to Janzek, "where there's smoke, there's fire."

"So, you saying he's dirty?" Janzek had asked.

Rhett had chewed that over. "Like I said, I can't prove anything," he had replied. "My take is, he ain't exactly dirty and he ain't exactly clean. How 'bout we just go with... *soiled.*"

Janzek let it go at that, figuring he'd make his own assessment soon enough.

Jimmie Driggers had been on the pad to Rutledge Middleton ever since the reputed suicide of a man named George Reed a year ago. Reed was indicted for running an investment-fund Ponzi scheme and Rutledge Middleton was one of the many disgruntled investors who lost his shirt on it.

After the hit on the mayor, Middleton had called up Driggers and placed another order from Ned Carlino: Find the owner of a late-model, black Mercedes, and frame him as the hit-and-run driver who ran down the mayor. It wasn't that tough of an assignment, Driggers thought at first, and he had come up with three possible fall guys. One was an out-of-work insurance salesman with two DUI's and three busted marriages. Another was an ex-NASCAR driver who won the Darlington 500 fifteen years ago and had a couple of top tens in other races, but basically was a second-tier driver who couldn't get a sponsor anymore. Another was a painting contractor from Moncks Corner.

Driggers's first choice was the ex-NASCAR driver. The only problem was that he had a rock-solid alibi, so he was out. His second choice was the guy with the DUI's and rocky marital history, Benny Terhune. Terhune hemmed and hawed when Driggers tracked him down and asked him what he was doing the morning the mayor was killed. Terhune finally 'fessed up and said he was banging a hooker at his house up in Hanahan. Driggers said he needed corroboration from the hooker and got her name and number from Terhune. Driggers then tracked her down and gave her three hundred in cash to forget she ever knew Terhune.

Right after that, Driggers arrested Terhune.

After Rhett heard that Driggers had made an arrest in the mayor's murder, he called Janzek.

"Jimmie Driggers arrested some guy, claims he's the guy ran down McCann," Rhett told Janzek.

Janzek was filling his tank at the BP on Calhoun Street.

"You're kidding," Janzek said, yanking the hose out of his gas tank.

"No, he claims he got a call from some guy who saw the whole thing and took down the license number of the Mercedes. Driggers says he ran the number and tracked down the owner. According to him, the guy had an alibi that didn't stand up."

"I don't know, Delvin, we checked out the cars pretty good."

"I know we did."

"So, what do you think?" Janzek said, getting into his car. "Sounds like bullshit to me."

There was no hesitation.

"Yeah, I can goddamn well guarantee you it is."

SEVENTEEN

JANZEK HAD JUST INTERVIEWED THE HIT-AND RUN-DRIVER WHO had allegedly killed the mayor.

He knew after two minutes there was no way. Benny Terhune was too specific about what he was doing at the time the mayor was killed. Provided way more information than Janzek needed. Janzek cut him off when Terhune started getting graphic about some aberrant B&D stuff he and the hooker were experimenting with the morning the mayor bought it.

As much as Janzek was convinced Benny Terhune was telling the truth, he knew Luke Morrison was lying. Morrison was the guy who said he'd taken down the Mercedes license plate number.

Morrison lived on Trapman Street—which Janzek thought was about the only thing he said that was true. He told Janzek he was walking to an office at Broad and State when he saw a black Mercedes going about three times the speed limit. Said he memorized the plate number but didn't give a credible reason why he would do that. Janzek asked him, "You just like memorizing license plates, Mr. Morrison?' Morrison said no, there was just something about the car going so fast, something told him it was headed for trouble.

Janzek's bullshitometer started wailing.

Morrison clearly could tell Janzek wasn't buying a word of it and asked if Jimmie Driggers could be in on the interview. Janzek told him no, because the interview was officially over and he started walking away.

Then, he stopped and doubled back. He asked Morrison why it had taken him so long to call the police. Morrison mumbled something about not wanting to get involved, but after a while, he realized it was his, "civic duty."

Still, the next day there was a front-page article about the mayor's alleged hit-and-run driver being arrested. Someone had leaked the story. Janzek had a good guess who had done that.

The poor bastard Benny Terhune hadn't been able to raise bail and was now bunking in a nine-by-twelve cell on Lockwood Drive.

But then later that day, a distraught Ginny Hooper apparently had an attack of conscience when she saw the paper. She claimed to be an out-of-work hairdresser from Goose Creek and called the police department to say that Benny had been with her from midnight the night before the mayor was killed until eleven the next morning. The cop who took the call asked for her address and said that a detective, Jimmie Driggers, would probably want to come over and take her statement.

She got all panicky when she heard Driggers's name and pleaded for someone else to come instead. The cop said he'd see what he could do, maybe he could send someone else. She said thank you and sounded relieved.

Rhett went to see her and felt she was a totally credible witness. Then Janzek did a follow-up interview with Luke Morrison, the supposed eyewitness who memorized license plates for a hobby. Morrison broke down and admitted halfway through it that he just wanted a little attention and, just like that, Benny Terhune was out on the street, a free man.

After the waste of time with Morrison and Terhune, Janzek decided to search Jefferson Davis's car again. The first time he did, the ME had been camped out in the front seat of the Davis's Mitsubishi and evidence techs were crawling all over it lifting samples, which made it tough for Janzek to do as thorough a job as he would have liked.

This time, though, fifteen minutes into it, he found a book of matches wedged deep into the driver's seat. On the back of the matchbook in tight, neat handwriting, it said *Fuel-6 Tues-RAM.* Janzek flashed to Rutledge Middleton right away as he remembered seeing the man's gold belt buckle with the blocky, engraved initials *RAM* the night Middleton came to bail out his miscreant son. There had to be other guys around with those initials, but his gut told him it was time to meet with Middleton again.

JANZEK WALKED OVER TO DELVIN RHETT'S CUBICLE. RHETT WAS on the phone. He motioned for Janzek to have a seat in the green chair, opposite his desk, that looked like a thousand overweight asses had flopped down in it over the years.

Rhett hung up and smiled at Janzek.

"Just out of curiosity, Delvin," Janzek asked, "who's your decorator? Habitat for Humanity?"

"You're not getting any fung shui vibes here, Nick?"

"Feng."

"Feng, fung, foo... whatever," Rhett said. "My Japanese is a little rusty."

"Chinese."

"That too," Rhett said, cocking his head to one side. "So, what's up?"

"'Fuel.' Ever heard of it?" Janzek said. "A bar, a restaurant, maybe?"

"Yeah, sure," Rhett said. "Up near my hood. Cannon and Rutledge."

Janzek wrote down the address in his notebook.

"Why you want to know?"

Janzek handed him the matchbook. Rhett studied it.

"I know what *Tues.* is too," Rhett said.

Janzek took the matchbook back. "Thatta boy."

"Hey, watch it."

"What?"

"Callin' me boy."

"Thatta *man*," Janzek said. "Okay, *Fuel* and *Tuesday*. What about *RAM?*"

Rhett shrugged and raised his arms. "Got me there."

"How 'bout Rutledge Ashley Middleton?" Janzek said. "Father of that kid up for the rape of the college girl."

"Okay, but how would he ever have run across the brother, Jefferson Davis?" Rhett asked. "Don't exactly run in the same social circle."

"I don't know yet," Janzek said, getting up.

"Hey, I did a little research."

"And?"

"And found out about that blue Boston police patch on your mantel."

Janzek rolled his eyes. "Oh, Christ."

"That's a big-time honor," Rhett said. "You don't get it for walking little old ladies across the street."

"Okay, I lied," Janzek said, standing up.

"The highest commendation a cop can get in Boston, And you were only twenty-eight when you got it."

"Twenty-nine."

"You know what they'd say up in Boston about that patch?"

"No, what would they say, Delvin?"

"*Wicked pissa.*"

"Christ, listen to you," Janzek said, starting to walk away. "Hey, how 'bout doin' research on our cases 'stead of lookin' into shit like that."

"Trust me, I am. Where you off to, man?"

Janzek looked at his watch. "Happy hour, up at Fuel?"

Rhett nodded. "You run across RAM, get him to buy you a cocktail."

JANZEK SHOWED A PICTURE OF JEFFERSON DAVIS TO THE bartender at Fuel. The bartender said he didn't remember ever seeing the man. Janzek asked him if he worked Tuesdays. He said no, a guy named Robert was the normal Tuesday guy. Janzek wrote down Robert's name and his cell phone number. Then he ordered a beer and went out to the back where there was a big, open brick terrace with tables, chairs, and a boccie court. There was a large table, which looked like it was actually three or four tables pulled together, where a big group of twentysomething girls were knocking back shots. From the College of Charleston, he guessed.

Janzek walked past them and sat down. One of the girls looked over at him, then nudged the girl next to her. The second girl looked over, then got up and walked over. She batted her eyes at him.

"You mind taking a couple pictures of us, sir?" she asked, holding up her cell phone.

Janzek smiled and took her camera. Sir... meant she thought he was at least sixty.

"Yeah, sure," he said, then got up and walked over to the table of girls.

"It's her bachelorette party," the one who had come over said, pointing to a big-breasted redhead who had just pounded a shot. "My name's Ali, by the way."

"Hi, Ali," Janzek said, trying to aim the camera.

"You got it upside down," she said, laughing.

"Oops," Janzek said, flipping the cell phone around. "Not the most tech-savvy guy around."

All the girls were looking at him now, dialing up their sexy looks

—pouty lips, popped eyes, hand on hips. He figured the photos were probably destined for Facebook pages.

"Okay, girls," Janzek said, trying to get them all in the picture, "squish together."

One hopped into another one's lap, one clamped her lips onto another one's cheek and froze it there, two did rapper-style, twisted-finger salutes.

Janzek started snapping.

"All right, good—yeah, that's it," he said. "A couple more—yeah, there you go, perfect."

He turned to Ali, smiled, and handed her back her cell phone.

"Thanks," she said, taking a look at the eight pictures he had shot. "You got some really good ones."

"Just call me Annie Leibovitz," Janzek said.

Ali looked at him with a big *huh?*

"Famous photographer."

"Oh, okay—hey, why don't you join us?" Ali said.

The girl next to her chimed in, "Yeah, come on, we're buyin'."

Janzek gave Ali a gentle pat on the shoulder.

"Thank you, girls," he said, "but I'm old enough to be your father."

Ali's friend turned to her and laughed.

"Trust me," she said. "You don't look anything like my dad."

Janzek walked over to a waitress wiping down a table and reached into his breast pocket.

"'Scuse me," he said, and the waitress looked up.

"Have you ever seen this man here?" he asked, handing her the photo of Jefferson Davis.

She looked closely.

"I think so," she said. "A week or so ago, sitting at that table over there"—she pointed— "with this really obnoxious white guy."

Janzek pulled a picture of Middleton, which he got from the website of Middleton's law firm, out of his pocket.

"Is this the really obnoxious white guy, by any chance?"

She didn't need to get too close to recognize him.

"That's him," she said. "Jerk was so rude."

Janzek nodded. "Thanks for your help."

"No problem," she said, sliding the cloth rag into an apron pocket. "We usually have really nice people here... that guy was such a douche."

EIGHTEEN

CARLINO AND THE NEW MAYOR, PETER POLLACK, WERE AT
Carlino's Sullivan's Island beachfront house, lounging around in their
bathing trunks, nursing stiff drinks. Carlino had bought the house
from Wendy Stanford, the John Deere heiress and divorced wife of
the former governor, Johnny Stanford. Stanford had been caught
cheating on his wife with his acupuncturist. The scandal had gone
national with a clumsy headline in the Enquirer: something really
tacky, 'Who Stuck Their Needle Into Who?'

"You ever been to Monte Carlo, Pete?" Carlino asked, feeling the
gentle, pleasurable buzz of 120-proof Jamaican rum.

"No, never have," Pollack said.

Unlike central casting's prototypical version of a southern politi-
cian, Pollack was not prone to long, windy stories, which invariably
started out, "Back when my *d-aa-ddy* was a young pup" or laced with,
"I reckons" and references to "colored folks." No, Pollack's MO was
that he actually got to the point fast and made no bones about the fact
that he had one thing on his mind: money.

"Well, there are two casinos in Monte Carlo," Carlino went on,
"the newer one, for the great unwashed, and the old one for the

elegant people of the world who can lose a million in a night and not let it bother 'em too much."

"Is that right?" Pollack said, shifting in his seat.

"Our casino is going to be like the old one," Carlino said.

"You mean, *if* you get the casino," Pollack said, not turning to make eye contact with his host.

Carlino wanted to bitch-slap the guy. Why did he think he'd been handed the mayor's job? "Oh, don't you worry, Pete, we'll get it."

"I guess we'll just have to see about that," Pollack said.

Carlino decided it was time to quit screwing around and get to the bottom line. "A hundred thousand dollars," he said simply.

Pollack turned to Carlino, stared him down for a few moments, then thrust out his beefy hand.

"I was just thinking," Pollack said, "what we really need in this town is a casino. Just like that one they got in Monte Carlo. The old one. Where a guy can drop a million bucks in a night and not sweat it."

Carlino shook Pollack's hand, wondering what would have happened if he had offered him only fifty thousand.

Pollack stood up, fighting back a triumphant smile. He was wearing something in the Speedo family that made Carlino want to gag.

"Got a bathroom in your pool house?" Pollack asked, pointing at the white-sided building with green trim.

"Sorry, there's a problem with the flusher. You gotta go up to the main house."

Pollack had a better idea. He walked slowly down the brick coping on the side of the pool to the shallow end and inched down the steps into the water until he was at waist level. Then he stopped.

He turned to Carlino and a smile slowly crept across his face as the water around him got warmer.

NINETEEN

Janzek had called Middleton four times in three hours. Middleton hadn't gotten back to him. Janzek called him a fifth time and stepped up the urgency in his message. Said if he hadn't heard back from him in an hour he was going to come down to Middleton's office and barge right in on him. He didn't care whether Middleton was in the middle of something or not.

A half hour later he got a call back.

"What is it now, Janzek?" Middleton said without identifying himself. "You know, your pushy Yankee shit doesn't fly so well down here."

Janzek ignored him. "I want to know about your relationship with Jefferson Davis."

Pause.

"Can't talk now," Middleton said. "I just got a call I been waitin' on. Call you back later."

"Hold on—" But Middleton had hung up.

Janzek knew Middleton hadn't gotten another call; he just needed time to concoct. Middleton struck Janzek as not the quickest guy on his feet, but someone who would need to craft a story, make sure it had no holes in it before he put it out there.

Janzek had been at his desk since five that morning, playing catch-up. Charleston was a small place, and Rhett had told him about how everybody knew everyone else's 'bidness.'

He figured it was time he learned a little more Charleston history. It might help him figure out where the bodies were buried. First thing he did was Google Rutledge Middleton III. What popped up first was an article about Middleton's connection to a man named Henry Reed, who seemed to be Charleston's answer to Bernie Madoff. Reed was a man who promised returns of twenty-five percent a year and, for a long time, delivered. But it turned out those returns were bogus: just incoming capital from new investors who had heard the scuttlebutt about this new financial visionary at some cocktail party and were falling all over each other to throw money at him. The article gave a list of prominent citizens who were, first, investors and later victims of Reed's scam. Rutledge Middleton was high on the list.

Back when the market tanked in 2008, the article said, many of Reed's investors had apparently panicked and tried to withdraw their capital. The first ones got out okay, but when it turned into a mass exodus, Reed ran out of cash. That's when it all fell apart and the feds came knocking on his door. Just as they were about to put him in handcuffs, the article stated, Reed checked into Roper Hospital, claiming that he was suffering from acute amnesia. If he couldn't remember his name or what he had for breakfast, Reed's attorneys had apparently advised him, how could he possibly know what happened to his clients' accounts? The feds just looked at Reed in disbelief like, *Really? This is how you're gonna play it?*

But Reed stuck to his guns and did a pretty convincing job of not having a clue who his wife was until one day he walked into his barn and blew his head off with a twelve gauge shotgun.

Janzek's cell phone rang, and he looked down at the number.

Finally. It was Middleton.

Middleton just started right in.

"I had to look up that guy you mentioned. Jefferson Davis," Middleton said, suddenly cooperative. "He was a guy who called and told me he got my name out of the Yellow Pages and needed a lawyer right away. Wanted to meet me, tell me about his case. So, I met him at a restaurant, and he said he was out on bail after getting arrested for drug possession" —sounded like Middleton was reading notes on an index card— "Told him I wasn't a litigator but could recommend one. He was appreciative, offered to pay me for my time, and that was it."

"So, let me get this straight," Janzek said, putting his feet up on his desk, "you went and met with this guy without asking him about his case beforehand?"

"Don't get pissy with me, Janzek. Sometimes I take on pro bono stuff," Middleton said. "He sounded like a candidate for that."

"How'd you determine that?" Janzek asked. "Because he was black?"

"I'll ignore that, and don't tell me how to do my job."

"I'm just asking. You trotted out to see this guy at a bar 'cause you were dying to help out your fellow man?"

"I don't need your sarcastic bullshit," Middleton said. "You asked, I'm telling. I had a twenty-minute conversation with him, and that was it."

Janzek swung his feet back down on the floor. "Did this guy, Jefferson Davis, have anything to eat?"

"What the hell kind of a question is that?"

"Just curious if was he lefty or a righty?"

No way a rightie would be sticking a gun out of the driver's side of the speeding Mercedes.

"No idea," Middleton said. "We didn't break bread together."

"Okay, thank you for your time. I ever need any free legal representation, I know where to go."

"Yeah, to hell." Middleton hung up.

Janzek was surprised the story was the best Middleton could come up with after having time to rehearse it.

Janzek had spent enough time with lawyers to know the first question out of their mouths was always something like, "What's the nature of your case?" Or, "What do you need me for?" They never took two steps out of their office without knowing exactly what they were getting into and how much they were going to charge for it.

Problem was, it wasn't something he could disprove or tie to the mayor's murder. He needed a lot more than a matchbook found in a dead man's car with Middleton's initials on it.

He was going over the conversation with Middleton again and didn't hear Delvin Rhett walk in.

"What's up?" Rhett said as he sat down.

Janzek put his feet back up on his desk and took a swig of luke-warm coffee. "Just had a conversation with my buddy, Rutledge Middeton."

"How'd that go?"

"'Bout what you'd expect," Janzek said, gesturing at his computer screen. "Article here's about how he got swindled out of two hundred fifty grand by some Ponzi guy."

Rhett took a pull on his coffee container and nodded. "Oh yeah, that guy Henry Reed," he said. "Just for the record, he never offed himself like it said in the report."

Janzek cocked his head and tilted his chair further back. "Really? How do you know that?"

"Well, not like I was at the scene or anything, but I just know. Guy didn't do it. Jimmie Driggers has a way of making the ME see things his way, even when it's pretty far-fetched."

Janzek leaned forward in his chair, and the two front legs hit the floor with a *thud*.

"Driggers caught that one, too?"

Rhett nodded.

"So what makes you think Reed didn't kill himself?"

Rhett stroked his chin.

"I'll tell you why. 'Cause a crime scene buddy of mine told me the angle of the gun was off. Meaning it was pointed down, hit Reed at about eye level. Half the buckshot ended up in his mouth."

Janzek nodded slowly. "Keep going."

"So, think about it," Rhett said. "No way he could have shot himself like that. I mean, would you ever take a heavy shotgun, bring it all the way up to eye level, and pull the trigger? No fucking way— you'd shoot upwards. Rest it on the floor or something. Not to mention, you'd have to have really long arms to even reach the trigger if you were holding it up like that."

Janzek was rocking back and forth now. "And?"

"He didn't, he was a short guy with short arms. Five-seven or so."

"And you never pointed this out to Brindle?"

"No, 'cause I screwed up. Made the mistake of asking Driggers about it instead," Rhett said, wincing a little, "I should have known better. I remember getting this look from him like, *Don't go playin' uppity nigger lookin' to prove yourself.* He didn't say that, but that's what his eyes were sayin'. Then he goes, in this really condescending tone, 'So, Delvin, you think someone snuck into Reed's barn, got a foot away from him, and blew him into the next county?'"

"Which was exactly what you were thinking, right?"

"Yeah, sure as hell seemed like it. Problem was I didn't have enough to go to Brindle with. I mean, what if the guy actually did pop himself, and I'm going around saying someone else did it. So now I'm this self-proclaimed expert, tellin' a guy who's been doin' it for twenty-five years that he's full of shit."

Janzek started nodding. "Yeah, I hear you," he said, "but your gut's telling you that's how it went down. Someone shot him close up?"

Rhett nodded, no hesitation. "That guy Reed made a lot of enemies."

Janzek's cell phone rang. He looked down and saw it was Middleton. Calling to apologize for telling him to go to hell, no doubt.

TWENTY

IT QUICKLY BECAME OBVIOUS THAT RUTLEDGE MIDDLETON WAS scrambling to do damage control. And that he could tell Janzek wasn't buying his story about going to meet with Davis. So, he was trying to spin it. Add a bunch of details to make it sound more plausible.

His revised edition—the one he had just told Janzek— was that he was going to Fuel anyway when Davis called. Claimed he was meeting his son there to try to talk him into going to law school. "Jesus," Janzek thought, "just what Charleston needed— a fuckhead like Quatro Middleton hanging his shingle at some law firm that hadn't checked him out." So, Middleton's story was that when Davis called and asked if he could meet with him, he figured he could kill two birds with one stone: see Davis after he had a heart-to-heart with his shit-for-brains son. The thing Janzek didn't buy at all was Middleton's spinning himself as a big-hearted guy out to help the little fellow. There were people who would be there in a jam, not looking for anything in return. Middleton was not one of them.

Janzek hung up with him and decided he needed to find out more about the man. Middleton was a long way from passing the smell test.

Best way he knew to get a read on someone was to follow them around for a while. See what a day in the life was like. He knew Middleton probably spent most of his days in his office, so he decided to see where he went after work. Maybe he had some dark secrets like the late mayor.

Middleton left his office at six o'clock and started walking north on Meeting Street.

Janzek was in an unmarked, white Dodge Charger. He turned the ignition key and followed Middleton up Meeting Street.

Two blocks up, Middleton walked into a three-story parking garage. Five minutes later, he drove out in a shiny black Audi 8000. But instead of the white button-down shirt and blue suit jacket Middleton was wearing before, he had changed into a blue linen shirt and a cream-colored suit with a stylishly narrow lapel. The man was gussied up for something.

Janzek followed him to a marina on Lockwood where Middleton got out of the car and walked toward a nearby gangplank. He no longer looked like a Tea Party lawyer but like a man going to a theme party where everyone was supposed to dress up like the late writer Tom Wolfe.

Janzek watched from his car as Middleton walked up the gangplank onto the biggest yacht in the marina. It was sleek and shark-like and flew a South Carolina flag below a U.S. one. Janzek noticed a few other men, standing and having drinks, on the stern of the boat. Perched on a deck above them was a helicopter painted an elegant, avocado green. A tuxedo-clad man in his twenties was circulating around with flutes of champagne on a silver tray.

Janzek watched as a few more men parked their cars and walked up the gangplank in the center of the boat and went onboard. He was struck by the nattiness of all the men, and something told him he was watching a parade of Charleston's power elite with maybe a sprinkling of wannabes thrown in. Ten minutes later, the boat started moving.

Janzek reached into his pocket for his cell phone. He fished it out and dialed.

Rhett answered."S'up, Nick?"

"You got a boat, right?"

"Yeah, why?"

"At the marina on Lockwood?"

"Uh-huh. The S.S. *Minnow*."

"Can you get here in five?" Janzek said. "It's a beautiful night for a cruise."

"The hell you talking about?" Rhett said. "I got work to do."

Janzek looked over at the liquor store he had spotted driving in.

"This is work, trust me," Janzek said. "I'll get us a six at the packie down the street. Make it a working cruise."

IT WAS DARK NOW. JANZEK AND RHETT WERE BOBBING ON THE Ashley River, a hundred yards away from the big boat. Janzek was looking through Rhett's binoculars as his partner nursed his second beer. Janzek's unofficial count was that there were about twenty-five men on board. No women.

"I heard rumors before about the owner, Coley Donaldson," Rhett said. "Happily married, but..."

"But what?"

"A boyfriend or two on the side."

Janzek lowered the binoculars. "You got my full attention, Del. What else?"

"Like I told you, Charleston is a small town," Rhett said. "You hear lots of stuff. You know, around the water cooler. Most of it's bullshit, but... a party with all guys and no women, I dunno?"

Janzek nodded, raised the binoculars up to his eyes and sighted in Rutledge Middleton. Middleton's jacket was off now, and he was talking to an older man.

"Is that Donaldson?" Janzek asked. "Talking to Middleton."

He handed Rhett the binoculars.

"Yeah, that's him."

"So, what do you hear about Middleton? You know, around the water cooler."

"Not much," Rhett said, taking another pull of his beer. "Just that he's old Charleston, and a guy you don't want to piss off."

Janzek lowered the binoculars, turned to Rhett, and raised his shoulders. "Oh, now you tell me."

Rhett laughed.

"Here's my take on the guy," Janzek said. "He's a lot of things— some of 'em criminal maybe— but one thing I'm not pickin' up on is the gay vibe."

"I wouldn't know," Rhett said, gesturing toward the big boat. "But something tells me that at least a few dudes up there might swing that way."

"Yeah, could be," Janzek said. "Question is, what's Middleton doing there?"

"You got me. Maybe tryin' to rustle up some new clients."

"I don't know, man," Janzek said, looking through the binoculars again. "I'd say he's definitely tryin' to rustle up something."

TWENTY-ONE

Janzek was in his office the next morning still thinking about what Rutledge Middleton was doing out on the boat. What little he knew about the guy was that whatever he did seemed carefully calculated.

He and Rhett had just had a meeting with Ernie Brindle and Peter Pollack, the new mayor. Janzek had been in similar meetings before up in Boston where the purpose was to somehow jump-start an investigation on a high-profile case that was badly stalled and treading water. The intent of most meetings that brass called up north was to give them the chance to do their best Vince Lombardi impressions. Rip into the troops and give them a good, old-fashioned locker-room ream-out. Like they were five touchdowns down and they damn well better get their asses in gear or they'd embarrass the shit out of themselves. Then—fired up—the troops were supposed to charge out of the locker room and win one for the Gipper.

Janzek caught himself. He was mixing too many coaches in his lame football analogy.

But, as it turned out, he was wrong anyway. Brindle and the mayor didn't go down that road at all. Brindle basically just wanted to find out what Janzek and Rhett had so far. Unlike Janzek's bombastic, earth-scorching chief up in Boston, Brindle just listened closely and asked a few intelligent questions.

As for the mayor, he just looked bored as hell. Kept stifling yawns and looking at his watch like he had a hot date or a tee time out at the local course. Still, even though Pollack seemed like this was the last place on earth he wanted to be, Janzek got the sense he was taking it all in by the series of little nods he kept doing. Like if you quizzed him afterwards, he'd have total recall of the whole meeting.

Afterwards, Janzek went back into his office and got on his computer. He saw that he had gotten a hit on a guy he considered a person of interest. The man's name was Wayland Young, and he had once been picked up with Jefferson Davis, his first cousin, on a charge of armed robbery. The two had gotten off that time, but Young, who apparently subscribed to the theory that practice makes perfect, hadn't been so lucky the next time. He had just started a five-year bit at Charleston County Detention for armed robbery and assault. Before finding out that Young was in jail, Janzek had managed to get an address for him, but when he went there, all he found was a charred foundation and a yard full of two-foot weeds. He went and talked to neighbors at the surrounding houses, but no one knew what had become of Wayland. Seemed like they didn't really want to know.

Janzek had made a few calls to prison officials and was now on his way to see Wayland at the county jail.

The jailer led the way back to a cell that smelled of gamey body functions dueling it out with Lysol.

Wayland Young was a thirty-year-old black man dressed like it was ten below instead of seventy-five in the shade. He was wearing a wool hat and a crusty, red parka. His face reflected life's many curve-balls, and was distinguished by a big, flattened-out nose and rheumy, yellow eyes. Like maybe he had a little Jamaican blood in him.

The jailer opened the door, and Janzek walked in.

Wayland was sitting on his bed. Janzek went over and leaned up against his stainless-steel sink.

He remembered the question the ME had asked him at the crime scene the day the mayor was killed. It was a good line, and he decided to borrow it.

"Goin' skiing, Wayland?"

Wayland gave him a look like he thought white guys had pretty gimpy senses of humor.

"My name's Nick Janzek, and I came here to see if I could make your quality of life a little better."

Wayland gave him a *yeah, right* look.

"You and your cousin," Janzek said. "I understand you guys were tight?"

"Which one?" Wayland asked, scratching his head.

"The dead one."

"That don't narrow it down much."

"Jefferson Davis."

Wayland didn't say anything.

"Let me lay it out for you, Wayland. I'll scratch your back if you scratch mine."

Wayland looked unfamiliar with the expression. Or maybe thought it had gay overtones.

"You tell me something Jefferson told you that helps me, and I put in a good word for you."

Janzek tapped the sink a few times and watched Wayland think.

"Okay," Janzek said, "let me put it in the form of a specific question: What did Jefferson tell you about runnin' down the mayor?"

Nothing.

Janzek pushed off of the sink and headed for the cell door. "Well, nice talkin' to you."

"Hang on, man. He tol' me he boosted a Mercedes to clip the mayor 'cause the guy was shankin' some dude's wife."

Janzek took a second to process that sentence, then turned back to Wayland and gave him a skeptical look.

"Let me ask you another question. You know how to read?"

Wayland looked offended. "Don't go insultin' me. 'Course I do."

Janzek nodded. "That's what I thought, 'cause you been readin' the newspapers, haven't you? Reporter speculating how the mayor's murder went down. Last chance, Wayland."

Wayland scratched his head again.

"Jefferson didn't tell you anything, did he," Janzek said, more a statement than a question.

Wayland just stared back blankly. Janzek turned to go, then looked back.

"Oh, and by the way... you should give it a rest."

Wayland blinked. "What you talkin' about?"

"Armed robberies ain't workin' for you, my brutha. When you get out, you oughta go into a new line of work."

At first, he thought going to see Young had been a complete waste of time. But then he thought again and realized it gave him a reason to go badger Rutledge Middleton yet again.

TWENTY-TWO

MIDDLETON CALLED NED CARLINO.

Carlino answered a lot of calls with questions. "How you doing on our little math problem, Rut?"

"That's exactly what I'm calling about." A bead of sweat inched down Middleton's chin. "There are a couple of happily married men on the city council. Only they're... not."

"You're being a little too oblique for me, Rut," Carlino said. "Break it down, simple English."

"Okay. I was out on Coley Donaldson's boat. It was a party for rich, old guys and young, good-looking guys. Know what I mean?"

"Hey, Rut, I don't have all day."

"Okay, I'll cut to the chase," Middleton said. "Turns out two married guys on the council have a thing for young guys."

"Really? Two?" Carlino sounded downright jubilant all of a sudden. "I knew I could count on you. Could be our fifth and six votes, huh?"

"Exactly what I was thinking," Middleton said. "Might be a job for your young English friend. He did a hell of a job getting Mona Tregalas to see the light."

"I'm looking up his number as we speak," Carlino said. "What were you doin' out on Donaldson's boat, anyway?"

"Cheap bastard got me out there to answer a bunch of legal questions for free," Middleton said, chuckling. "Or, for all I know, maybe he thought he could lure me out of the closet."

"Sounds like you were the only straight guy there," Carlino said, looking down at Trajan's number. "So tell me, what are the names of our two new casino backers?"

JANZEK DECIDED TO SHOW UP AT MIDDLETON'S OFFICE unannounced. Screw it, he thought, it beat calling the guy five times until he finally called back with some cocked-up story.

Middleton's receptionist was frosty. "Sorry, sir, but Mr. Middleton is all booked up today."

Janzek gave her a smile he had a pretty good track record with. "I just want to see him for ten minutes," he said, "quick and painless."

"Sorry, he could see you next Friday at eight thirty."

So much for the smile that had opened doors in the past. "Miss—"

"Ms.," she corrected him. "Ragsdale."

"Ms. Ragsdale," he said, stepping it up. "I'm not looking to make a dentist's appointment here... tell him I need to see him."

She glared back at him.

"I'm not going to let you just barge in on him."

Janzek held up his hands. "Okay, then how 'bout... could I trouble you for a piece of paper?"

She frowned, then reached to a stack of computer paper and handed him a sheet.

"I s'pose you need a pen too?"

Janzek reached into his breast pocket, pulled out his trusty Fineliner, and started writing.

"If you'd be so kind as to walk this into him," he said as he finished the quick note, then signed his name at the bottom of the piece of paper.

He looked up and caught her trying to read it upside down. He folded it up.

"Do you have a spare envelope, Ms. Ragsdale?"

She reached into the top drawer of her desk, got an envelope, and handed it to him.

"Thank you," he said, stuffing the piece of paper into the envelope and licking the edge. He sealed it, then wrote in big, blocky letters, *Rutledge A. Middleton III, Esquire.*

Ms. Ragsdale walked it in, then came back out a few minutes later and said Middleton would see him, but he needed to "make it quick."

Middleton didn't look up when Janzek walked in. He had Janzek's note in front of him.

It read, *I saw you out on Mr. Donaldson's boat and have a question or two.*

"What do you want?" Middleton said. "I've been very tolerant of your frequent intrusions, but it's getting to the point—"

"How about a nice, 'Have a seat, Detective, take a load off.' Where's that Southern hospitality *y'all* are so famous for?"

Middleton flicked his hand toward a chair. Janzek sat down.

"Okay, I'll get right to it. I had a long conversation with a man by the name of Wayland Young."

Janzek studied Middleton for a reaction.

Nothing.

"Wayland, as you may know, is the cousin of the man who ran down Mayor McCann—"

"Wait a minute," Middleton held up his hands, "Not only do you not have anyone in custody for the mayor's death, but you also have no definitive proof that it was anything other than an accident."

"You know that's bullshit," Janzek said. "I just had a nice, long chat with this guy Wayland at Charleston Detention. He told me—quote-unquote—Jefferson 'boosted a Mercedes and clipped the mayor 'cause some lawyer paid him to.' So I said to Wayland, 'some lawyer?' And he goes, 'Yeah, Middleburg or something.'" Janzek smoothed out his pants. "I think that might be close enough for a jury."

"You know, Janzek, you kill me. Until you got here, we had a police department that operated by the book. They'd go around, gather up their evidence, make a case, and put the bad guy behind bars. But you go around hassling people, making absurd accusations with absolutely no evidence."

"I got a book of matches that says you hired Jefferson Davis to hit —and I use the word literally—the mayor of Charleston."

"Okay, then, tell you what you do: You take your little book of matches to the DA and see if he wants to come after me. Let's see if you can make your little half-assed claim stick. Come on, Janzek, go ahead—do it."

"Just out of curiosity, what *were* you doing out on that boat the other night, Mr. Middleton?"

Middleton just shook his head and scowled. "So, I guess you don't want to talk about the DA anymore? 'Cause you know you ain't got squat," Middleton said with a sneer. "That boat—in case you didn't know—is owned by a man by the name of Coley Donaldson. He and I are good friends who go way back. You'll find out if you ask around, he's a very powerful man around here. The kind of man who eats guys like you for breakfast."

Janzek looked at his watch. "Well, thank you, Mr. Middleton, that's all very interesting. I promised Ms. Ragsdale I would only take ten minutes of your time, and the last thing I want to do is upset her. But... you can be sure I'll be getting back to you very soon."

He walked out of Middleton's office, thinking that if he was a boxing referee, he'd have to give that round to Middleton.

TWENTY-THREE

TRAJAN CHECKED OUT THE GIRLS IN THE COLLEGE OF Charleston library and decided they were just as advertised: about the best-looking women on any campus he'd ever been to. He had heard that out of the entire student body, only 40 percent were guys. Which meant that the place was 60 percent female. Which was obviously pretty awesome if you were a guy.

He had just clicked off with Ned Carlino when he saw a kid come out of the Java City snack bar in the library and saunter across the vast room. The kid looked like a cross between Ashton Kutcher and the young guy from *The Office,* whose name he couldn't remember.

Trajan pushed himself out of the thick leather chair he was sitting in and walked up to the kid.

"Yo," he said.

The kid's eyes met Trajan's.

"Got a minute?" Trajan asked. "Like to talk to you."

"Sure," the kid said. "What about?"

"My name's Trajan. I work for a modeling agency." He handed the kid a card that said his name, number, and *High Fly Modeling*

Agency at the top. "We're on the lookout for new talent. Would you be interested?"

"Sure," the kid said. "Awesome."

"Cool. What's your name?"

"Matt."

"Okay, Matt, here's what we're doing. This Thursday at six, me and another guy from my company are having tryouts at our office over on East Bay. Can you make it?"

"Sure, that's cool," Matt said. "What do we need to do?"

"Nothing, really; we're just gonna want to take some pictures, see how photogenic you are."

Matt nodded. "Pays pretty good, right?"

"Anywhere from a hundred to three hundred an hour if we sign you up."

"Whoa," Matt said, rearing back, "awesome."

"Perfect, so we'll see you Thursday at six. The address is on my card."

Matt looked at it and nodded. "Awesome, see you then, man."

Trajan smiled at the kid and realized he better get used to hearing the word 'awesome' in every sentence.

TWENTY-FOUR

CARLINO NEEDED A BAGMAN. POLLACK HAD CALLED HIM A couple times and asked him where his hundred-thousand-dollar "campaign donation" was. Problem was, Carlino had gone back up to Philadelphia for a few days. He was walking around his office on the top floor of the Hammersmith building on Pennsylvania Square, which had a jaw-dropping view of the city in three directions. His wife, the long-suffering Janice Carlino, was waiting for her husband out in the reception area.

Carlino thought for a moment, then dialed Middleton.

As he waited for Middleton to pick up, he kicked himself again for paying Pollack more than he probably had to. He figured he could have been able to get away with just fifty thousand. But then he soothed himself with the thought that the difference was only a day's worth of profit at the casino.

"Hi, Ned," Middleton answered.

"Hey, Rut. I forgot to tell you, the mayor and I had a meeting of the minds. All we need to do now is make a little delivery to him. I'm going to let you be in charge of that."

"Sure, no problem, I'll take care of it," Middleton said.

"The fewer people in the loop, the better. Think you can handle it?"

"Yes, of course, Ned."

"Good," Carlino said. "So now that the mayor and Mona Tregalas are on the team, we got four down, two to go. I got my guy Trajan on the case of those two nancy boys who were out on the boat."

Middleton did his little *heh-heh-heh* laugh. Nancy boys, he'd never heard that one before. "That Trajan does a hell of a job, huh?" Middleton said.

"Yup, never failed me yet," Carlino said, watching a helicopter fly by at eye level a few hundred feet from his office. "I want to get this vote out of the way so we can get going, start building the goddamn casino."

"I hear you."

"All right, so let's wrap it up this week."

"I'm on it," Middleton said.

"Okay, keep me posted."

"Will do."

Middleton hung up and flashed to Janzek, the only possible fly in the ointment.

Then he had a thought. If he could somehow manage to get Janzek to the top of some really rich, powerful guy's shit list, maybe the guy could exert enough leverage to get Janzek fired from the police department.

The more he thought about it, the more he thought Coley Donaldson might just be the man. Donaldson had a reputation for vendettas, after all. Like the time he got a cop abruptly terminated for arresting him on a DUI. Poor guy never knew what hit him.

Middleton looked up Donaldson's office number and dialed it. He got ready to work his way up the ladder to get to the great man himself. First, the receptionist. Then, his assistant. Then, maybe a detour to the troubleshooter. Then, finally, to Donaldson himself.

The troubleshooter was a guy named Teddy Burns. Donaldson

probably paid Teddy a couple hundred thousand a year just to make low- and mid-level decisions for him. The shit Donaldson couldn't be bothered with. Middleton figured Donaldson had it all set up so he didn't have to talk to anybody he didn't want to.

It was usually fifty-fifty that Middleton would get through to Donaldson when he called him. Not that he called him a lot.

But those times when he did get through, Donaldson faked it, made it seem like they were best friends. Well, they had gone to Porter-Gaud together back in high school. Donaldson graduated from there and went on to Yale, Middleton to Clemson.

This time Donaldson picked up.

"Hey, Rutledge," Donaldson said. "How ya' doin,' old buddy?"

"Real good, Coley," Middleton said, "thanks for taking my call"— like he was on with some radio talk-show guy. "That was fun out on the boat. Hey, just wanted to let you know"—he lowered his voice —"there's this new detective in town, guy by the name of Nick Janzek, likes to nose around. Anyway, he knew all about the cruise the other night."

Silence. Like they had been cut off.

Then: "I don't really know why you're bringing this to my attention, Rutledge." Donaldson's tone had just done a complete one-eighty.

"Well, I just thought..." He was scrambling now. "He's a guy from up in Boston."

"I don't give a shit if he's from fucking Turkistan. The hell's that got to do with anything?" Then Donaldson went off on him. "So, let me get this straight. You're implying that I should be worried that some detective knows I went on a boat ride with some friends? Is that it, Rutledge?"

"No, I just—"

"You just what? Are you suggesting I have something to be ashamed of? Is that what this is about? Well, I can assure you, if that's what you're thinkin', you're badly mistaken. And if either you or some fucking detective from Boston doesn't like it—well, then, fuck

him, fuck you, fuck 'em all—" then his tone went back to courtly—
"Anything else on your mind... old buddy?"

"No, I guess not, Coley. I didn't mean to—"

Click.

Middleton had heard Donaldson had a temper but had no idea
that he turned into such a raving f-bomber when he got pissed.

He suddenly felt like the world's punching bag.

He decided to call Jimmie Driggers. Take his frustration out on
him. Middleton had put Driggers on the payroll a year before the
mayor was killed. He had told Driggers about the mayor's love shack
on Grove Street, having heard about it from a client whose wife had
been entertained by the mayor there. His client had had a PI bird-dog
his wife around.

Back then, Jimmie Driggers had gone up to Grove Street with the
intention of breaking in, find out what he could. But, it turned out, he
didn't need to break in. There was an unlocked window on the
ground floor. Driggers spent a half hour there one afternoon when he
knew Mayor McCann was at a city council meeting. He found what
he was looking for right away. A cell phone was sitting on top of a
cable TV box. He suspected the mayor might have at least two cell
phones. This was probably the one he didn't want his wife to know
about. He turned it on and pushed *contacts*. Sixteen names popped
up— all women. He looked around and found a stack of business
cards in the top drawer of a dresser. Among the cards were two real-
tors, an attorney, a decorator, an antiques dealer, and the head of the
Historic Charleston Foundation. All of them were women.

Driggers then spent the better part of the next three months
monitoring the comings and goings of women at 201 Grove Street
from across the street in his unmarked, white Impala. He ran the
license plates of the mayor's visitors, dug around a little, and found
out that ten out of the sixteen women in the mayor's secret cell phone
were married. He checked into all of them. One of them was named
Erica Cannon. Her husband caught Driggers's attention.

Driggers's cell phone rang and he answered.

"You come up with another pigeon for the mayor's murder yet?" Middleton asked. "I mean, that first guy was fuckin' pathetic."

"I know, I know," Driggers said. "It's not that easy, Mr. Middleton."

Driggers, five years older than Middleton, had made the mistake of calling him by his first name when they first met. Middleton quickly made it clear that was in no way acceptable; he was Mr. Middleton. No cop was ever going to be calling him by his first name.

"I actually think I may have found the perfect guy," Driggers said. "Name's Pat Cannon. His wife was one of the women doing— ah, having sex with— the mayor. So, the scenario is this: her husband —this guy Cannon— finds out about their affair, gets crazy jealous, then goes out, gets drunk, and on the spur of the moment runs down the mayor."

Middleton had to think about it for a second. "I don't like it," he said. "Doesn't sound any better than your first fiasco with that Terhune guy."

"Wait, hang on," Driggers said, "hear me out—"

"Well, hurry the hell up."

"Okay," Driggers said. "First of all, the guy's got motive. The mayor's doin' his wife. And two, the guy's got a record. Nothing major, but a couple of misdemeanors. Started a fight in a bar back in 2011, then another time, punched out a guy from a towing company who put a boot on his car. Used to work for that company Blackbaud but got fired when his boss read about him in the paper. And three, the clincher: He's got a five-year-old black Mercedes five hundred."

Middleton thought for a second.

"Okay," he finally said, "I guess it might work. But this time, don't go screwin' it up, huh?"

"Don't worry."

"I worry," Middleton said. "What's the guy's name again?"

"Pat Cannon."

Middleton did his little *heh-heh-heh*. "I think you mean... *Patsy* Cannon."

TWENTY-FIVE

TRAJAN WAS SITTING ON A BENCH IN A BEAUTIFUL, HISTORIC courtyard of the College of Charleston campus between Calhoun and George Streets.

He still couldn't get over it. One hot chick after another.

But he wasn't there for the girls.

He stood up when he saw a guy coming toward him on an orange skateboard. The guy had a three-day growth, blond, shaggy hair, and a finely chiseled face.

Trajan shot up from the bench and put up his hand.

"Hey, dude," he said. "Got a minute?"

The guy hopped off his skateboard.

"Sure, what's up?"

"Name's Trajan," he said, putting his hand out.

The kid shook it.

"Matt," the kid said.

Christ, was everyone named Matt at this college? Trajan wondered.

"I work for a modeling company and we're looking to sign up some new talent."

Matt smiled a big, goofy, surfer-dude smile.

"Really, so what do I have to do?"

"Nothin', man, just look pretty," Trajan said, handing Matt his card. "We're having interviews next Thursday at our office. We'll want to take some pictures too. You doing anything around six?"

"I was," Matt said, reading the card, "but not anymore. This is where we go? One-fourteen East Bay?"

Trajan nodded. Matt beamed. He was like an eight-year-old kid who had just spotted a big, red Schwinn under the Christmas tree.

"Awesome," Matt said, giving Trajan a fist bump, "first GQ, then Hollywood, right?"

Dream on, Trajan thought, as Matt number two got on his skateboard and sailed off down the brick pathway.

TWENTY-SIX

Janzek and Rhett were at a bar on America Street at eight at night. Janzek was the only white guy there. He had taken a shine to a local microbrew called Coast and was down to his last sip.

Rhett had introduced him to the bartender, Calvin, and they'd just had a nice conversation with two guys sitting at the next table. Delvin had gone to high school with one of them. The other guy at the table asked Delvin who he liked in the USC game on Saturday. Before Delvin could answer, Janzek jumped in, "No question about it —Southern Cal, ten points over UCLA." The guy looked at him like he was an alien but explained patiently that—in this neck of the woods, anyway—USC meant University of South Carolina. You know, the Gamecocks. Then he added his reasons why the 'Cocks were going to "whoop-up" on poor Ole Miss.

"Yeah, let's hope they do," Janzek said limply, deciding to let Delvin field sports in the future.

They were talking to each other alone now. "So... took a few months off before you started here?" Rhett asked.

Janzek reached for his beer and took a long pull. "Well, kinda."

"Needed a little break, huh?"

"Yeah, my wife died, and..." Janzek didn't want to go there and slipped into a thousand-yard stare.

"What happened?"

"I developed a little drug problem, let's just say."

"But you were a super star up there."

Janzek chuckled and shook his head. "Where'd you get that?"

"Read it."

"Don't believe everything you read."

"Come on, Nick, you had a solid gold sheet. Brindle told me."

Janzek just took a sip of his beer.

"How long?" Rhett asked.

"How long what?"

"How long 'til you got clean?"

"Too long."

Rhett chuckled. "You're not a very easy interview, Nick. Hey, what about Whitey Bulger and your old man?"

"What about 'em?"

"See what I mean."

Janzek sighed. "Okay... Whitey had my old man shot. Or maybe did it himself."

Rhett—in mid sip—stopped. "Jesus. Really?"

Janzek nodded. "Yup. And that's all I know so don't ask me any more questions. I was only sixteen." He was eager to change the subject. "We got a hell of a lot of moving parts on our case. First, we got Middleton but no apparent motive. Not like his wife had a thing with the mayor."

"Yeah, she was too busy with the golf pro."

"We don't know that for a fact," Janzek said. "But could be that Middleton had something to do with the Madoff wannabe you told me about, the guy who caught the load of buckshot in the face."

"Could be."

"Best thing we got on him are his initials on that matchbook."

"Yeah, the Jefferson Davis link."

Janzek nodded as he watched Delvin kill what was left of his white wine.

"The brothers all right with you drinkin' that pinot grigio shit?"

Rhett laughed. "Gotta admit they look at me a little funny. Like how my friend looked at you when you were talking USC beating UCLA."

Janzek leaned closer. "Hey, Delvin, I got news for you... USC—in the other forty-nine states anyway—means University of Southern California."

"Maybe so, but you're in the Palmetto State, my man."

"Yeah," Janzek said, patting Rhett's arm, "but where I come from, we don't have to share our professional football team with another state."

"You're brutal, man," Rhett said, then looking away, "So you think...what...Middleton is like the tip of the iceberg? A front man or something?"

Janzek was nodding before Rhett got the whole question out. "Yeah, that's exactly what I think. He's in the equation, for sure, but not the brains. My gut's telling me there're a lot of people in the mix here. Thing just feels like a monster gangbang. Trick is to work our way up the food chain, figuring Middleton's definitely not the guy on top."

Janzek started peeling the Budweiser coaster that his beer was sitting on.

"'Cause if he was the guy on top," Janzek went on, "we'd be closing in on him by now. Hey, I'm not too worried, never been a first-forty-eight-hour guy anyway."

"Good," Rhett said. "'Cause we're into the second week now."

Janzek now had the Budweiser coaster peeled down to *weiser*. "So, I gotta ask you a few things about your little town here," he said. "I been here almost two weeks and I'm still trying to figure the place out."

"Takes a while," Rhett said. "So, what's the question?"

"Okay, first, what's all the noise about oysters?"

Rhett squinted. "What do you mean?"

"Well, people 'round here treat 'em like they're sacred," Janzek said. "I can't stand the slimy little bastards. Look like..."

"What?"

"I don't how, like what someone hawked on the sidewalk."

"Oh, that's pretty, Nick."

"Plus, you gotta work your ass off to get that shit out of the shell."

Rhett shook his head. "I hear ya there. Me? I can take 'em or leave 'em."

"Okay, another one," Janzek said, leaning closer to Rhett. "When someone says south of Broad, that basically means where the rich people live, right?"

"Yeah," Rhett said, "and white as vanilla ice cream."

"And what's with all the horse-drawn carriages? That gets old pretty fast. All that *clippity-clop* and horse shit all over the place."

"Supposed to be quaint, Nick."

Janzek shook his head.

"'Nother one... so I'm walkin' down the sidewalk last Sunday and this guy, out of the blue, says, 'Good afternoon, sir,' and tips his hat. And I'm thinking, *o-kay*? Then the next block this old lady looks up at me and says, 'Beautiful day,' and almost curtsies. I'm thinking, what the hell do they want from me and clamp my hand on my wallet."

Rhett beat the table with his hand. "That's classic, man," he said. "What can I tell ya', just Charleston folks being friendly. Just the way we are. Not like you prune-ass Yankees."

"It got me all suspicious, like, what the hell are they after?"

"Get over yourself, Nick," Rhett said. "Hey, you run across Bob Doyle yet? He lives in your neck of the woods."

"The actor Bob Doyle?"

"Yeah, him. He lives here. Matter of fact, I saw him walking down King Street the other day in his pajamas," Rhett said. "Guy's kinda out there, I hear."

"No shit. I'll keep an eye out for him."

"Yeah, you'll see him around. Not exactly the Hollywood type.

Owns the Riverdogs"—the minor league baseball team— "and supposedly has a company buyin' up half the real estate in town on the down-low. Company's called Elyod Realty."

"What kinda name is that?"

"His last name spelled backwards."

Rhett finished off his wine and stood up.

"Where ya' goin'?" Janzek asked.

"After that shit you gave me about drinking pinot grigio, I'm getting me a *man's* drink."

"Okay, whatever it is... get me one too."

Rhett was back in a few minutes with two martini glasses. He handed one to Janzek.

"Thanks, but I'm not exactly a martini kind of guy."

"This is not exactly a martini."

"Looks exactly like one. Olive and all."

"Come on," Rhett said, "just try it."

Janzek eyeballed it, put it up to his lips, and took a sip.

He nodded, then took another one.

"Not bad," he said. "What the hell is it?"

"A Charleston Dirty," Rhett said. "Bombay gin, vermouth, and oyster juice."

Janzek winced and pushed it away. "Oh, Christ, why didn't you tell me?"

"Hey, you said you liked it."

A group of three black guys walked in. Blue-collar, working class guys. Construction or maybe from the big Boeing plant a few miles to the north.

Janzek saw Rhett look over.

"See that big guy with the baseball cap?" he whispered.

Janzek nodded.

"That's Jefferson Davis's brother," Rhett said. "Name's Ronnie."

Janzek took the man in. Broad shoulders, looked fit. Intelligent too.

"Looks like he took a different road from his brother. Job, wife, kids, the whole nine?"

Rhett nodded. "Pretty much. There was a third brother—"

"Was?"

Delvin nodded.

"Jesus, the poor parents," Janzek said, shaking his head. "Two out of three."

"I know. Different father, though," Delvin said. "The mother's a real sweetheart. The third brother, the oldest, was the star. Got a full boat to Annapolis, played football there. Ended up in Iraq, a major in the Marines at like twenty-seven. Got killed by a land mine over there."

"Christ," Janzek said, grabbing Delvin's empty glass. "Married? Kids?"

"No kids. Wife, though," Rhett said. "A white chick from an old Charleston family. I can pretty much guarantee you, them getting married and all didn't sit too well with the south of Broad crowd."

"I hear you. What was her name?"

"Name *was* Maybank," Rhett said. "Geneva Maybank. Her married name is Crane. The brother she married was Marcus Crane."

It clicked.

"*Ho-ly shit,*" Janzek said. "I met her. She was the one on our list, owns the bookstore."

"Oh yeah, you're right. I never put it together," Rhett said. "Damn, that chick's a dime."

Janzek nodded.

"Yeah, ol' Marcus did all right for his black-ass self."

Janzek nodded. "Goddam Iraq. What a waste of good soldiers." He shook his head and stood up, his martini glass in one hand and Rhett's in the other.

"'Nother Charleston Dirty?" he asked. "My new favorite drink."

"Fuck, yeah," Rhett said and smiled. "Brothers gonna love it."

"What's that?"

"You waitin' on me and all. My very own Stepin Fetchit."

TWENTY-SEVEN

Out of the twenty-two kids who Trajan had given his card out to, twenty showed up at the recently leased office of High Fly Models. Trajan had gotten a bartender from a site called *Go Charleston* for twenty bucks an hour. The bartender was making a lot of things like Scotch and coke, and bourbon and Red Bull. It was not a group of seasoned, sophisticated drinkers.

The main thing, though, was the bar was fully stocked and the boys all looked eager.

The surfer-looking Matt came up to Trajan with a beer in his hand.

"Trajan, my man," he said, lassoing Trajan with a high five. "'S up, dude?"

"Hey, Matt, welcome. It is Matt, right?"

"Yup," he said. "Hey, I met Mr. Mellor, your southeastern coordinator. He took a few snaps of me."

Joe Mellor had a very impressive card that identified himself as *Vice President-Southeastern Coordinator* of High Fly Models. Below it was his number, then *Los Angeles. Philadelphia. Charleston.*

"That's great," Trajan said, "so what happens next is Joe and I make our recommendations, then email out photos to our guys in the L.A. office. They ultimately make the final call on talent."

"Cool," Matt said, sweeping the blond hair out of his eyes. "So, when do we find out?"

Trajan took a pull of his Black Label on the rocks.

"Couple days," Trajan said, seeing the cute college girl he had picked up, approaching.

"Hey, Shawna," he said, taking her in, "you look—" he started to say *hot*— "fabulous."

"Thanks," Shawna said.

He could see Matt thought so too.

"Oh... ah...Shawna, this is Matt."

Matt put his fist out to her for a bump.

"Hey," he said.

She ignored his fist. "You're in English 305 with me."

"Oh yeah, right," Matt said, nodding. "I knew you looked familiar."

Trajan watched the guy who was a cross between Ashton Kutcher and the guy in *The Office* shuffle toward them.

"Hey, Trajan," the kid said, putting out his hand to do an old-fashioned shake, "cool party."

"Thanks, Matt. Oh... Shawna, this is Matt."

Shawna shot the second Matt vampy eyes and nodded. "Spanish class," she said.

"Yeah, I know," Matt said. "Hola."

Trajan smiled up at Shawna and decided that both she and the second Matt were keepers.

TWENTY-EIGHT

QUATRO MIDDLETON WAS CRUISING THE EAST SIDE OF Charleston in his beloved Mustang. The east side was what people called 'in transition,' but there were still a lot of abandoned, falling down houses and high crime areas. Quatro had driven the mean streets plenty of times before, trying to score weed, which had always been easy, but now his mission was a different one: He was in the market for a big, scary-looking black dude. He pulled up to two guys in their twenties sitting on the front steps of a run-down, two-story building that had a distinct right-to-left lean to it and trash strewn all over the front yard. He rolled down his window.

"One of you dudes want to make a quick fifty?"

The one with an Afro comb stuck into the side of his do jumped up and started coming toward him.

"Get your faggot cracker ass outta here, motherfuckah."

Quatro started to explain but gunned it instead.

He drove over to Nassau Street and saw a big, heavy guy shuffling along the sidewalk like he was just walking, no particular destination in mind. Quatro pulled up next to him.

"Yo," he said.

The guy was about forty and had holes in his jeans that weren't meant to be stylish.

"Hey, man, how'd you like to make fifty bucks in an hour doin' nothing?"

If the guy thought Quatro was propositioning him, he didn't show it. Or care.

He walked up to the Mustang and cast a large shadow over it.

"What do I gotta do?"

"Hop in, my brother, and I'll fill you in."

Quatro knocked on the door of the duplex building on Pitt Street and turned to the big guy behind him.

"You ready, Lindale?"

Lindale nodded and looked appropriately scary.

A girl Quatro had never seen before opened the door. He brushed past her, Lindale right behind him.

"Hey, wait—"

"Where's Chelsea?" Quatro asked.

Chelsea Watson, the woman he was accused of raping, was watching TV in the living room with a Mac in her lap.

She looked terrified at seeing the two; her eyes darted away from Quatros'.

Quatro turned to the other girl who had followed them in. "Get the fuck outta here."

She beelined out the front door.

Quatro turned to Chelsea who was shaking like a pine tree in a stiff wind.

"Don't worry," Quatro said with a cruel smile, "nothing's gonna happen to you... unless, of course, you don't do what I say."

Quatro turned to Lindale, who stepped forward.

"If you don't," Lindale said, "I be payin' you a visit ina middle of the night. Nobody likes it much when I come through their window at two a.m."

Quatro was particularly proud of the lines he had come up with for Lindale.

"So whaddaya say, Chels, we gonna let bygones be bygones?" Quatro asked.

She stared at him, fear and hatred in her eyes.

"Just leave me alone, please," she said. "I'll tell 'em I was drunk and made it all up."

Quatro flashed the cruel smile again, an expression he had picked up from his father.

"Exactly what I was gonna tell you to say."

He took two steps toward her, leaned down, and kissed her hard on the lips.

"I think we have an understanding," he said.

She couldn't get any words out.

He turned and walked out. Lindale lumbered along behind him. His job was done.

TWENTY-NINE

Mayor Pollack had gotten a key and a note in a FedEx envelope.

The note said, *Go to locker 65 in the MUSC men's locker room. The combination is 1-5-7.*

Not that Pollack needed to justify it, but he had actually kind of come around on the casino, thought it would be a good thing for Charleston. It was going to be a pretty classy operation from the plans that Monarch had presented, not to mention all the jobs it was going to create. Some six hundred of them. Plus, all the taxes the casino was going to pay. In fact, Charleston was pretty damn lucky to get it. It could have gone to Charlotte, after all, and Savannah was doing their damnedest to get in on the running.

Then he thought about all the medical care that his autistic son required and the fact that his wife, Marlene, had a major jones for designer dresses and diamonds. Come to think of it... when it came to the casino, there really wasn't much to think about.

He paid fifteen bucks at the front desk to get a one-day pass for the MUSC gym. He went into the massive cardio room and spent six and a half minutes on the treadmill, which got him huffing and puffing pretty hard on account of his three-pack-a-day Marlboro habit. Might as well get something for the fifteen bucks, he figured.

He saw a few people check him out. He wasn't sure whether it was because they recognized him as the mayor or because he was wearing khakis, a chemise Lacoste, and his snappy new white bucks on the treadmill. After getting off it, dripping sweat, he asked for directions to the men's locker room. His heart was beating faster, both from the walking machine and the anticipation about what awaited him in locker number 65. As he fumbled with the combination lock, he wondered how many times his mayoral predecessor had been in the position of accepting largesse from well-heeled taxpayers.

Probably never, Pollack thought with disgust. McCann was such a flaming straight arrow. Except with the broads, of course.

Finally, he got all three numbers lined up. *1-5-7*. Only a nine was missing from the year that he was born poor, the son of an inconsequential nobody from nowheresville, North Carolina.

The lock snapped open, and he pulled open the door. A worn gym bag sat there. In faded white letters right below the rusted zipper, it said *Porter-Gaud*, the tony, private day school in West Ashley where he couldn't afford to send his kids. Until now, anyway. He grabbed the handle and slid the bag out.

He walked out of the locker room, passing several naked, blubbery bodies that didn't look to be in much better shape than him.

He walked outside and went down into the garage below. He got into his CR-V and looked around. Nobody. He opened the zipper and saw two neatly folded white towels on top.

He lifted up one of the towels. Below it, in large stacks, were hundred-dollar bills. Twenty-four of them, to be exact, six across and four high.

For a few moments, Pollack simply ogled the beautiful green stacks, which smelled vaguely of sawdust. As he patted one of them, he decided this was a little secret he didn't need to share with Marlene.

THIRTY

TRAJAN AND THE SECOND MATT WERE AT A BAR ON UPPER KING Street. It was the day after the cocktail party at the makeshift offices of High Fly Models.

Trajan had previously gone through all of the photos of the guys from the college with Joe Mellor after everyone left the party.

He and Joe had ruled out the first Matt–the surfer– because he was kind of goofy and clearly as heterosexual as Trajan was. There were a couple of obvious gay guys who had come to the party. Nice guys, Trajan thought, but none of them quite fit the bill. Then there was a contingent of hard-to-tells.

But, as Joe had pointed out, you didn't have to be gay to be a hustler. Look at that guy in *Midnight Cowboy,* Joe said, but Trajan had no idea what he was talking about since the movie was way before his time.

They had narrowed the field down to two. They had decided that Trajan would be the one to sign them up.

Trajan looked across at Matt the surfer and told him he was sorry to have to tell him, but he hadn't made the cut as a model. Matt took it quite stoically. Wasn't like his life depended on it, he said.

"But," Trajan said, "here's the good news and, hopefully, it might be of interest to you."

Matt leaned forward in his chair.

"We also have this little side business." He had to tread lightly at this point. One kid had punched him in the face a year ago when Trajan told him what he wanted him to do. "You know how on Facebook you have friends?"

Matt nodded. That was the first step: get 'em nodding.

"Well, we have a similar concept. It's called 'companions.'"

Matt nodded again.

"For a fee, ranging from one hundred to two hundred dollars, we pay a 'companion' to attend a social event or dinner or whatever it may be, with what we call a 'sponsor.'"

Trajan paused. Matt hadn't registered a frown or any other form of discontent with the suggested arrangement so far.

In fact, Matt seemed seriously interested. Trajan could tell because he heard Matt start tapping his foot under the table when he mentioned the money.

"Now, whatever happens after the social event, dinner, or whatever—what we call the 'rendezvous'— well, that's entirely between the companion and the sponsor. It's none of our business. It's a free country, after all."

"Sounds good," Matt said. "Where do I sign up?"

"You just did—" just one more little hurdle—"but just to make sure we're on the same page... you'd be good with either a female *or* a male companion, right?"

Matt went into rapid-blink mode.

"Ah—"

"We've been told that our sponsors— male and female alike— are very generous after the 'rendezvous.'"

Matt stopped blinking, but the tapping got faster and louder. Then he looked down, sighed, and looked back up. "Yeah, sure, count me in," he said.

Trajan slung his hand across the table.

"Welcome aboard, Matt! So, what are you doing this Thursday?"

THIRTY-ONE

Janzek had a uniform cop named John Bruns shadowing Rutledge Middleton. Bruns was parked right outside Middleton's office, trying not to nod off. Nothing happened the first day. Middleton got in at nine, went to a restaurant for lunch at 12:30, left at 5:45, went home.

But the second day, Middleton went to his parking garage just up the block on Queen Street and drove over the bridge to Route 17. Bruns followed him for twenty miles all the way down to a town called Harpersboro, where Middleton took a right on a back road, then went down a long, straight driveway with perfectly manicured live oak trees on either side of the driveway. Bruns wrote down the name that was emblazoned on a faded brass plaque at one of the two large pillars on the eight-foot-high stone wall that ran along the road for two hundred yards on either side.

Pinckney Hall. 1802 it said. Then below, in smaller letters: *911 Wade Hampton Road.*

Bruns had phoned Janzek as he tailed Middleton down Route 17 and then again after Middleton disappeared down the long driveway.

"Place looks like something out of an old movie. It's a plantation, I guess," Bruns said as he gave Janzek the address.

Janzek looked it up in a reverse directory and saw that it was owned by a man named Edward J. Carlino.

He Googled Carlino and spent the next two hours reading about him.

Turned out, he was All-World, first-string varsity.

A lawyer who had won a ton of high-profile cases in New York and Philadelphia and—judging by the cases—probably billed himself out at two grand an hour and got a hundred-thousand-dollar retainer.

Janzek figured that what he made in a year, Carlino probably made in a week.

The big question, Janzek wondered, was what was a heavy hitter like Carlino doing with Rutledge Middleton?

Janzek read on and found out that Carlino had won three big cases for what sounded like Philadelphia mob guys involved in a number of blue-collar and white-collar crimes. Not to mention him being defense attorney on four homicide cases. In another article, he found out that one of the homicides was a Tony Soprano-style, old-fashioned garroting. The names of the suspects were Salvatore "Bad Kitty" Carlino, Richard Carlino, and Frank Silvestre. Turned out Bad Kitty, Richard, and Frank were, respectively, Ned Carlino's uncle, brother, and cousin.

That was all he could find out about Carlino, but it was plenty, and his appetite was seriously whetted. Then he remembered something. He called up his former partner in Boston, Pete Schiff.

"Hey, man, it's me."

"Who the fuck is *me?*"

"Janzek."

"I know, just bustin' your balls," Schiff said. "What's doin' in Charlotte?"

"Charleston."

"I know, just bustin' your balls again."

"Okay, you busted my balls twice now, cut the shit," Janzek said. "What's the name of your FBI buddy who transferred down to Philly, specialized in fraud and white-collar shit?"

"You mean Doakes?"

"Yeah. What's his first name?"

"John."

"Got a number?"

"Hold on a sec," Schiff said. "Here you go. Two-one-five, nine-oh-one, four-three-four-four. That's his cell."

"Thanks, man," Janzek said, "I'll split the reward with you."

"Reward?" Schiff perked up.

"Just busting your balls."

JANZEK CALLED JOHN DOAKES AND GOT HIM RIGHT AWAY. THEY spent almost an hour on the phone. Doakes read him a DOJ document that revealed Carlino had a substantial interest in a thoroughbred racetrack outside of Philadelphia. Carlino had also been charged with bribing a public official— in this case, a Pennsylvania state senator. Reading between the lines, it was apparent that the payoff was to get the senator to wield his influence in getting slot machines at Carlino's track.

Doakes emailed him the document, along with a few others.

Janzek read it and found out that the bribery charge was ultimately dropped, the track got their slot machines, and Carlino and his partners sold the track for one hundred sixty-five million dollars a year later. Only two years before they had bought it for fifty million.

RUTLEDGE MIDDLETON, NED CARLINO, HENRY NEBLE, AND Caleb Prioleau were in the library of the main house at Pinckney. Middleton had proudly told the other three about leaving the hundred-thousand dollars in the Porter-Gaud gym bag for the mayor. Like he wanted to impress them how cloak-and-dagger it all was. But Carlino just looked at it as a lot of wasted effort. Why didn't he just go to the mayor's office and drop it off, or if he was going to do all the key business, why not put the bag in a safe deposit box at his bank, then get the key over to the mayor?

Then Neble chimed in. "Yeah, what were you trying to do, Rut, make it a scene out of a James Bond movie?"

Midddleton felt like bitch-slapping him.

The fourth man—Caleb Prioleau— was another guy Middleton had grown up with. He was from an old Charleston family and had inherited the family's insurance and construction company. He was a local guy who actually had real money. His company, Peninsula Construction, was going to get the contract to build the casino, and a huge contract it was going to be. Theoretically, the job was going to have three other companies bid it, but in reality, Prioleau's company already had it wrapped up. The quid pro quo was that Prioleau was going to smooth the way for the permitting process with his buddies in the building department once the casino got voted in.

Their business done, Middleton could see that Neble was itching to go down to the guesthouse and have a tumble with one of the girls. But then Prioleau, rich windbag he was, started jawing about "his movie." A subject they were all bored to death with.

"So, gentlemen," Prioleau said, like a father announcing the birth of a child, "Suzie and I wrapped the movie, and I've got a DVD of it for all of you."

Middleton and Neble tried to muster enthusiastic expressions. Carlino couldn't be bothered. He was a man who didn't need to fake anything anymore.

"The movie"—called *Beaufort*—was a pet project of Prioleau's and his wife, Suzie. It took place in Beaufort, South Carolina, seventy miles from Charleston, and was a semi-biography about the relationship between Prioleau's great-grandfather and a loyal, beloved black man who worked for him. It was meant to be an epic saga of the Old

South including duck hunting, cotton picking, slave lynching, and Prioleau's great-grandfather's apparent penchant for being a world-class wencher.

Prioleau opened a manila envelope and handed DVDs to the three others.

Carlino had read a thumbs-down preview of the movie and knew it was going to bomb.

"Thank you, Caleb," Carlino said. "I'm sure this will end up being a collector's item. I just hope that between the Sundance Film Festival and the Academy Awards you're going to have enough time to build me a nice hotel casino."

Carlino's sarcasm flew right over Prioleau's head.

Jeter, Carlino's butler, walked out of the kitchen. He was holding his hand over the mouthpiece of a wireless phone.

"Phone call, Mr. C," Jeter said. "Said his name is Detective Janzek, Charleston Police Department."

Carlino smiled at Middleton, who had perked up like a bird dog with a scent.

"This should be interesting," Carlino said.

Carlino motioned to Jeter to bring the phone over.

"Give him my best," Middleton muttered under his breath.

"Hello," Carlino said.

"Yes, hello, Mr. Carlino," Janzek said. "My name is Nick Janzek, detective with the Charleston Police Department."

"Hello, Detective, it's a pleasure," Carlino said, coming danger-ously close to winking at Middleton. "What can I do for you?"

"I'm investigating the murder of Mayor McCann and talking to as many people as I can. Just wondered when it would be possible to come by and ask you a few questions?"

Carlino looked over at Middleton.

"About what?" Carlino said. "What do you want to ask me?"

"Just a few routine questions."

"Sure, how's tomorrow at three? My office is at twenty-two State. I'll be back in town by then."

"Sounds good. I'll see you then."

"I look forward to it, Detective."

Carlino handed back the phone to Jeter and looked at Middleton.

"Know that old expression, *Keep your friends close and your enemies closer?*"

THIRTY-TWO

"Red Truck Books, this is Geneva."

"Hi, Ms. Crane, it's Nick Janzek, Charleston Pol—"

"Yes, Detective, as I told you, I never met a detective before, so it would be hard to forget you," Geneva said. "You calling to check on my supply of Bernard Cornwell novels?"

"Nothing I'd like better than to read a good book right now. But I got my hands full at the moment. I wondered if I could buy you a cup of coffee. Just need to ask you a few more questions."

"Not about the mayor, I hope?"

"No," Janzek said, "but if there's anything you care to add on that subject—"

"There isn't."

Janzek looked at his watch. It was 11:30.

"I've got a better idea," he said, segueing into what he had planned all along. "Could I buy you lunch? There's that place, Virginia's, up near you. My partner told me it's good."

"It is and I would love to," Geneva said. "Is this like a date, Detective?"

Janzek sighed. "It's like a date, but different."

"So... you mean... a business date."

"Well, yes."

"Aw, shucks."

"Is 12:30 good?"

"Sure, I'll see you then."

SHE ORDERED THE CRAB CAKES AND HE DID TOO.

They had already done five minutes of small talk.

Him: How's business?

She: Thank God for E. L. James.

He: You sell sex books at the Red Truck, Ms. Crane?

She: You betcha. As many as I can. Pays the rent, you know. Caught any bad guys yet on the Mayor's murder?

He (exaggerating considerably): No, but we're getting close.

She: Is that your standard answer?

He: Yes.

Then she told him about her coup of getting a famous author to come plug his latest book at the Red Truck.

"So, after years of begging and pleading with the cranky old bastard, I finally got him to come."

"You're kidding," Janzek said. "I'll be there. When is it?"

She gave him the information, and he wrote it down in his book.

"You like his stuff? It's pretty autobiographical, you know," she said.

"Yeah, I do. I could swear we had the same father. Tough old bastards you can never please."

"Did your father have anything to do with you becoming a detective... Detective?"

He laughed. "That would require a very long answer." He went silent for a few seconds. "Hey, how 'bout we just be Nick and Geneva instead of Detective and Ms. Crane?"

"Okay, sounds good to me," Geneva said. "What did you want to ask me?"

He twisted the white cloth napkin in his hands. "This is kind of hard," he said, "and I don't mean to just spring it on you. But, what can you tell me about Jefferson Davis?"

Her eyes danced around before lighting on Janzek's. "Wow, so obviously you know about... Marcus and me?"

He nodded.

Geneva looked around the room, then her eyes came back to him again.

"Jefferson and Marcus were—" she laughed. "I started to say black and white, but that doesn't quite work, so I'll go with another cliché: night and day. I mean, Jefferson—believe it or not— had a good heart. Misguided and messed up? For sure. He tried a bunch of straight jobs after he got back from Afghanistan but was basically a war casualty. Then it was like he forgot everything he ever learned over there. Lost his discipline. Couldn't show up for work on time. Got into crack. It's an old story. Marcus, well—maybe you heard— he was the diametric opposite. Would have made general in the Marines, everyone said. Driven. Obsessed. But nice too, though not without his own demons. You probably would have liked him."

Janzek could see tears forming in her eyes. He waited a moment so she could compose herself. "So, do you know who Rutledge Middleton is?"

Geneva rolled her eyes.

"Yes, of course I do. A colossal asshole." She put her hand up over her mouth. "Oops, sorry, where's my breeding?"

Janzek laughed. "I think you nailed it," he said. "How would Middleton and Jefferson have crossed paths?"

Geneva blew a strand of hair off her forehead.

"I don't know exactly," she said. "What I heard, though, was that Jefferson and this other guy got pulled over for some traffic thing, and the cops found a crack pipe and enough crack to make 'em think they were dealers. Maybe they were, for all I know.

Anyway, the other guy's girlfriend got Middleton's name from the Yellow Pages, and Middleton got them off with just community service."

"Middleton told me he never represented him."

Geneva wiped her mouth with her napkin.

"Then he's not just an a-hole, but a liar too," she said. "Jefferson had a few other scrapes with the law, and Middleton represented him." Geneva leaned forward. "Can we talk about something else? Rutledge Middleton's about my least favorite subject in the world. And talking about Jefferson just makes me profoundly sad."

"Just one last question."

"Okay, shoot."

"Was Jefferson right- or left-handed?"

"That's an odd one," Geneva said, pausing to think. "Left-handed... yeah, definitely. I remember sitting next to him at dinner once, our hands kept bumping into each other."

"Thanks," Janzek said. "So, what would you like to talk about?"

"Why don't we talk about you? Where you from? Ever married? You know, a quick bio."

"Boston... once... and it's a pretty dull story."

Geneva laughed. "I don't believe that. How do I know your marriage ended badly?"

He wrapped the napkin tighter.

"I don't know, how do you?"

She shrugged. "I just do."

Janzek ended up telling her the whole story. She just kind of coaxed it out of him, little by little.

He told her about meeting Caroline when she was a bridesmaid at the wedding of a college friend. How all her friends thought it was kind of strange when they first started going out. He was, after all, a cop. To them, that was a blue-collar job at best, and she was on the fast track at an old-line publishing house in Boston. Surely, the two didn't have a lot of high-minded literary discussions, her friends chuckled.

But the fact was, he and Caroline were completely, totally, madly in love.

Then that terrible night in May. Janzek was still working the case from eight hundred miles away and had his former partner, Zeke Jacks, interviewing possible suspects and poking around as best he could. Declan O'Brian, his former chief, had gotten wind of Janzek's never-ending search and, according to Jacks, was now calling Janzek, "the Fugitive," referring to the movie where Harrison Ford relentlessly pursued the one-armed man. Janzek chuckled when he heard that. There were worse men to be compared to.

He told Geneva about what had happened to Caroline. She put her hands up to her mouth and her eyes got big. "Oh my God, I am so sorry."

"Thanks."

He could tell she had questions but was too sensitive to ask them.

"So a little over a year after it happened, I was down here for a wedding and really liked it," he said. "It was time for me to put some distance between me and Boston."

Janzek looked down at his watch. It was 2:20.

"Oh, Jesus," he said, putting his credit card on top of the bill. "I am so sorry. I've been rambling on forever."

He paid the bill and they got up from the table. They went outside, and she turned to him.

"I enjoyed it," she said. "Let's do it again."

"I'd like that," he said and gave her a kiss on the cheek.

THIRTY-THREE

Trajan and Joe Mellor walked into Carlino's office on State Street.

The receptionist couldn't take her eyes off Trajan.

Carlino came out and shook hands with them and led them back to his office. He pointed to the two hunter-green leather chairs facing his desk.

"So, gentlemen, catch me up on the world of Fly Boy Modeling."

"It's called High Fly, Ned." Trajan knew Carlino knew the actual name. Just liked to mess with him. "So, our guy Matt had a... date with Mr. Thorne McKenzie. And Joe, gifted shutterbug he is, got a couple of brilliant shots of the dream couple in what you might call... a compromising position." Trajan put a manila envelope on Carlino's desk. "Nothing too risqué, mind you, but photos Mr. McKenzie would probably not want Mrs. McKenzie to see."

"Or worse," said Mellor, "the boys in his golf foursome."

Carlino was beaming ear-to-ear. "I love a nice romantic tale," he said. "And what about Tim Anderson?"

Thorne McKenzie and Tim Anderson were two old-school Charleston guys who had sworn that they would never let a casino come to their beloved Charleston. Carlino had originally thought that McKenzie and Anderson were untouchables because McKenzie had a pile of money and Anderson seemed to be that rare commodity—an honest man.

But, it turned out, they both liked pretty boys, as Rutledge Middleton had discovered when he was out on Coley Donaldson's boat.

"Tim Anderson met another one of my young protégés," Trajan said, "and I understand that they had a lovely weekend down in Savannah. Of course, as far as Tim's wife knows, he went on a hunting trip at a plantation up near a place called Tryon."

"Congratulations, boys," Carlino said, mentally shifting McKenzie and Anderson from the con side of the casino vote to the pro side. "Good job, as always."

"Thanks," Trajan said, "and I was thinking, just in case you ever need a replacement for any of your girls out at Pinckney Hall—"

"Matter of fact, I do," Carlino said. "You got somebody good? My girl Vruska turns out to be way more into cocaine than men, and it's turning into a problem."

"I've got this incredible new girl," Trajan said. "Twenty-one, but light-years older than her age. She's a little bored with college life and boys who sit around getting drunk at the frat house. I think she'd fit right in. Just let me know."

"You know," Carlino said, putting his feet up on his desk and lighting a cigar, "you boys definitely deserve a bonus."

He reached into the top drawer of his desk and pulled out a large, leather-bound checkbook. He wrote out a check for both of them for ten thousand dollars each. It was a drop in the bucket. A couple hours' worth of profit, he figured, once the casino was up and running.

THIRTY-FOUR

CARLINO HAD HIRED THE DECORATOR SISSIE BURBAGE OF THE Tradd Street Burbages and told her he wanted the look of his office to be "Charleston understated." He didn't want to come on like some tacky carpetbagger from the north and shove it in everybody's face how rich he was. He wanted to be thought of as a man of taste, discrimination, and moderation. Even though *moderation* really wasn't in his vocabulary.

The receptionist announced Janzek's arrival. Carlino walked out to the reception area. Janzek was flipping through a glossy magazine called *Charleston Style.*

"Sorry I don't have a *Gardens & Gun* for you, Detective," Carlino said, referring to a local magazine. Then he thrust out his hand. "Ned Carlino. Nice to meet you."

"Hello, Mr. Carlino. Nice to meet you too."

Carlino started toward the back. "Come on back. You want coffee, water, or something?"

"Water would be great," Janzek said.

The receptionist kicked into gear.

Janzek followed Carlino into his wood-paneled office, and

Carlino motioned to one of the two green leather chairs facing his big, antique, partners desk.

Janzek sat down.

"Thank you, Gwen," Carlino said, as the receptionist brought in two bottled waters. "So, what did you want to talk to me about, Detective?"

Janzek dove right in. "I read about Monarch Hospitality's proposed casino and hotel for the city, Mr. Carlino, and know you're involved in it. I also know how opposed to it Mayor McCann was."

"You don't pull any punches, do you?" Carlino said, unscrewing the cap of his water. "I like that. You're like me. Guys down here trip all over their dicks, trying to be polite."

Janzek smiled. "So, I was just curious about your relationship with the former mayor?"

"Relationship?" Carlino said, taking a quick sip. "I never met the man. So I guess you could say we had no relationship."

"But did you ever talk to him?"

"I had a couple of conference calls with him," Carlino said, putting down his water bottle. "Are you thinking I might know something about what happened to him? Is that it, Detective?"

"No, I'm just going around asking people questions. Doesn't necessarily mean a thing."

Carlino's eyes hardened.

"Let me tell you how it is, Detective. Charleston was, and is, going to get that casino, whether Jim McCann voted for it or not." Carlino put his hands together and leaned back in his chair. "It's good for all Charlestonians, for all the jobs it's gonna create, the tax base— and, hell, even as a place to have a little fun on a Saturday night. I don't know whether you've noticed but this town can be a little stiff."

Janzek took a hit on his water. "But I heard there aren't enough votes in favor."

"All that matters, Detective, is when it's time for the vote, there will be," Carlino said. "I'm just trying to get the word out, 'cause the more people know about it, the more they'll get behind it. I mean, the

Monarch is going to be a five-star hotel, and the casino will be as classy as any place in the world."

"I'm sure it will be, Mr. Carlino, but the way I hear it, there's still a little bit of the Bible Belt mentality down here. The Holy City, churches on every block. You know, people think bingo's a sin, and how gambling and prostitution go hand in hand. I don't need to tell you, you've heard it all before."

"Yeah, and it's ridiculous," Carlino said. "We got the lottery here, don't we?"

"That's the *state* of South Carolina."

Carlino took a long pull of his water and finished it.

"How long you been in town, Detective?"

"Ahh... little shy of two weeks."

Carlino burst out laughing. "Well, hell, no offense, but you don't really know *anything* about this place, do you?"

"No, I guess I don't," Janzek said. "But, I'm a pretty quick learner."

"I bet you are," Carlino said, "and like a Canadian Mountie, you probably always get your man, too. Right, Detective?"

Janzek locked onto Carlino's eyes.

"Most of the time," he said. "How long have *you* been in Charleston?"

"Bought my place out on Sullivan's about five years ago. Then a plantation down in Harpersboro couple years back."

"They tell me Charleston people don't really start accepting you until you're at least second generation," Janzek said.

"Yeah, well, it's not easy. I think they accept me," Carlino said. "Least the ones I care about."

"That's all that matters. Mind telling me about your relationship with Rutledge Middleton?"

Carlino didn't even hesitate.

"Sure, he's an attorney I use for some of my legal work that he's better equipped to handle than me. He's wired into the Charleston elite and a friend of mine too."

Janzek leaned forward in his chair.

"Were Middleton and Mayor McCann friends, as far as you knew?"

"As far as I know, no, not particularly," Carlino said, scratching the back of his head. "You keep circling back to McCann. Like I said, maybe you think I had something to do with what happened to him. Is that it, Detective?"

Janzek looked down at his empty water bottle.

"Would it be possible to get another bottle of water?" Janzek asked. "I don't know why, I'm just really thirsty."

Carlino hit the intercom button.

"Gwen, another couple of waters, please?"

"Thanks," Janzek said. "Does your brother, Richard, or your Uncle Salvatore ever visit you down here?"

Carlino eyed him coldly, like suddenly he was getting sick of Janzek's questions.

"I asked you a question before that you never answered," Carlino said. "I'm asking you again: Do you think I had something to do with what happened to McCann?"

"It crossed my mind," Janzek said, "but then a lot of crazy stuff crosses my mind."

Carlino frowned.

"Okay, so in answer to your question, my brother's been down on his boat a couple times to visit. Why?"

"What about Frank Silvestre? He's your cousin, right?"

"No, he hasn't and yes, he is," Carlino said. "What are you getting at?"

Janzek straightened up in his chair. "All three of them were charged with murder at one time or another, isn't that right?"

Carlino's eyes narrowed.

"Yeah, and all three of them were acquitted. They all have nice, clean records."

"Maybe because they had a really good lawyer," Janzek said, glancing out the window, then coming back to Carlino. "What evidence did they have in Philadelphia to think you bribed that senator to get slot machines at your racetrack?"

Carlino smiled. "I admire a man who does his homework," he said. "As far as your question goes, they had absolutely no evidence. Because it never happened. It's very simple: It's called envy. A lot of other people wanted slots. I made the best case why my track should get them. Lots of sour grapes after I got 'em. You know how it is, people make up a lotta bullshit stories."

Janzek nodded, like he was out of questions.

"Now I have a question for you, Detective." Carlino smiled and settled back in his chair. "Where you from, anyway? I'm not hearin' any southern in your accent."

"Boston, born and bred."

"No shit. I went to Harvard Law," Carlino said, leaning forward. "Probably hung out at a few of the same bars. On second thought, the ones I went to were probably long gone by the time you were old enough to drink."

"I don't know about that. Bars in Boston tend to stick around a long time. Cambridge is a great town, huh?"

"Oh yeah, I loved it. More damn colleges... and college girls. Where'd you live, anyway?"

"Out in Brighton," Janzek said. "Had a little place up in New Hampshire too."

"Is that right?" Carlino put his hands together and leaned back again. "Ever do any hunting up there?"

Janzek paused. "Yeah, a little."

"Well, hell, man, you ought to come down to my place, it's about forty-five minutes from here. I got every bird known to man down there. Quail, ducks, pheasants, doves—if it flaps or quacks, I got 'em. Why don't you come on down and help me get rid of all that goddamn quacking."

Janzek smiled. "Well, yeah, maybe. That's awful nice of you."

"You could get there late and leave early. Not miss any work," Carlino said.

"I appreciate the invitation," Janzek said, standing up. "I also appreciate you seeing me on short notice. Answering my questions and all."

"Happy to meet a fellow Boston guy," Carlino said.

Janzek shook Carlino's hand and left.

He had never shot a bird in his life.

THIRTY-FIVE

MIDDLETON WAS MEETING WITH CALEB PRIOLEAU. PRIOLEAU, as usual, seemed more interested in the ridiculous movie about his whoring great-grandfather than the eight-hundred-million-dollar casino building project. At the ten per percent margin he was going to clear, Middleton thought, Prioleau would be able to make a movie about every single one of his worthless, inbred relatives if he wanted.

"So, listen to this," Middleton said to Prioleau. "We got a call from the guy who owns Tanger Outlets. He offered to move the whole kit and caboodle down from North Charleston to the casino site."

"What the hell's Tanger Outlets?"

"For Chrissake, Caleb," Middleton said, "that huge outlet mall up in North Charleston. They got all the blue-chip tenants. Brooks Brothers, Polo, Eddie Bauer, Nike, you name it."

"Too far to drive," Prioleau said. "Besides what's wrong with that Brooks Brothers on King Street?"

"Nothing. Except everything's double the price."

"The fuck do I care," Prioleau said. "You watch that DVD?"

Christ, he just couldn't get off his damn movie.

"Yeah," Middleton said. "I liked it okay. But, obviously... no one else did."

Prioleau's jaw went into free fall.

MIDDLETON'S NEXT MEETING WAS WITH HIS ACCOUNTANT: THE purveyor of bad news. At least he had been for the last couple of years. Between bad real estate deals and the Ponzi guy, Henry Reed, Middleton had lost about a third of his net worth. Which wasn't all that much to begin with.

Stuart Price, his CPA, put an optimistic spin on Middleton's finances when they met. He accentuated the positive. Just imagine all the loss carry-forwards you've got, he said. For the next ten years at least. Middleton was pretty much over his losses by now. In fact, he took the Ponzi debacle a whole lot better than Ned Carlino did. Of course, Carlino had twenty-five million in it, instead of the measly hundred thousand that Middleton had. Which was why Carlino had taken the extreme measure he had. Getting his brother and the other goombah down from Philly.

Middleton chalked it up to being an Italian thing— how vengeful those damn guinea bastards always got when someone fucked them over.

The other big loser on the Ponzi thing, Middleton knew, was the shipping guy in Savannah who had gotten totally wiped out. Served him right; greedy fucker kept pumping more and more money into the fund. Then when it blew up, he was basically out on the streets of Savannah. The story Middleton had heard was that he— his name was Jake Pike—ended up in Charleston with just the shirt on his back.

To the guy's credit, though, he had landed on his feet. What happened was, since nobody in Savannah wanted to know a broke Jake Pike, he moved to Charleston where he didn't know a soul. Pike was a good-looking man— probably around fifty-five or so— and an old school guy with good manners and the courtly southern gentleman thing going for him. So, what he did was walk around the streets south of Broad on Saturday nights, where you could look through a window or into the courtyard of a house and see a cocktail party in full swing. He picked big cocktail parties—forty, fifty people —then he'd walk in, all confident and charming like he owned the place.

Not only was Jake Pike handsome and courtly, but he had a few snappy lines and before too long, a list of women's phone numbers.

One of them was a rich widow.

Four months later, she and Jake got married in a small ceremony at the Episcopal Church on State Street.

Only in Charleston, Middleton thought.

He called Quatro after the meeting with Stuart Price.

Middleton's ducks—if not quite in a row—were definitely starting to line up. He had to just make sure that his fuckup son hadn't blown the relatively simple job that he had given him.

Quatro picked up right before the second ring. "Hey, Dad. Whassup?"

"Do you *have* to talk like a Negro?"

"Sorry, so, ah, what's going on, Dad?"

"That's marginally better," Middleton said. "Did you talk to that Watson girl?"

"Yeah, all taken care of."

"What did you do?"

"Got this big, black dude to go to the girl's place with me and convince her she was drunk and I didn't do anything wrong."

"So, she's not going to press charges?"

"Not unless she wants the black dude crawling through her window in the middle—"

"Just answer the question for Chrissakes."

"No, sir, she's not going to press charges."

"Good," Middleton said, "that oughta piss off my friend Detective Janzek. Watching his case go up in smoke."

"Just happy to help the team, Dad."

Middleton sighed. "Best way to help the team is to keep your ass out of bars."

THIRTY-SIX

"Mr. McKenzie, please," Carlino said to the woman who had just answered the phone at McKenzie Investcorp.

Carlino knew that Thorne McKenzie not only owned a company listed on the NASDAQ but also had a substantial piece of the Tennessee Titans football team.

"Yes, and may I tell him who's calling?"

"Ned Carlino."

It took her a while to come back to him.

"Sorry, Mr. Carlino, he's in a meeting. Is there any message?"

"Yes, tell him I'm a good friend of Matt's and need to speak to him right now."

McKenzie came right on. "What do you want?" he said in a snarly voice.

"Just your vote on my casino, Mr. McKenzie. Then once it's built, maybe I'll put you and Matt up in the presidential suite for a couple of nights."

"Fuck you, Carlino," McKenzie snapped.

"So, are you saying you're going to vote against the hotel-casino?"

Carlino listened to McKenzie's labored breathing.

"Are you okay, Mr. McKenzie?"

"I'll vote for the goddamn thing," McKenzie said finally.

"Thank you, and when you do, I'll burn all the pretty pictures I have of you and Matt."

The phone went dead. Carlino imagined McKenzie throwing it across the room and it shattering into a hundred pieces against a wall.

He dialed Tim Anderson next.

He had heard Anderson was retired. Middleton described him as a professional do-gooder.

Trajan had given Carlino Anderson's phone number, which he had gotten from Anderson's "companion."

It rang three times.

"Hello."

"Mr. Anderson?"

"Yes, who's this?"

"My name is Ned Carlino. I—"

"I know who you are," Anderson said. "Why you calling me?"

Carlino decided to have a little fun. "Perhaps you've heard, my company is involved with the proposed hotel-casino, and I'm hoping I could get your vote in favor of the project."

"Forget it," Anderson said, "not in this lifetime. There are a million reasons to vote against it and not one to vote for it."

"I bet I can come up with one."

"Trust me, you can't. I'm pretty busy right now, so—"

"Matt Johnston."

"What did you say?"

"I said, 'Matt Johnston.' That's the reason why you're going to vote for the casino, Mr. Anderson."

Nothing at the other end.

"Mr. Anderson?"

"I'm here."

"Can I count on your vote?"

Anderson choked out something, but Carlino couldn't make it out. He sat back in his chair and smiled.

"Thank you, Mr. Anderson, I'll take that as a yes."

THIRTY-SEVEN

Janzek got a call at the station.

"Hello, Nick."

It was Geneva Crane.

"Oh, hi, you beat me to it," he said. "I was going to call you."

"Yeah, likely story."

"No, I really was. I was going to ask you if you wanted to go to some galleries with me this Friday. They have this thing on the first Friday of the month where they stay open late."

He needed a break. He had been working twelve- to thirteen-hour days ever since he got to Charleston.

"Yes, I know, and some of them serve wine and cheese too," Geneva said. "Sounds like someone's idea of a cheap date?"

"Wait a minute, I also want to take you out for dinner afterwards. I was thinking about that place on upper King, the Average."

She laughed. "I think you mean, the Ordinary."

"Yeah, that's it. Pretty dumb name."

"How about this instead? We go to the galleries but then to my friend's for dinner afterward. Her name's June. You'd like her, she's got this cool, old house down on Stoll's Alley."

"Sounds good—let's do it. The Ordinary can wait."

"There's only one little hitch," she said. "June's good friends with Rutledge Middleton's wife, so it's fifty-fifty they'll be there."

"Even more reason to go. I still have a bunch more questions for him."

"Nick, this isn't a business—"

"I'm kidding. I'll pick you up at 6:30. Where do you live?"

"Thirty-Six Savage, not far from the galleries. Why don't you just park, come get me, and we can walk. June's house is about five blocks south of Broad."

"Deal," he said. "Looking forward to it. How about I get a bottle of wine?"

"That would be nice. See you then."

Janzek hung up and walked down to Delvin Rhett's cubicle. Rhett was on his phone but waved Janzek into the chair opposite him.

"Thanks a lot, Detective," Rhett said into the phone. "Yeah, yeah, I will. You ever need a favor in Charleston, you know who to call."

Rhett hung up. "Holy shit, man," he said. "I called that guy in Philly you told me to call back. Doakes. Asked him a few more questions, then he hooked me up with another guy who was like the local Ned Carlino expert. Told me Carlino's Uncle Salvatore got off on a murder-one charge, even with a goddamn eyewitness. Carlino took the witness apart on the stand. Plus, two of the jurors, it turns out, were bought off. One of 'em's working with the DA's office right now. DA's trying to get a retrial."

"Good job, anything else?"

"Just that if you want to prove that black is white, you go to Ned Carlino. You want to prove that up is down, you go to Ned Carlino. This cop was telling me Carlino's got a whole network of crooked pols who owe him 'cause he got 'em off for one thing or another. Between that and the family—and I use the word loosely—he gets what he wants in Philly served up on a silver platter."

Janzek's foot started tapping.

"Feds ever go after him on any RICO charges?"

A wide smiled creased Rhett's face.

"Funny you should ask. They tried to nail a couple of councilmen for giving out city contracts to some Carlino family corporations. Same thing, though— they got nowhere."

Janzek's foot tapped faster. "Like trash-hauling companies, maybe?"

Rhett nodded. "Exactly, and a big cement outfit."

"So, then what? Carlino moved his whole operation down here?"

"Yes and no," Rhett said. "It doesn't look like he brought the family along. Like he's using local companies as his partners. Peninsula Construction for one, a company owned by a guy named Caleb Prioleau. Supposedly, Prioleau's got the inside track to build the casino and hotel. Guy's got a lot of juice in this town."

"You got some good intel," Janzek said. "Now, listen to this."

Janzek told Rhett about his meeting with Carlino the day before. How they danced around each other for forty-five minutes. How Carlino asked him down to his plantation to help reduce the duck population.

And how fishy it all sounded. Like Carlino wanted something out of him.

They were wrapping it up when a man with a bulbous nose, thinning, mousy brown hair, and a suit that swam on him walked in.

"Well, well, my man, Jim-mie," Rhett said. "Long time no see."

Jimmie Driggers didn't even look at Rhett, just Janzek.

"We haven't had the pleasure," Driggers said to Janzek. "I'm Jimmie Driggers."

Janzek stood up and put his hand out.

"Nick Janzek... heard a lot about you, Jimmie."

"Likewise," Driggers said, shaking his hand. "Been so damn busy, I never got a chance to welcome you."

"Thanks," Janzek said, "how you making out on your end?"

Driggers went around the chair Janzek was sitting in and sat down.

"Just what I was coming to tell you boys," Driggers said, lacing his fingers together. "After that fuckup with the phony eyewitness, I looked into a woman the mayor was bangin' and in the course of it, tracked down the guy who did it."

"Killed the mayor, you mean?" Janzek asked.

"Yeah."

Janzek caught Rhett's eye.

"Name's Pat Cannon," Driggers said, "the husband of a real estate broker, Erica Cannon. Seems she spent more time flashing the mayor her ta-ta's than showing houses."

"What I love about you, Jimmie," Rhett said. "Your way with words."

Driggers looked over at Rhett. "Shit. Barely noticed you there, Delvin."

"Mean 'cause I blend in with the wallpaper?"

Driggers glanced at the brown wallpaper, sniffled a laugh, then turned back to Janzek.

"So anyway, this guy Cannon's a real bad actor."

"What'd he do?" Janzek asked.

"Assault charge arising out of a bar fight in 2013," Driggers said. "Then last year he punched out a guy from a towing company who put a boot on his car. Seems like old Pat has himself quite the temper, likes to resort to violence to take care of shit."

"That's not exactly my definition of a *real bad actor*," Janzek said.

Driggers's lower lip slid up over his upper one.

"It isn't, huh? Well, what about him telling a guy in a bar he's gonna kill the guy who's bangin' his wife?"

Rhett leaned forward and put his elbows on his desk. "That guy wouldn't happen to be the same one who took down the plate number of the hit-and-run-driver, would it?"

Janzek wanted to high-five him.

"Go fuck yourself, Rhett," Driggers said. "No, dude's the real deal. I talked to the wife, who told me she and Cannon had a big fight the morning the mayor bought it. Told me he went storming out of the house, tires squealing out the driveway. Fifteen minutes later, the mayor got hit."

"So, what are you gonna do, Jimmie?" Janzek asked.

"What do you think? Bring the guy in, book him. First-degree, premeditated. Why? You got a better candidate?"

"Nothing solid," Janzek said. "A few leads."

"Know that guy Rutledge Middleton?" Rhett asked.

Janzek wanted to stuff Rhett's tie in his mouth.

"Heard the name, why?" Driggers said.

Janzek shot a glower at Rhett. Rhett caught it.

"Just a guy that... we looked at." Rhett said. "Crossed him off our list."

It was an okay recovery.

"Whatever," Driggers said, turning to Rhett. "You guys oughta go find the guy who did that brother. Stonewall Jackson... or whatever his name was."

"I think you mean Jefferson Davis," Rhett said.

"Yeah, him."

"So, you mean, that's like the booby prize," Rhett said. "You got the trophy? That it, Jimmie?"

"Always such a fuckin' wiseass," Driggers said, getting up to leave. Then to Janzek: "Good luck with fuckin' Urkel here."

"Good luck with your collar," Rhett said.

"Thanks, but I won't be needing any," Driggers said and walked out of the office.

Rhett glanced at Janzek after Driggers was out of earshot. "Sorry about bringing up Middleton."

"That's all right," Janzek said. "Just my gut's telling me we ought to keep it quiet until we got enough to hang him."

"So, you're not buying this Pat Cannon thing?"

"Not for a second. Driggers is clearly desperate for a collar, and any warm body will do. Seen that movie a million times. Collar equals promotion, promotion equals money—the usual drill."

Rhett nodded. "So, you thinkin' it's not that he's dirty, it's just about clearance?"

"I don't know yet," Janzek said. "I can't tell whether he really buys this Cannon guy did it or is trying to distract us away from our suspects."

Rhett nodded.

Janzek looked out his window.

"I mean, if I was a guy in a jury box," Janzek said, turning back to Rhett, "and Driggers ran that Cannon story by me, I might just buy it."

"You mean, if you didn't know about Middleton and Jefferson Davis and Carlino?"

"Yeah, exactly."

"But you do."

"Yeah. I'm just trying to get into Driggers's head."

"You mean, figure out whether he's dirty or just... stupid?"

Janzek laughed. "How 'bout just barking up the wrong tree."

"I'm goin' with dirty."

"You might be right."

Janzek leaned back and put his hands behind his head. "I didn't tell you about my date tonight, did I?"

"About time you had some fun, man," Rhett said. "Been workin' your ass off. You need a break. Who is it?"

"Geneva Crane."

"Holy shit."

Janzek nodded. "So, what else do you know about her?"

"Well, like I said last time, top ten of best-looking women in Charleston. Maybe top five." Rhett blinked a few times.

"Come on, Delvin, I can see your brain clankin' away. What else? Don't hold out on me."

Rhett's eyes flickered.

"Just like I said, Charleston high society wasn't real thrilled, her marrying a black guy. Even one like Marcus."

"So, did something happen?"

"No, not that I know of. Not like I get the stiff cards to their parties. I just heard maybe she got a little—what's the word?"

"Ostracized?"

"Yeah, exactly. Kinda like what happened to the British guy."

"What British guy?"

"A pretty well-known writer, s'posedly. Twenty years back or so. Came to town as a man, then one day turned into a woman. Then the crazy bastard marries a black dude. None of the old guard was real cool with any of it, as you might imagine."

JIMMIE DRIGGERS ARRESTED PAT CANNON AND FORMALLY charged him when Cannon provided no solid alibi. Cannon told him after the fight with his wife that he had taken a long drive up Route 26—halfway to Columbia—trying to cool off and figure out whether his marriage was worth trying to salvage or not.

Cannon vehemently denied that he had anything to do with the mayor's death and claimed there'd be some kind of mark on his car's bumper if he hit someone who weighed 180 pounds.

Cuffing him, Driggers said, "No, 'krauts make real sturdy bumpers," and threw him into a cell on Lockwood Drive.

THIRTY-EIGHT

At 6:30, Janzek went straight from the station house to Geneva's house on Savage Street. It was about ten doors south of Broad Street. She lived in a typical Charleston single with a ground floor and a second story, covered piazza.

Janzek pressed the buzzer, then a few seconds later heard footsteps.

Geneva opened the door, and it was confirmed: she definitely lived up to Rhett's top-five ranking.

She was wearing long pants, a teal green, collarless top, and very little makeup. She didn't need to. Her high cheekbones and striking brown eyes were enough, but then there were also her big, sensuous lips and long, lean body.

"Wow," he said, "look at you."

She leaned forward and gave him a kiss on the cheek. He was glad she wasn't a double-cheeker. He wasn't big on that. Way too French.

"Ready to go get some *cul-chah*?" she said.

"I can definitely use some," he said as she walked down the two steps to the sidewalk.

He followed her.

Five minutes later they were at a gallery on the corner of Broad and Church.

They walked in and went along one side of the gallery, looking at the paintings. They were mostly landscapes and paintings of Charleston houses.

Pointing to one, he caught her eye and wobbled his hand from side to side.

"You're being generous," she whispered, walking away from it.

He followed her over to a table that had white wine in tiny plastic cups along with a row of Triscuits and processed cheese on a cardboard tray.

"Very elegant," she whispered.

He nodded, took two cups of wine, and handed her one.

"Mouton Rothschild, ninety-three?" she asked.

"Ernest and Julio last month," he said, taking a sip and wincing. "A little on the vinegary side."

He picked up a Triscuit and ate it. "Why ruin a perfectly good Triscuit with Kraft cheese?"

She nodded and walked over to the other side of the gallery. More landscapes and several Impressionistic pictures of cows.

Geneva leaned in close.

"Now I remember this place. Not one of my favorites."

He beckoned her with his hand.

"So then, let's go, on to the next. Maybe we'll get a wine upgrade."

She grabbed his arm as they walked outside.

They went into another gallery on the same block. More landscapes and cows.

"Seems like every artist has to do his rendition of the South Carolina low country—marsh grass and water," he said.

She smiled and nodded as they watched a group of four young people in their late teens, early twenties, come in.

Geneva nudged him. "See those kids," she said. "From the

college. Word got out they can get drunk for free and walk around with booze on the streets legally."

Janzek smiled as he watched one boy pour a small cup of white wine into another cup. Right up to the top. "You learn some very useful stuff in college."

He watched a boy and a girl toast each other with their thimble-sized plastic cups.

"Why don't the gallery owners just roll out a couple of kegs of PBR?" he asked.

"What's PBR?"

"Where you been, girl? Pabst Blue Ribbon. The king of rotgut beer."

She pulled him toward the door. "Somehow, I don't think that's the image the owners here are trying to promote. Let's go across the street, there's a good gallery on the next block."

They walked out, crossed the street, and went down a block. Janzek looked up at the name. It was called the Ella Fitzmorris Gallery.

"The owner here, she's got great taste," Geneva said, walking in.

She nodded to a nice-looking, well-dressed woman across the room, who waved back.

"That's her," she whispered.

Janzek spotted a landscape that was not of the Charleston low country. In fact, it looked like it could be in Maine or somewhere in New England.

It was of several old, clapboard, colonial houses on the ocean, then behind them were small, bright-colored sailboats in a race.

"I love that one," Janzek said, pointing to the painting. "My old stomping grounds."

"How do you know?"

"It's gotta be New England," he said.

"Stonington, Maine," came a voice from behind him.

He looked around. It was the owner.

"I really like it... how much is it?" he asked.

"Thirty-two hundred dollars," she said. "The artist's name is Ben Lester. He's got a way with water and boats, don't you think?"

"Not too shabby with houses, either," Janzek said. "I'll take it."

Geneva looked a little surprised.

"My apartment walls need help," he said, then turning to the gallery owner, "Can I pick it up tomorrow?"

"Absolutely," said the owner.

***

TWENTY MINUTES LATER, GENEVA PUSHED THE DOORBELL AT June Porcher's house on Stoll's Alley.

"Now, just to prepare you, since you haven't been in Charleston long," Geneva said, "people in this town like to drink... think in terms of gallons."

And before Janzek had a chance to respond, June Porcher was at the door. Janzek was surprised—she was quite a bit older than Geneva. Late forties, he guessed; tall, willowy blonde, killer smile.

"So nice to meet you, Nick," she said. "Welcome."

"Well, thanks," he said, handing her a bottle of wine he had just bought at a nearby wine shop. "Here you go. Thanks for having me."

June took the bottle and smiled. "Oh, that is so kind of you. Thank you so much. Come on in and I'll introduce you."

Geneva went in first, and Janzek followed her.

The first person he saw across the room was none other than Rutledge Ashley Middleton III, Esquire.

THIRTY-NINE

MIDDLETON WAS STANDING IN JUNE'S TASTEFULLY DECORATED living room, holding a glass of something clear. A big hunk of lime was floating on top of his drink like something that had just fallen out of a tree.

Middleton glanced up and saw Janzek. It was like he was seeing a charging rhinoceros bearing down on him.

Next to Middleton stood a short, perky brunette and another couple.

June did the introductions, unaware of the history between him and Middleton.

Middleton cut June off and said, "We've met," when she tried to introduce them. He was a little more cordial toward Geneva, but not much. Wendy Middleton, the perky brunette, was friendly, and the other couple, George and Sandy something, smiled and said "nice to meet you" in unison.

"You two go out to the porch and get drinks," June said. "I've got a cute, young mixologist out there."

Janzek followed Geneva out back. She turned to him and smiled. "You might want to make it a double," she said.

He nodded and ordered from the bartender, who looked barely old enough to drink.

As the bartender handed them their drinks, Janzek heard a voice off to one side. "Well, look who it is."

He turned to see Becky Hall from the apartment below his. She was with a tall man who was wearing glasses that looked good on him.

"Oh, hey, Becky, long time no see."

"I know," she said with a fluorescent smile. "Weird.... I never see you in the building, but here you are."

"Yeah, it is weird," he said, turning to Geneva. "Oh, hey, this is my friend, Geneva. Geneva, this is Becky."

The two women smiled and said hello, then Becky turned to the man next to her.

"And this is Sam," she said.

Janzek shook his hand and said hello.

"So, everything good with you?" Janzek asked Becky.

"Yeah, I guess," she said, "working too hard, not getting paid enough. You know the drill."

"That's Charleston," Geneva said.

"No kidding," Becky said, turning to the bartender. "All right... well, it's time to give this nice man something to do." Then to Janzek: "Catch up with you back inside."

"Will do," Janzek said.

An hour and two drinks later, Janzek was sitting between Wendy Middleton and Becky at the ten-person dinner table.

Wendy put away three and a half glasses of red wine before dessert rolled around and was clearly an experienced and highly accomplished flirt.

A couple of times when Janzek said something that Wendy laughed at, Rutledge Middleton shot razor-edged daggers at her.

Janzek turned to Becky. "So?"

"So?" she said.

And they both laughed.

"She seems nice, your date," Becky said. "Beautiful too. Pisses me off."

He laughed.

"But I figured you'd find somebody," she said.

He nodded. "You and Sam been going out long?"

"Yeah, a few times."

"Seems like a nice guy."

Becky nodded and said, "Well, glad you found her, Nick."

Then she turned back to the man next to her.

His name was Edward, and he was a loud, blustery guy who kept bending Becky's ear about the proposed casino coming to town. Edward was— stridently—opposed to it.

After a while, Rutledge Middleton overheard their conversation and rammed his way into it from across the table. He was, of course— vociferously—in favor of it.

"Come on, Edward," Middleton said, "get more enlightened. This town could use another economic engine. We still got unemployment that's way too high, plus the casino will be paying a couple million in real estate taxes and a lot more in state taxes."

Edward killed his wine and wiped his mouth with the back of his hand.

"Are you kiddin'?" Edward glared at Middleton. "You're saying that, in addition to all the riffraff the goddamn cruise ships dump onto the streets, now we want to go after the Vegas crowd?"

Middleton looked like the accusation was a personal slap in the face.

"For Chrissakes, have you ever been out of Charleston in your life?" Middleton said. "Monarch is a first-class operation. Five-star hotels, the best in the business. They're going to be gearing the casino to the highest level of clientele."

"Clientele?" Edward said. "What are you talking about? More like degenerate gamblers."

"You have no idea what you're—"

Geneva cut Middleton off. "What do you really know about Monarch, Rutledge?" she asked calmly.

Middleton turned to her with his small, contemptuous eyes. "Well, for starters, they're a very successful company," he said. "Their stock price doubled in the past year and a half."

"Maybe you didn't know, but they've had literally dozens of lawsuits for human rights violations?" Geneva said.

"Who the hell cares about that?"

"Any minority person trying to get a job, for one," Geneva said. "Their hiring practices are atrocious, and the company has a long history of being racially biased. In the entire company, minorities comprise less than a half percent of their employees. A little while back, there was a lawsuit against them where the plaintiff won a thirty-million-dollar judgment. And guess what happened?"

"I have no idea."

"Poor man disappeared. Never to be heard from again. Lucky for Monarch, though, they never had to pay him a nickel."

Nine sets of eyes were on Geneva.

"How do you know all this, Gen?" June asked.

"I heard stories about Monarch," Geneva said, "then I went and did a bunch of research. We don't need a company like that in Charleston."

"You don't know what you're talking about," Middleton said, flashing his trademark sneer. "That's all speculation and unsubstantiated charges. Company's got a great reputation."

Geneva raised her hand and jabbed with one finger. "Yeah, for racism and discrimination."

Then Edward chimed in. "And when you say, 'highest level of clientele,' that sounds like a pretty low bar to me."

Middleton was seething now. "You ever been to Monte Carlo, Edward?" he asked, remembering what Carlino had told him. "Seen the casino there?"

"No," Edward said. "And I have no interest in going."

"Well, I can tell you it's a totally different class of people than the so-called 'Vegas crowd' you were talking about."

"The aristocracy of the world, I suppose?" Edward said.

"And the cognoscenti?" Geneva piled on.

"And don't forget James Bond," June said, trying to lighten the mood. "He used to hang out there, right?"

Middleton looked like he wanted to strangle all three of them.

"What do you think, Nick?" Wendy Middleton asked out of the blue, swinging her substantial cleavage toward him.

Middleton shot his wife a look like he wanted to drag her out to the car and lock her in it.

"What the hell would he know?" Middleton fumed. "He's a cop who just got to Charleston five minutes ago."

Janzek just smiled. "You are so right. I don't know the first thing about casinos in Monte Carlo," he said. "James Bond, on the other hand, I know him cold."

Everybody laughed but Middleton.

Conversations veered off in other directions, and after fifteen minutes, the group went back to the living room after a detour by the bar. Janzek noticed the kid bartender was running low on just about everything.

Then June cranked up some tunes, and she and Edward started to dance on the heart pine floor. June had some nice moves on her. Edward, fifty or so, was a frenetic arm thrasher and not in June's league.

Janzek was sitting between Geneva and Wendy Middleton in a sofa. Wendy was emitting white-hot heat you could almost see. She was pressed up close against Janzek, seemingly oblivious to his date's presence on the other side of him.

Wendy powered through her latest red wine, then stood up.

"I think I must have a hole in my glass," she said, going toward the bar in back. "Save my seat, Nick."

Geneva waited for Wendy to get out of earshot, then shook her head.

"I'm sorry, but I warned you—"

"Stop, I'm having a great time," he said. "And you're right, these people sure as hell know how to knock back their cocktails."

Wendy walked back in.

"All right, people—" she had her arm around the waist of the bartender— "step aside. Me and Junior here are gonna show you how to cut a rug."

The kid looked like he was up to the challenge.

June smiled and went over and turned up the volume.

It was the Stones. "Sympathy for the Devil."

Wendy got the bartender out onto the dance floor and started shaking her stuff. She knew what she was doing. She was singing along too:

"Please allow me to intro-duce maa-self, I'm a man of wealth and taste—"

The girl could dance like Lady Gaga, but her singing wasn't in Jagger's league.

Then, the next song came on: A Four Tops oldie and, and as if someone had flipped an invisible switch, the bartender amped it up a notch. He wasn't bad for a white guy.

Janzek was mesmerized, watching the two.

Out of nowhere, the bartender— sweat flying off him— suddenly whipped off his shirt like he'd been just dying to do it all night. He was ripped like a Calvin Klein model.

Wendy's eyes went wide and lascivious, and her jaw seemed to unhinge.

Then, June and Edward, who had temporarily cleared the living-room dance floor before, got back into it. Edward's thrashing ratcheted up like his arms were in danger of flying out of their sockets. Then, without warning, Edward yanked his shirt off too. Buttons went flying.

His flabby, hairless body was not pretty. He had a Buddha belly where the bartender had six-pack abs.

June, a sexy dancer in her own right, seemed to be in her own little world— a continent away from Edward's. She kept her shirt on.

Janzek saw Becky and Sam across the room. Becky caught his eye, shook her head, and roared with laughter.

Geneva poked him. "A regular three-ring circus we got here."

"My first rager in Charleston," Janzek said. "Something I'm never gonna forget."

FORTY

NED CARLINO, HIS BROTHER RICH, AND CHRIS MARTONE WERE finishing up a late dinner at Hall's Chop House on King Street.

"I still don't get them charging eighty-five bucks for a steak, Neddy," Rich Carlino said to his brother. "I mean, in this little burg?"

"Let me ask you a question, Rich. Was it good?" Carlino asked.

"Yeah, it was good."

"Let me ask you another question. Did you pay for it?"

"No."

"So, quit your bitching," Carlino said.

Rich held up his hands. "Okay, okay. Just sayin'."

"I'm beginning to like your little burg, Ned," Martone said.

Ned didn't get why his brother thought it necessary to bring along Martone. Guy ate like a caveman. It was like having the maid over for cocktails.

"Well, good, Chris. I'm glad," Carlino said.

"'Cept that guy—the greeter, I guess you call him—too damn friendly," Martone said. "Keeps saying, 'We're so happy to have you here as our guest tonight.' Or coming over, putting his hand on my shoulder when I'm in the middle of a bite and saying, 'You enjoying your dinner, sir, is everything to your liking?' Fucking guy a fag or something?"

Ned shook his head. "Hey, Chris, lower your voice. This isn't the goddamn Badda Bing or something," he said. "Guy's the son of the owner."

Rich looked over at Martone and shook his head.

"Yeah, keep your stupid fuckin' comments to yourself," Rich said, like Martone was a twelve-year-old.

Carlino gave his brother a nod. "Did I tell ya? The emperor came through like a champ."

"Who's the emperor?" Rich asked.

"Trajan."

"Why you call him that?"

"You know the Roman emperor... Trajan?" Carlino asked.

"Never heard of him," Rich said.

Carlino looked at his brother and shook his head. "We did go to the same high school, right, Rich?"

Rich wiped his mouth looking quizzical. "Yeah, why?"

Carlino knew his brother would be on the back of a garbage truck if it wasn't for him.

"Never mind," he said. "So anyway, we got ourselves two more votes."

Rich pumped his first. "That about wraps it up, huh?"

"Just need a few more," Carlino said, lowering his voice and leaning toward Martone. "So, Chris, your next job, assuming I get it set up, is going to be way different from that guy in the barn. Only similarity is you're gonna use a shotgun again and it's gonna look like an accident."

Martone nodded, though Carlino knew he was more comfortable with his Glock.

"So, I'm gonna try to get this guy down to the plantation," Carlino went on. "Then, the next morning you, me, Rich, and the guy will go on a little hunting trip."

"So, who's the guy? The target?" Rich asked.

"His name's Janzek. A detective, Charleston Police Department."

Martone's eyes lit up. "Sweet," he said. "I love whacking cops."

Carlino looked back at his brother.

"You remember when Dick Cheney shot that guy?" Carlino said. "Down in Texas, duck hunting."

"Sort of," Rich said. "Bush's vice president, right?"

"Very good," Carlino said.

Rich shook his head. "I don't know, man."

"You don't know what?" Carlino asked, his patience with his brother waning.

"That's a little dicey. Wouldn't it be better if Chris just follows him somewhere in town here. Takes him out with a bullet to the back of the head?"

Chris Martone's eyes got big. "Yeah, or I could blow him out of his fuckin' shoes with one of my bombs."

Carlino turned to his brother.

"I'll tell you why, Rich, 'cause that way we'd get every cop in South Carolina on the case, goin' after a cop killer. My way, there's just a simple, routine investigation and the verdict ends up being it was just an unfortunate and tragic accident." Carlino took a long sip of his red wine.

"Besides, my way is so much more creative."

"You really think the guy'll come down to Pinckney?" Rich asked.

"I think it's a possibility."

"Why?"

"'Cause it's a golden opportunity for him to poke around, see if he can get something on us. Guy's definitely got me in his crosshairs."

"Perfect," Martone chuckled. "Then I'll get him in mine."

FORTY-ONE

Janzek was in his office at seven the next morning. A little hungover but not too bad, considering he only got four hours of sleep.

He and Geneva had left June's house at around 12:30, then walked back to Geneva's. After they rehashed the dinner party, they started kissing like teenagers on her living room couch.

He left around two and was in bed by 2:15. He had called Ernie Brindle the day before and said he and Rhett needed to get together with him. Brindle was out of the office all day and couldn't meet with them. So, they had an eight o'clock scheduled for this morning. Rhett got there at ten of eight, then together they walked down to Brindle's office.

Brindle had a big container of Black Tap coffee in his hand. He looked like he'd already polished off five of them, he was so amped up.

"Come on in, boys," Brindle said with a smile. "So, I just heard, we got the guy. Driggers filled me in."

"The wrong guy," Janzek said.

"*Fuu-ck*, are you kidding me?" Brindle said, throwing up his hands. "Again?"

"Yeah, no way Driggers's guy did it," Rhett said. "This thing's way bigger than some dude running down the mayor 'cause he had a wandering johnson."

"Jesus, Delvin, will you speak fuckin' English," Brindle said, shaking his head. "So then, what the hell do you two got?" He sipped his Black Tap. "I can see Jimmie getting a little overzealous, but he usually gets the guy."

Rhett shot Janzek a look. Brindle intercepted it.

"What's that look s'posed to mean?" Brindle asked.

"Nothing," Rhett said.

"Ernie," Janzek said, "I can guarantee you, Driggers's guy didn't do it. Like we told you before, Rutledge Middleton is up to his ass in this thing, and we got a strong hunch he's Ned Carlino's boy. You know who Ned Carlino is, right?"

Brindle's eyes got big. "Yeah, fuckin' heavy hitter. You sure?"

"We can't give you hard evidence right this minute," Janzek said, "but we're getting close."

"Close is not gonna do it for me."

"It's all we got right now," Janzek replied.

Then he and Rhett laid out everything they had. First, the matchbook in Jefferson Davis's car that tied him to Middleton. And, even though they couldn't match the Mercedes key in Davis's pocket to the Mercedes used in the hit-and-run, they told him they were certain Davis was behind the wheel. Janzek finding out that Davis was left-handed backed up the eyewitnesses' report of seeing him aiming a pistol out the window right before he hit McCann.

Then they outlined everything they had dug up about Ned Carlino, including how Carlino had bought off Philadelphia pols to get slot machines at his racetrack and how similar that was to what they suspected Carlino was doing in Charleston, except now on a far larger scale. Janzek told Brindle about their suspicion that Carlino was somehow influencing people to vote for the billion-dollar casino, which Mayor McCann had been dead-set against.

Then, finally, they filled him in on Carlino's association with known racketeers and murderers, half of whom shared the same last name.

That got Brindle's full attention.

"Jesus Christ, that's just what we need, a bunch of mobbed-up Philadelphia goombahs coming down here and setting up shop," he said, shaking his head. "Hey, what do you have on the Watson girl rape?"

Janzek looked at Rhett. Rhett's eyes dropped to the floor.

"All we got is the classic, 'he said, she said,'" Janzek said.

Rhett looked up. "Yeah, except there are three *he*'s."

Brindle shook his head. "Consensual is their story?"

Janzek and Rhett nodded.

"Well, you guys are really knockin' it out of the park," Brindle said.

"Ernie," Rhett said, soberly. "I want to say something."

"Okay," Brindle replied. "Then say it."

"I don't know about Driggers."

Janzek tried to catch Rhett's eyes. Head him off at the pass.

"What the hell's that s'posed to mean?"

Rhett exhaled. "I think he may be... dirty."

Brindle's eyes narrowed. "Are you fucking kidding me?" he said. "Jimmie Driggers has got almost thirty years on the job. More collars than just about anybody in the history of the department."

Rhett held up both hands. "Hey, last thing I want is to get jammed up with you, Ernie, but I gotta tell you what I think."

"That's your whole problem, Delvin. Sometimes you shoot your mouth off before you think," Brindle said. "I'm gonna just pretend this conversation ended when you told me about Carlino."

Janzek's cell phone rang. He looked down at the number.

"Holy shit, speak of the devil, it's Carlino," he said. "I'm gonna take it."

Brindle nodded.

Janzek hit the green button on his cell. "Hello."

"Hey, Detective, it's Ned Carlino," Carlino said. "So, I just had a guy drop out of one of my shoots down at the plantation. I know it's last minute and you're a busy man, but maybe you could come down tonight after work, then we go out first thing tomorrow morning. You could be back there in the late morning catchin' bad guys."

Janzek almost blurted out a yes.

"I appreciate the offer. I am pretty busy, but can I get right back to you?"

"Sure, let me know as soon as you can. If you can't do it, I gotta get someone else."

"I understand, call you back shortly."

"Okay."

Janzek hung up.

"What the hell was that about?" Brindle asked.

"Carlino wants to be my new best friend," Janzek said. "Asked me to go duck hunting at his plantation tomorrow morning."

"You're kidding? What's that all about?"

"I think I should go."

"Why?" Brindle and Rhett said in unison.

Janzek scratched the back of his head and tapped a pen on Brindle's desk.

"Carlino wants me to come down there so he can figure out what we got on him. You know, ply me with a few drinks, maybe I let a few things slip."

Brindle looked at Rhett, then Janzek. "So, you figure the opposite's gonna happen, is that it?"

"Yeah, I get stuff out of him instead."

"I think you're dreaming," Brindle said.

Janzek threw up his hands. "What do I have to lose?"

"Oh, I don't know, your life, maybe," Brindle said. "I think it's a bad idea, Nick."

The way Janzek heard it, that wasn't exactly a no.

AFTER NED CARLINO HUNG UP WITH JANZEK, HE OPENED HIS *Wall Street Journal* and read it, then his Charleston newspaper. If the *Journal* took him a half hour to get through, the *Post & Courier* took three minutes. Five, max. It was usually pretty lean on content.

But not today. The headline read: PRO-CASINO GROUP A FEW VOTES SHORT. Carlino tossed the paper on the floor in disgust, pulled out his cell, and dialed Rutledge Middleton.

Middleton answered.

"I want you to talk to the editor of the local rag" Carlino was revved up. "Tell him he's got a lawsuit on his hands unless he prints a retraction of today's headline."

"I haven't seen it yet," Middleton said. "What's it say?"

Carlino read him the headline.

"Shit like that feeds on itself," Carlino said. "People on the council read it and think, maybe they should change their mind and go against it."

"I understand," Middleton said, "but we have all the votes we need."

"Yeah, we do, but a couple of them are soft. I don't need shit like this getting them to rethink their vote."

"I hear you," Middleton said. "I'll call the owner. What exactly do you want me to say to him?"

"Tell him his jerk-off reporter is just speculating," Carlino said. "Tell him the reporter doesn't have a clue who's for it and who's against it. Guy maybe had a quick conversation with a few of the assholes on the council."

"So, what would be the grounds of a lawsuit, Ned?"

"Fuck if I know, you figure it out," Carlino said, getting even more worked up as he stared down at the headline. "Get 'em to write another story, a new headline, something like, 'pro-casino group optimistic on next week's vote.'"

"Okay, I'll get on it."

Carlino hung up, reached down for the paper, balled it up, and hurled it in his wastebasket.

FORTY-TWO

Janzek was in his office with Rhett. They had just left Brindle's office.

"I think we can safely assume Carlino didn't ask you down there 'cause he needs a guy who can shoot straight."

"Yeah, like I said, he wants to probe me, see what we got. I got the sense the guy's real methodical, probably a hell of a chess player. Doesn't make a move until he's figured out his opponent's next three."

Rhett glanced out the window.

"I think he might be looking to feed me information," Janzek said. "So he can get us to go in a whole different direction."

Rhett turned back to Janzek and tapped two fingers on the arm of his chair.

"Or," Rhett said, eyebrows arched, "what Brindle was saying."

"You mean, get me down there to take me out."

Rhett nodded. "Exactly. Somewhere on his own turf or out in the middle of nowhere. Figures you know too much. Plans to make sure you don't go home vertical."

Janzek shook his head. "Ain't gonna happen," he said. "No way in hell. Carlino knows if something happens to me every cop in Charleston will be crawling up his skivvies."

Rhett threw up his arms. "Okay, but don't say we didn't warn you."

Janzek shook his head. "Tryin' to take me out has way too big a downside."

"Maybe."

Janzek looked out his window. "Oh, and another thing..."

"What?"

"I'm gonna plant a bug," Janzek said. "Try to find out what Carlino and the boys are up to."

Rhett shook his head so hard his hair moved. "Now you're goin' way off the reservation, Nick," he said. "You can't fucking do that. It's totally inadmissible, anyway."

Janzek just sighed.

"Seriously, you can't—" Rhett said.

Janzek held up his hand, took out his cell phone, and dialed.

It rang a few times.

"Hello, Mr. Carlino"— he paused—"yeah, okay, Ned—hey, I'd like to take you up on your offer. See if I can still hit a flying object. I just need directions."

He got a pen out and started writing.

"Got it. I'll be there around seven or so... yeah, me too. Looking forward to it."

He hung up and looked at Rhett. "Never hunted a day in my life. Not really a big fan of guns."

Rhett smiled and shook his head. "Ever occur to you maybe you're in the wrong business."

Janzek's cell phone rang. He looked at the display but didn't recognize the number. He held up his hand to Rhett. "Hang on a sec... hello."

"Detective Janzek?

"Yeah."

"Hey, my name's Charlie Crawford. I'm with the Palm Beach Police Department, Palm Beach, Florida."

"Yeah, Charlie, what can I do for you?"

"I'm trying to track down a fugitive from down here, a guy by the name of Roy Jenkins. Word is, he may be up there somewhere. He's an art forger, a pretty damn good one. Ring a bell at all?"

Janzek thought for a moment. "Can't say it does. But I can ask around. Check with some people who might have run across him."

"I'd appreciate it. He's also wanted for assault."

"Gimme a day or two to get back to you, Charlie. I got your number here."

"Thanks, man."

Janzek clicked off and heard loud, thudding footsteps. He looked toward the door.

It was Jimmie Driggers, and he wasn't happy.

"What the fuck is this?" Driggers said. "We're putting my suspect on ice because you two don't think he did it?"

"Is that what Brindle told you?" Janzek asked.

"Yeah, and it's fuckin' bullshit," Driggers said. "I mean, he's saying if Cannon's all we got, then maybe we go with him. 'But, give it another week, Jimmie, see if we do better.' Which is really fucked 'cause I'm tellin' you, Cannon fuckin' did it."

"Problem is, Jimmie, nobody else thinks so," Janzek said.

"I don't see you geniuses coming up with someone better."

Janzek shook his head. "News flash, Jimmie," he said. "It's not about coming up with *someone better*, it's about coming up with the right guy."

"Don't get all high-and-mighty with me. Like I said, Cannon's the guy."

"And you got a confession out of him?" Rhett asked.

"'Course not," Driggers said, "but so what—what does that mean?"

"Means everyone but you thinks Cannon ain't the guy," Rhett said.

Driggers's eyes went from Rhett to Janzek, his expression like he was talking to two crack-addled lowlifes. Then he stormed out of the room.

Janzek stood up.

"Where you goin'?" Rhett asked.

"Go buy me some hunting gear."

FORTY-THREE

A BLACK GUY IN A DARK SUIT WAS WAITING FOR JANZEK AS HE
got out of his car at Pinckney Hall. "Good evening, sir, I'm Jeter," the
man said. "You must be Detective Janzek?"

The man smiled and flashed two rows of snow-white teeth and
one gold crown.

"How you doin', Jeter," Janzek said, looking around. "Beautiful
place you got here."

The black man nodded. "The rest of the fellas are over in the
guest house, having themselves a libation," he said, pointing to a two-
story brick house with ivy-covered walls and fluted columns at the
front entrance. "That's where you'll be staying, sir. I can take your
bag over there, if you'd like."

"No, that's fine—I got it."

"Okay, well, have yourself a nice time, sir."

"Thanks, Jeter."

Janzek nodded, got his well-traveled L.L. Bean duffel bag stuffed
with new hunting gear out of the car, and walked over to the
guesthouse.

He opened the door and walked in. He saw two men talking to

three women. None of the women were their wives, that was clear. For one thing, they were half the men's ages. For another, no husband would ever let his wife dress like these women were dressed.

One of the men looked a lot like Carlino, except taller. He glanced over at Janzek. "Wild guess," he said. "Detective Janzek?"

Janzek walked over to him. "Yeah, hi, Nick Janzek," he said, putting out his hand.

"Rich Carlino. My brother's—um—taking a little nap."

The other man next to him laughed.

"Chris Martone," the other one said. "I'm an old friend, and this is Justine, Ashley, and—sorry, I forget..."

"Vruska."

Janzek nodded to all three women. They were all in their early twenties, he guessed, and, in Delvin-speak, "dimes."

"So, you found the place all right?" Rich asked.

Janzek nodded. "Yeah, only one wrong turn."

"Kinda in the middle of nowhere, huh?" Martone said.

He had a pretty serious accent. South Jersey, Janzek guessed.

He heard a door open and saw Carlino come out. Right behind him was a six-foot-tall blonde. A double-dime.

"Thought I heard your voice," Carlino said with a big smile.

He went up to Janzek and gave him a bear hug. Janzek definitely wasn't expecting that on their first date.

"Welcome to Pinckney." Carlino said.

"Thanks."

Carlino looked over at William at the bar.

"Well, what are we waiting for?" Carlino said. "Let's get you a drink, my friend."

He and Janzek walked over to the bar.

"This is William," Carlino said. "Man makes the best drinks in South Carolina. Maybe the world."

William smiled and nodded.

"I'll just have a beer," Janzek said. "Got a Heineken, maybe?"

"Yes, sir," William said, pointing to the green bar stick, "tap or bottle?"

"Tap's good. Thanks."

"So," Carlino said, "I figured we'd go out at six in the morning. Reveille at five thirty, then a quick breakfast."

Janzek nodded as William handed him the Heineken draft.

"Sounds good to me."

"So, why don't we go relax a little, have a chat with the ladies," Carlino said, walking back to where the others were seated.

JANZEK HAD JUST FINISHED HIS SECOND HEINEKEN. HE WAS thinking how his social life had really picked up. This was the second night in a row where he was going to be having dinner at an actual dinner table. A very different crowd from the night before, to be sure, since the women in the line-up tonight weren't there for their minds and intellects. From what he could tell so far, none of the people here drank as hard as the ones from the night before. Although the one named Chris and the girl Ashley seemed to be giving them a pretty good run for their money.

Carlino's brother, Rich, and Justine had disappeared shortly after Janzek arrived and had just reemerged from what Janzek assumed was a bedroom. A fancy bedroom, he imagined. King-sized beds, crispy sheets, a mirror on the ceiling, maybe. The opposite of his bedroom on Queen Street.

Turned out, though, the women weren't going to be joining them for dinner.

The four men walked up to the main house at 8:15 and ate the best lamb chops Janzek had had in a long time. They talked a lot about football. The Eagles and their Superbowl win, in particular.

After dinner, they all went back to the guesthouse. Chris Martone and Vruska— drinks in hand— disappeared immediately, then Carlino gave Janzek a little wave and walked out of the room—

this time with Ashley. Five minutes later, Rich Carlino got a bottle of champagne and two glasses, put his arm around one named Carla—Ned Carlino's double dime—and they were gone.

"Guess it's just us," Justine said, putting her hand on Janzek's arm. They were sitting at two bar stools. William was at the other end, trying to blend into the mahogany paneling. Which, at six-eight, was no easy trick.

"So, where'd everybody go?" Janzek said.

Justine laughed. "Gee, I wonder," she said, moving closer. "You're very cute, you know."

"You mean, for a cop?" Lame, he knew, but he was pretty far outside his comfort zone.

"No, that's not what I meant," she said, and leaned across and gave him a kiss on the lips, then pulled back. "How'd you get that scar?"

"Misunderstanding with a bear," he said, looking to kill the subject.

"Really?" She pulled back from him and gave him a look that made promises.

"Wanna go back there?" she said, gesturing with her head.

He hesitated.

"Well, I do, but I'm not going to."

She cocked her head to one side.

"You a happily married man or something?"

He shook his head. "No, but I have a... girlfriend."

She laughed.

"So? I have a boyfriend."

"Yeah, well, maybe I'm just crazy."

"But that's your answer and you're stickin' to it?"

He nodded.

"I gotta tell you, you definitely are crazy, but I guess I admire you for it."

FORTY-FOUR

Janzek was in bed.

Alone.

His watch alarm had just gone off.

It was three in the morning.

He slipped out of the sheets of his king-size bed. Turned out there was no mirror on the ceiling. He was wearing just boxers. He went and got the two bugs out of the pocket of his duffel bag, then got his cell phone and clicked the flashlight switch.

He walked to the door of his bedroom and slowly turned the knob.

Then he went down the hallway. He was glad there were no squeaking floorboards in the elegant herringbone hardwood floor.

Inside the large living room, the only other light came from the three antique slot machines all in a row on a long, dark wood bench. Janzek wondered if they were relics from Carlino's racetrack outside of Philadelphia.

He looked around for the table that he had targeted earlier in the night. It was between two big leather chairs and a leather sofa. He thought it was the first place anybody would think to sit. It was in the middle of everything and also close to the bar. He knelt down next to the table and reached up under it. He felt a spot in a corner and stuck the first bug there. Then he put his hands on two sides of the table and shook it noiselessly. He didn't hear anything drop and reached up under. The bug was still there.

Next, he walked over to the secondary spot he had decided on. It was under the overhang of the bar itself. He reached back about two feet and stuck the bug there. There was no way that anybody sitting at the bar would stumble across it, it was that far from the edge. The only person he thought would notice it was someone cleaning the room. And that would almost have to be if they were looking for it. He turned toward the hallway and walked back toward his bedroom. Then suddenly, he heard a noise. It was someone flushing a toilet. He stopped dead in his tracks and waited.

He really didn't want to have to pretend he was sleepwalking.

He didn't hear anything more.

He tiptoed back to his bedroom and slid back under the sheets.

HE WOKE UP TO THE SOUND OF SOMEONE KNOCKING ON HIS door, then a loud voice.

"Rise and shine." It was Carlino. "It's five thirty, Nick. Bacon, eggs, and bourbon waiting for ya."

He got dressed in the shirt and jacket he had bought the day before at Half Moon Outfitters. He smoothed out the creases as best he could so they didn't look brand new. Then he pulled on his Levi's, which had a lot of mileage on them. He checked his clothes out in the mirror, decided he could pass for a hunter, and walked out into the living room where the other three were chowing down at a table off in one corner.

Chris Martone looked at him funny when he walked up to the table.

The women apparently didn't feel it necessary to get up and break bread with the hunter-gatherers.

"Sleep all right, Nick?" Carlino asked.

"Yeah, good. Thanks."

"Solo, huh?" Carlino said.

Janzek nodded.

Chris Martone looked at him like it didn't compute. "Your dick busted or something?"

Janzek forced a laugh and took a bite of the thick bacon.

"So, Ned tells me you're new on the job in Charleston?" Rich said.

"Yeah. And the first day the mayor gets killed."

"No shit," Rich said. "You caught the guy yet?"

"Nah, not yet."

"But you got an idea who did it?" Rich asked, throwing down a big forkful of scrambled eggs.

"Yeah, pretty good idea," Janzek said, polishing off the strip of bacon.

"Detective Janzek *almost* always gets his man," Carlino said.

"Glad to hear it," Rich said.

Janzek noticed four identical flasks at the end of the table.

"So, I guess that's the bourbon you were talking about?" Janzek said to Carlino, pointing at the flasks.

"Yeah, a little custom inherited from old man Pinckney. He walked me through the whole hunting thing after I signed the contract. Told me you need to have a little 'bracer' on cold mornings before goin' out. But I got the feeling he had a 'bracer' even when it was ninety degrees."

Ten minutes later, the four got up from the table. Janzek followed the others and picked up the last remaining flask.

A few minutes later, the four of them were getting bounced around on a dirt road in a green Ford 250 club cab. Chris Martone was driving, Rich Carlino riding shotgun, Ned Carlino and Janzek in the back.

Janzek asked Carlino if he had dogs, since the way he heard it, hunting dogs were supposed to sniff out the birds, then go retrieve them once they fell out of the sky. Carlino explained that the old man who trained them had died, and he hadn't replaced him yet. So the dogs were staying in their kennel.

"Beautiful country," Janzek said to Ned Carlino.

"I know, beats the hell out of the streets of Philly," Carlino said.

Janzek nodded. "How much do you lead the birds?"

"You asking me?" Carlino said, "Shit, only time I ever hit 'em is when I close my eyes."

"Just aim at their beaks," Rich Carlino said from up front.

"Thanks," Janzek said, watching him take a pull from his silver flask.

Ned Carlino took out his flask, rolled his head back, and chugged. He shook his head and winced.

"Christ," he said. "Whoever said this was a good custom?" He smiled at Janzek. "Come on, if I'm doing it, you have to. Down the hatch."

Janzek unscrewed the top and sniffed it. It smelled strong.

He took a pull. He never did well with straight bourbon. Or any booze, first thing in the morning.

"Jesus," he said, shaking his head.

Carlino laughed.

Rich Carlino pulled over.

"Just saw a covey up ahead," Rich said. "You see 'em?"

"No," Carlino said, "right or left side?"

"Left," Rich said. "Let's go check it out, maybe there's another one in there."

Janzek figured out a covey meant a flock of birds.

All four of them got out of the pickup with their shotguns raised.

Rich and Chris Martone let Janzek and Carlino go ahead of them.

Janzek heard the heavy, shuffling steps behind him. All four of them had their shotguns in ready position.

There suddenly came a flapping and a *whooshing* sound to their right, and a covey of quail flew up out of the bushes. Rich and Chris Martone swung on the birds and fired.

One of them was hit and dropped back into the bushes.

"Nice shot," Martone said to Rich.

"Thanks," Rich said. "I think we got more in here."

Janzek walked forward beside Carlino.

Then another covey of quail flew up out of a thicket.

All four of them raised their shotguns and fired. Janzek missed. But two quail fell to the ground ahead of them.

"Way to go!" Rich said to his brother. "You guys mind getting 'em? Might be more still in here."

"Sure," Carlino said. He started walking and Janzek followed him. Then, without warning, Carlino turned and started running back to the other two.

It hit Janzek like a baseball bat to the gut. He was a sitting duck, just twenty yards in front of them.

He charged into the bushes and immediately heard the simultaneous explosion of two shotguns. He hit the ground and rolled to his right, dropping his shotgun, trying to put a big magnolia tree between him and the men behind. Then he got up and started running through the bushes—crouched low— going as fast as he could. He heard another blast, then the buckshot ripped into the brush a few feet to his left.

"Get him, for Chrissakes," he heard Carlino yell.

He heard the bushes rustling behind him and, still in a crouch, ran into a stand of trees. He got to a crevasse, fell forward, but caught himself just as he was about to fall to the ground. Then he heard two more shotgun blasts and felt a sudden jab of pain in his left shoulder. It felt like he had been stung by a swarm of bees.

He saw another stand of trees ahead and ran for it.

"Come on, for Chrissakes, get the son of a bitch," he heard Carlino shout again. But this time his voice came from farther back.

Janzek ran faster, his heart pounding.

He came to the edge of a shallow stream and didn't hesitate: He ran through it, the water only up to his ankles. Then he scrambled up a bank, looked out, and saw an open field.

He ran onto it but realized he made an easy target there. At least shotguns were only good at fairly close range. He knew, though, the men had backup weapons. He turned and looked back, but there was no one behind him. He didn't slow down and ran as fast as he could to the other side of the field. Suddenly, he heard the *crack* of gunfire, and the ground near him kicked up. He turned his head and saw Martone and Rich Carlino holding pistols with both hands. He heard another shot and then a bullet *thunked* into a tree just ahead.

He ran into the woods, going full speed, weaving, and dodging trees.

It felt like he was halfway through a marathon. He hadn't run like this since he played sports in college.

Sweat was pouring off him. He bent over, feeling like he was going to throw up.

He looked down at the cuffs of his pants. They were shredded and ripped; burrs and a crooked twig were stuck to one leg. His Merrell's were crusted with mud and soaked through from the brackish stream. He turned his head and looked at his shoulder that had caught the buckshot. There were little red welts all over the back and side of his shoulder. A foot to the right and up a little, it would have been his head.

Then he heard branches cracking, like an elephant was charging.

He looked back and saw Chris Martone fifty yards back and heard a burst of automatic weapon fire.

He turned and ran, running so fast he couldn't keep all the tree branches from slapping him in the face.

He ducked under a big branch of a pine tree, then jumped over a tree stump but hit it with his left toe.

It hurt like hell, but he kept going.

Then he saw another stream up ahead. It was much wider and

deeper. He looked back and saw Martone, a little further back now, running but not shooting.

He gauged the width of the stream and figured that, by the time he got to the other side, Martone would be on the near side and would have an easy shot at him. He saw a stick floating down the creek. Based on its speed, the current was moving fast.

He dived in, then turned so that he was going downstream with the current. Staying underwater, he kicked and stroked with his arms.

He was running out of breath, but he kept going.

The water was brackish, and he couldn't see a thing. He just tried to stay underwater for as long as he could.

He slashed and kicked furiously one last time, then came to the surface.

He inhaled deeply and went under again, heading down stream.

A minute later he came up.

Then he inhaled a third time and went back under.

When he came up this time, he looked back behind him. The creek had become a small river, and he was in the middle of it. A long pine limb was bearing down on him. He caught it, then let it go off to one side of him.

He looked back again but didn't see anybody.

He paddled to a bank of the river, grabbed a slippery root, and pulled himself up.

He was breathing in short gasps, and his shoes sloshed with water as he started to run.

Then suddenly, not more than fifty yards away, he saw two men with rifles.

FORTY-FIVE

Turned out, they were boys. One of them reminded him of the kid who played banjo in *Deliverance*.

The boys were out hunting squirrels in the back of their house, which was really more like a cabin with a big silver trailer off to one side of it. Janzek asked them if he could use their phone, and the boys led him inside. His cell, having been underwater for the better part of the last fifteen minutes, was a goner.

He introduced himself to the boys' father who said his name was Roy Dan Creech. He showed Creech his soggy ID, then he dialed the phone. It was an old Trimline from at least twenty years ago. Didn't matter, it worked fine.

"Delvin, it's me," Janzek said. "You called it. Carlino and his mutts tried to kill me."

"Jesus, are you all right? Where the hell are you?"

"Yeah, I'm fine, I got no clue where I am." He looked over at Roy Dan Creech, who started to say something.

Janzek held up his hand.

"Hang on, I'm gonna put Mr. Creech on. It's his house, he'll tell you how to get here." Then he added. "Get down here as fast as you can. For all I know, those guys are closing in."

He could hear Delvin slam a door. "All right, I'm leaving right now. I'll get some guys."

"Hold on, here's Mr. Creech," Janzek said.

Creech gave Rhett directions.

Janzek walked around the house and looked out the windows. Nothing out there but chickens and a scrawny-looking horse.

He went back and grabbed the phone out of Creech's hand.

"Sorry, I gotta speak to him," he said, then to Rhett, "I'll call the sheriff or whoever's got this jurisdiction, get him here too."

"Yeah and see if Creech's got a hunting rifle for you," Rhett said. "I'm on my way, probably thirty-five minutes. I got a good idea where you are."

Rhett hung up. Janzek had never heard Rhett so jacked up in their short time together as partners.

JANZEK WAS LOOKING OUT THE WINDOW, CREECH'S DEER RIFLE up against his shoulder, when two cop cars pulled up twenty-five minutes later.

Janzek put the hunting rifle down to his side.

He walked out onto the porch, holding up his ID in his right hand.

"Nick Janzek, Charleston Police," he shouted. "Violent crimes unit."

Three uniforms and an older guy with a gray mustache walked toward him.

The older man holstered his pistol, the other three kept theirs ready.

The older man was the local sheriff.

Janzek explained what had happened. It was a lot for the sheriff and his deputies to process. The sheriff asked him several questions and made him repeat himself in a few places.

A few minutes later, Janzek heard a siren, and a minute after that Rhett wheeled up and jumped out of his unmarked Crown Vic. Four uniforms followed in a black-and-white right behind him.

Rhett went right up to Janzek. "They never showed up?"

Janzek shook his head.

"And you're okay?"

"Yeah, fine."

Rhett turned to the sheriff and introduced himself.

Then the sheriff, his deputies, and the police got in their cars. Janzek got in with Rhett, who followed the sheriff and his men along a backwoods road to Pinckney Hall.

Ten minutes later, they were bumping down the long allée to Pinckney Hall, the perfect rows of live oaks lining either side.

Janzek saw the erect figure of Jeter walk down the steps of the house. He wondered whether Jeter just sat on the porch all day long with a pair of binoculars up to his eyes.

Janzek got out of the car before Rhett had come to a full stop, Rhett's spare Glock in his hand.

"Where's Carlino?" Janzek asked Jeter.

Jeter looked at Janzek differently than when he'd first arrived. His dark, squinty eyes were hostile now.

Rhett and the sheriff came up behind Janzek.

"In the guest house," Jeter said, looking around at the seven heavily armed law enforcement officials.

"Follow me," Janzek said, walking down the brick path to where he had recently spent the night.

Rhett caught up to Janzek and the other seven men were right behind them.

Janzek got to the door and turned to the sheriff.

"Why don't you and your guys go around back? I'll whistle, then we all go in."

The sheriff nodded and went around the left side of the house.

Janzek gave them enough time to get to the back, put two fingers in his mouth and whistled.

He put his hand on the doorknob, and nodded to Rhett, who nodded back.

Janzek swung it open and he and Rhett, in a crouch with both hands on their weapons, charged in. The three uniforms were right behind them.

"All right, everyone—freeze," Janzek said. "Weapons on the floor."

Carlino was sitting in one of the leather chairs, his brother and Chris Martone in the couch, watching *Morning Joe*. Three of the four women were at the breakfast table having breakfast.

They all put their hands up.

"What the hell's this?" Carlino said, alarmed. "Put the guns down, will ya'? We're not armed, for Chrissakes."

FORTY-SIX

CARLINO PATIENTLY EXPLAINED TO THE SHERIFF AND RHETT that he, his brother, and their friend, Chris Martone, were very concerned about what had happened to Janzek after he ran off into the woods so unexpectedly. The only explanation the three of them could come up with was that because of the liquid breakfast he had— four shots of bourbon plus polishing off the flask in the pickup—that he was too drunk to know what he was doing. It was scary, Rich Carlino added, when Janzek ran off into the bushes at the same time the other three were firing on a covey of quail. It was just lucky none of them hit him, he added.

Janzek looked at them in disbelief, then his eyes darted first to Rhett, then the sheriff.

"You do realize this is complete bullshit," Janzek said, baring his shoulder. "And, fact is, one of them *did* hit me. On purpose."

The sheriff looked at Janzek's shoulder. "Looks like you're gonna survive."

"Only 'cause I ran my ass off when they started shooting."

"That's absurd," Carlino said, shaking his head.

Janzek heard a door open. Justine was dressed in blue jeans and a white-collared shirt, the sexy, revealing look long gone.

"Oh, Nick, thank God you're all right," she said, coming up to him. "I was so worried."

"What the hell are you talking about?" Janzek said.

"When you got up in the middle of the night," Justine said. "I didn't know what happened to you."

"Don't gimme that, I slept by myself."

The sheriff stepped toward Justine. "Tell me what happened last night, ma'am?"

She glanced over at Janzek but didn't make eye contact.

"Well, he and I were in bed and about two in the morning he got up—"

Janzek exploded. "This is bullshit. I was never in the same bed—"

The sheriff held up a hand to Janzek.

"Hang on," he said. "I want to hear what she has to say."

"Exactly what Carlino told her to say." Janzek said.

The sheriff stepped toward Janzek.

"This is my jurisdiction and I'm calling the shots," he said, then turning to Justine. "Keep going."

"Well, like I said, he got up and didn't come back," she said, blinking. "I didn't know where he went, so I came out here and saw him—" she had it right down to the sigh and dramatic pause—"he had a bottle in front of him, a shot glass in one hand and a joint in the other."

Janzek laughed derisively. "Come on," he said to the sheriff, "you don't believe this shit?" Janzek pointed at Carlino: "That guy wrote the whole script for her."

"That's an outrageous accusation," Carlino said.

The sheriff stepped toward Rhett.

"I want to talk to you," he said, and the two started walking to the other side of the room.

Janzek followed them.

The sheriff turned and held up his hand to him.

"Just me and your partner."

"Come on, what the—"

Rhett held up his hand. "It's cool, Nick," he said and walked away with the sheriff.

The sheriff started talking very earnestly to Rhett. Rhett said something back.

Then Janzek looked over at Carlino. Carlino smiled at him. He was enjoying himself. Janzek looked at Justine. She was sitting on a bar stool, looking down, not about to let him catch her eye.

The sheriff and Rhett walked back over.

"Detective, we're all gonna leave now," the sheriff said. "You're gonna go back to Charleston with your partner. Me and my boys back to our station."

Carlino stood up and walked toward the sheriff. "Wait a minute, Sheriff, what are you talking about. You're gonna let this man—" pointing at Janzek—"get off making these crazy allegations just 'cause he's a cop? Barges into my house ready to shoot up the place. I demand action be taken. This is a goddamn travesty."

"Please, Mr. Carlino," the sheriff said, putting his hands up, "let's just forget it ever happened. We're gonna take off, let you and your guests get back to what you were doing."

Carlino turned to Janzek. "I'm not gonna let you get away with this," he said. "You can't just come here, take advantage of my hospitality, and invent some paranoid plot. Trust me, this isn't the end of it."

"Trust me," Janzek said and walked toward the door, "it sure as hell isn't."

FORTY-SEVEN

"That guy Carlino's good, really good," Rhett said, as he drove down the allée out of Pinckney planation. "If I didn't know you, I might just buy that chick's little performance."

Janzek snorted a laugh. "Yeah, she had a good director."

"That sheriff," Rhett said, pulling out onto the two-lane road, "he said I oughta tell Brindle to put you on administrative leave."

Janzek shook his head.

"That's 'cause he's in on it," Janzek said. "Guarantee you, bought and paid for by Carlino, just in case something like this ever happened."

"Yeah, that occurred to me," Rhett said. "But how we ever gonna prove it?"

"We're not," Janzek said. "An envelope at Christmas is a pretty tough thing to prove."

Rhett nodded. "So, fill me in on the whole thing, blow-by-blow."

Janzek spent most of the ride back to Charleston telling Rhett what had happened since he first arrived at Pinckney Hall, a little over ten hours before, until Rhett showed up at Roy Dan Creech's house.

Rhett made the suggestion that Janzek go to Ernie Brindle right away and get his story on the record. He had a feeling that there could be some serious fall out, that Carlino was the type to want to capitalize on the whole incident. Do everything he could to make Janzek look bad and discredit him, including get him thrown off the mayor's murder, if possible.

Janzek agreed.

Then Rhett looked over at him. "I want you to know, just for the record, I wasn't just sittin' around while you were out there getting shot at," he said. "I got something you're not gonna believe."

"Let's hear it."

"You know how I was never buying that guy, Henry Reed, was a suicide?"

"Yeah, the trajectory of the shotgun, right?"

"Among other things. I mean, the fact that he waits to kill himself when he's facing a much softer sentence than originally. That makes no sense," Rhett said. "I mean, if he was going to kill himself, why wouldn't he do it when it looked like he was going up for twenty years instead of just six-to-eight. He was out on parole then, too."

"I hear you," Janzek said. "So, what exactly did you find out?"

"Well, I figured I'd go talk to Reed's wife, find out what I could," Rhett said. "I mean, it sounded like Driggers spent all of about five minutes on the damn case."

Janzek nodded and looked out his window at the rows of car dealerships along Highway 17.

"So, I had to work her a little—you know, ratchet up the Rhett charm. Broad wasn't giving me anything at first. Just a bunch of three-word answers. So, I ask her where she was when her husband did it."

"'Inside the house,' she says. She heard the shotgun. So I asked what she did at that point. 'Went to the window,' she says. So I ask her, then what happened? And she goes, 'Two men came out of the barn.' I'm like, *What? Two guys were in the barn?* And she nods. So, I ask if she got a good look at them. She goes, 'Good look? I took pictures of them with my camera phone. Didn't Detective Driggers show 'em to you?'"

"*Ho-ly* shit," Janzek said.

"Wait, that's not the half of it," Rhett said, reaching into the inside pocket of his jacket.

He pulled out an envelope and opened it up. There were four pictures in total. They were of Rich Carlino and Chris Martone coming out of a barn and going to their car.

"Wow," said Janzek, "these guys get around."

The only problem was, Rhett told Janzek, Mrs. Reed was so scared of the two men coming after her that she decided to drop the whole thing. Said she'd deny she'd ever taken the four photos too.

"Meaning we got dick," Janzek said.

Rhett nodded. "Until we got 'em behind bars," he said, driving into the police lot on Lockwood, "and she knows they're not gonna come pay her a visit."

Janzek went directly to Brindle's office. He knew Rhett's suggestion of going into damage-control mode was the right way to play it. On his way there, he flashed back to the bugs he had planted, his ace in the hole. He imagined they could be picking up some pretty incriminating stuff.

He described everything that happened at Carlino's plantation to Brindle except the planting of the bugs.

"For Chrissakes, Janzek," Brindle said, pushing his chair back. "What the hell were you thinking?"

"Sorry," Janzek said, "guess it was a bad idea. Shoulda listened to you and Delvin."

Brindle looked at the bloodstains on the shoulder of Janzek's shirt and pointed.

"You okay?"

"Yeah, fine." Janzek touched his shoulder gingerly. "What's a little buckshot?"

TURNED OUT, RHETT WAS RIGHT AGAIN.

At three o'clock, Brindle received a five-page, messengered letter from Rutledge Middleton.

It purported to recount what happened at Pinckney plantation.

It started with an account of the first meeting between Janzek and Ned Carlino in Carlino's office; how Carlino thought Janzek seemed like a nice guy and how Carlino was always a big supporter of cops to begin with. In the course of their conversation, the letter read, Carlino happened to mention that he had a plantation and asked the detective if he liked to shoot birds, and the detective said he did. And because he was so partial to law enforcement officers, Carlino invited Janzek down for some hunting when another guy dropped out and had to cancel at the last minute.

Janzek had accepted and driven down that night—last night, to be exact. Immediately, he had started drinking heavily while smoking a joint and talking somewhat abusively to the four female, "house guests."

Then, Carlino related, in the course of the evening Janzek had gotten friendly with one of the women by the name of Justine, and she and Janzek had ended up in bed together. Then there was a detailed description of what Justine had encountered when she woke up in the middle of the night and Janzek wasn't in bed. How she got concerned about him and went out and found him in the living room at two in the morning.

He had taken a bottle of Maker's Mark from the bar and was drinking shots, in between tokes on a joint. Then he had become verbally abusive to Justine for no apparent reason when she sat down next to him. She was concerned because he was "raging incoherent-ly," and he insisted that she drink with him. He tried to force her to smoke some of the joint, but she adamantly refused. After about an hour, she finally got him "calmed down" and coaxed him back to bed, where he proceeded to snore loudly. Some hours later—she didn't quite know when—there was a knock on the door, and Janzek got up and left.

It went on to say that Justine had heard later from Chris Martone that the detective immediately started drinking again before going hunting. She wasn't sure whether he had smoked more weed at that time, she said, but suspected he might have.

Next came the collective recollections of Chris Martone, Ned, and Rich Carlino. They gave their versions of what happened at the breakfast table, then in the pickup truck, and finally when they got out of the truck to hunt for quail.

Suffice it to say, Middleton's account went on, *Mr. Carlino did not feel that Detective Janzek's conduct was in keeping with that of an officer of the law, and further, was both disruptive and dangerous to himself and the others present.*

The last paragraph said, in effect, that although Carlino had grounds to press for disciplinary action to be taken against Janzek, that because of Carlino's profound respect for law enforcement, all he was going to ask for was an apology from Janzek. He added that he was well aware that there were "bad elements" in every line of work. Though Carlino felt that his hospitality had been taken advantage of, he was "confident that a continuation of good relations between him and the Charleston police force would be ongoing."

Janzek looked up at Ernie Brindle after he finished reading it and shook his head.

"I mean, you gotta be kidding me, Ernie," Janzek said. "I can see Carlino laughing his ass off after he wrote this piece of shit. And I guarantee you, this is all Carlino, Middleton didn't write a word of it."

He thought about the tapes again and how much he needed them.

"Yeah, but this could turn into a huge PR disaster," Brindle said.

"You can see what's going on here. If this guy wants to, he could feed this thing to the press and turn it into a big fucking nightmare."

"You're forgetting one little thing, Ernie."

Brindle raised his arms.

"I know, I know, that it's all concocted, it's all bullshit."

"Well, it is."

"I know that, but they got a lot of witnesses, and according to Rhett, one of the girls is pretty damn credible."

"Like I said, 'cause Carlino wrote her lines."

Brindle closed his eyes, like he'd just gotten a stab from a bad migraine.

"Listen, Nick, you gotta go apologize to the guy."

Janzek's mouth dropped.

"Really, Ernie? And while I'm asking him for his forgiveness—this guy who shot me—should I also promise I'll never say a mean thing about him?"

FORTY-EIGHT

JANZEK LISTENED TO CARLINO AND COMPANY VIA THE BUG under the table in Carlino's guesthouse. The quality of the audio wasn't perfect, but it was good enough.

"No," Carlino's voice said, "you can't do anything now. You do, and all of a sudden, his story about us trying to take him out looks pretty credible. Plus, the guy's gonna be watching his back real carefully."

Janzek could just picture Rich Carlino and Chris Martone nodding as his little silver microcassette recorder recorded their silence.

———

JANZEK CALLED GENEVA AT RED TRUCK BOOKS.

"Hi," she answered.

"I need to ask you a big favor. Could you arrange a meeting with your ex-mother-in-law, Mrs. Davis? I need to ask her something important about her son, Jefferson."

There was a pause.

"How 'bout this instead," she said. 'Oh hi, Geneva, how have you been? It's been too long, and I've missed you terribly. Particularly our little sessions on the couch.'"

"Sorry," Janzek said. "Hi Geneva, how have you been? I've missed you terribly. Particularly our little sessions on the couch."

"Good boy, much better," Geneva said, as she put books she'd just gotten from the UPS driver on their respective shelves. "First, she's not my *ex*-mother-in-law, she'll always be my mother-in-law. Second, it's going to be tough. She doesn't like to talk about Jefferson."

"Would you mind trying anyway? It's really important."

"Sure, I'll try. But I can't promise you anything."

"I understand."

"That's it? No invitation to go have another nice lunch or something?"

"Sorry, I'm—"

"I know, a workaholic."

"Yeah, but I'm working on it."

"Good boy. I'll try Dorothea and get back to you, okay?"

"I appreciate it."

"You're gonna owe me big."

She called him back two hours later and told him—as she'd predicted— that at first Mrs. Davis said she didn't want to talk about Jefferson. It was too painful, still too raw. Then Geneva gave her a gentle twist of the arm, told her how hard Janzek was trying to catch her son's killer, that finally she agreed to meet with him. But she had insisted that Geneva be there.

Janzek picked her up at the Red Truck a little before seven.

"And how was your day?" she asked, getting into his car.

"If I told you, you wouldn't believe me," he said, checking out her skirt that showed a lot of leg. "But seeing you makes me kind of forget it."

"Aw, that's sweet, Nick," she said. "You're gonna like Dorothea, by the way."

DOROTHEA DAVIS LIVED IN A NEAT, WHITE CAPE ON DUNNEMAN Street in Wagener Terrace, about twelve blocks north of the crosstown. Her backyard backed up to the Citadel campus.

They were sitting in her living room, which was dominated by an old Yamaha piano covered with family pictures. Most of them were of Marcus Crane and Jefferson Davis in uniform.

"Mrs. Davis, I'm trying to find out the identity of the man who murdered your son and would appreciate any help you can give me," Janzek said. "Can you tell me how Jefferson knew Rutledge Middleton?"

"I don't know, exactly," she said, looking down at the floor.

"Any light you can shed on anything, Mrs. Davis, will get me closer to finding his killer."

Dorothea Davis raised her head slowly.

"You're not really interested in finding Jefferson's killer, are you? All you care about is who killed the mayor."

"We're doing everything we can to solve both," Janzek said. "We're pretty sure their deaths are related."

Dorothea Davis sighed and looked back down at the dark carpet.

"Jefferson needed a lawyer. Someone recommended Middleton, I guess."

Janzek glanced over at Geneva.

"I know the detective, Mama. Like I told you, he's a friend of mine," she said. "He's a good man who's trying to get to the bottom of all this."

Dorothea looked at Geneva, and suddenly, she looked unspeakably sad. Janzek saw a tear in her eye. Geneva got up from her chair and went over to Dorothea. She sat down next to her and hugged her.

"Please help me find your son's killer, Mrs. Davis," Janzek said.

She looked at him. Her eyes were filled with tears, and her head slumped into Geneva's chest.

"You know how Jefferson wanted to go to college," Dorothea said to Geneva, "to be like Marcus?"

"I heard him talk about it," Geneva said, nodding. "Never knew it went anywhere."

"He told me he mentioned it to Rutledge Middleton," Dorothea said. "Told me Middleton promised he'd talk to somebody or write a letter for Jefferson. To someone he knew high up at the Citadel."

Janzek glanced over at Geneva and saw her fists tighten.

"Best I could tell, that's where it ended," Dorothea said. "I just think it was something Middleton promised Jefferson to get him to do stuff for him."

Dorothea stood up and walked across the living room into the kitchen. She came back in dabbing at her eyes with a paper towel, stopping in front of Janzek.

"It was so cruel," she said. "Jefferson would come by my house all excited. Told me how Middleton used his influence once to get a kid into Clemson and another into the Citadel. How they both had good careers now. One was an engineer."

Janzek saw Geneva's eyes darken and her chest heave.

"But how in God's name was Jefferson, a boy with a record, ever going to get into one of those places?" Dorothea said. "I was going to say something to him, but I didn't want to ruin his dream. And, truth was, I wanted to believe it too."

"That bastard," Geneva said.

"I never told you that before, honey?" Dorothea said.

Geneva shook her head while Dorothea sniffled quietly.

"Mrs. Davis, did Jefferson ever mention the name Carlino to you? Either Ned or Rich Carlino?"

Dorothea Davis dabbed at her eyes again.

"I—I don't remember," she said. "Sounds kind of familiar. He spoke to a man named Chris, I know, a few days before he was killed."

Janzek leaned forward.

"Did he say what Chris's last name was," he asked, "or why he called?"

Dorothea hesitated, then shook her head. "Sorry."

"Was it Chris Martone?" Janzek asked.

"Sounds familiar," Dorothea said.

Janzek pressed. "Did Jefferson maybe have another cell phone which might have had messages on it from back then?"

Dorothea tensed, thinking hard, like she wanted to do whatever she could to help. "Sorry," she said, finally, "only phone he had was the one you found in his car."

Janzek reached across and patted her wrist. "That's okay."

No one spoke for a few moments.

Finally, Janzek stood up. "Whoever killed your son, ma'am, we're gonna get him. I promise you that."

This time he didn't regret making the promise.

Dorothea Davis nodded slowly and looked up at him.

"Thank you."

"Thank you," Janzek said. "I appreciate your help, I really do."

Geneva walked back over to Dorothea and wrapped her arms around her again. Not saying anything, the two just slowly rocked for a few moments. After a while, Geneva broke the clinch, took her hand, and softly stroked Dorothea's face.

Then she stood up.

"Take care of yourself, Mama," Geneva said, walking toward the door.

"Thank you for seeing me, Mrs. Davis," Janzek said and he followed Geneva out the door.

Halfway down the path to the street, Geneva turned to him.

"So you know who Nick Carlino is?"

"You mean besides being a rich guy from Philadelphia who tried to kill me?"

"He tried to kill you?"

"I'll tell you all about it," Janzek said, walking to his car. "What do you know about him?"

"Ned Carlino is the largest stockholder of Monarch Hospitality, that company trying to get the casino here. Remember me talking about it at June's? He's the guy pulling all the strings."

"*Ho-ly* Christ," Janzek said. "So that's what this is all about."

"Must be," Geneva said. "So, tell me what happened?"

His mind was going in twelve directions.

"I planned to tell you at dinner," he said. "We have a reservation at the Average."

Geneva laughed. "You're never going to get it straight, are you? The Ordinary."

"Yeah, whatever," Janzek said, lost in thought. "This whole thing is starting to finally add up."

THE DINNER WAS BELOW AVERAGE FOR A PLACE THAT HAD SO much hype.

Janzek was telling Geneva all about what happened at Pinckney Hall earlier in the day.

She said, "Oh my God" several times and gripped his hand tightly more than once—one time so hard he thought she was going to break the skin. He finally got to the end. Geneva's mouth was open and she looked stunned.

"That is so incredible," she said. "And there's nothing you can do?"

He flashed to the tapes and smiled. "Oh yeah... there is."

"GOOD, 'CAUSE YOU SHOULD TOSS THAT GUY IN JAIL AND THROW away the key," Geneva said. "Not to mention how his company has such a sordid history."

"I remember you saying, for racism and human rights violations, right?"

"Exactly."

"Well, let me tell you, Carlino himself's got a pretty nasty history too."

"Who's surprised? I've been waging my quiet, little war against the whole casino thing. I think maybe it's time to step it up a little," Geneva said, shaking her head. "Let me see that shoulder of yours."

He had to think how he was going to show it to her.

He unbuttoned the top three buttons of his shirt.

"Wow, I get a striptease?"

He laughed, then took the collar of his shirt and pulled it down over his shoulder.

She leaned forward.

"Oh God, you poor baby. It looks like you got a really bad case of the measles. All those red spots. Did it bleed?"

"A little."

"Did you cry?"

"A little."

She laughed, kissed him on the cheek, and carefully pulled his shirt back over his shoulder. "But seriously, you could have been killed."

"No kidding, that was the whole idea."

"Then you wouldn't have been able to take me out to dinner."

"Or do a lot of other things."

They were back on her couch. "You're a hell of a kisser, you know," he said, coming up for air.

"You're not too shabby yourself."

"I'm way out of practice." He brushed a strand of hair away from her eyes.

"Shut up and kiss me again," she said, leaning into him.

It was like a switch was flipped and it suddenly became way more intense. Their hands started wandering and exploring. She reached over and turned off the lamp on the table next to them.

"Let's just fumble around in the dark," she said.

He didn't respond, because he was on a mission: To unhook her bra.

And she wasn't fighting it one little bit.

FORTY-NINE

His mental alarm clock went off at five in the morning.

He looked over at Geneva lying next to him. Her taut, muscular back with the sheet halfway covering her perfect, arched ass. He listened to her quiet breathing, more like a kitten, and looked down at the right side of her beautiful face, half on and half off the plump white pillow.

He was tempted to nudge her, wake her up, make love again. The morning was his favorite time.

He got up, put his clothes on, and started to walk out of the bedroom door. Then he turned, walked back over to Geneva, and leaned down and kissed her.

He was at his office at six. A half hour later, Rhett showed up.

"You know," Rhett said, sitting down in Janzek's office, "it's not like we're getting overtime."

"Yeah, I know," Janzek said. "Maybe we'll get back to normal hours when we wrap this thing up."

Rhett stretched out and took a long pull from his Black Tap coffee container.

"Yeah, if that ever happens," he said. "Don't forget we still got the rape, too."

"Yeah, I know, I been thinking about that too," Janzek said, as he watched a sly smile light up Rhett's face. "What?"

"How was your date last night?"

"Fine. Why?"

"'Cause I do believe you're wearing the exact same clothes you were wearing yesterday."

Janzek fought off a blush. "Yeah, so?"

"Just sayin'," Rhett answered. "I *am* a detective, you know."

"Okay, wiseass," Janzek said. "So, listen to what I found out last night about Ned Carlino."

First, he told Huger what Dorothea Davis had told him, then what Geneva said about Carlino and Monarch Hospitality. While they were talking, Janzek Googled Monarch on his computer.

"Says here they've had twenty-three lawsuits from former employees, plus the ACLU and the National Labor Relations Board." He skimmed a little further down the page. "Take this name down: Stan Warnecki, Department of Justice, Washington."

"Who's he?"

"He prosecuted Monarch on one of the cases. Got a thirty-million-dollar settlement, but then the plaintiff just— *poof*—vanished. Back in 2015—" He scrolled further down. "Here we go—says Edward H. Carlino owns four million two hundred thousand shares of Monarch stock."

Rhett was working his iPhone.

"Stock closed yesterday at twenty-two and a quarter," Rhett said, then, looking up, "That's a shade under a hundred million that Carlino's stock is worth."

Janzek nodded.

"So that means, hold on," Janzek was working the calculator on his phone, "that means for every quarter point Monarch stock goes up, Carlino's net worth increases by a million bucks."

"Correct," Rhett said, nodding back at him. "Meaning, that guy who won the lawsuit was gonna take a couple mil out of Carlino's pocket. Which, I'm assuming, is why he disappeared."

"And why McCann got hit, since he was gonna take a lot more than a couple million out of his pocket, assuming the casino got shot down."

They were both nodding now.

"We gotta get this guy, Delvin."

"Yeah, and all his lap dogs too. Like Middleton."

"Especially Middleton."

"You're not letting this get personal by any chance, are you Nick?"

"Oh yeah, definitely."

"You know what it says in the manual."

"Fuck the manual."

Janzek and Rhett talked about ways of getting to Carlino. They agreed that what they needed most of all was a weak link. Janzek told Rhett he had gone ahead and planted the bug. At first, Rhett gave him a look like Janzek was a naughty child in need of a serious spanking, then Janzek told him that was a big part of the reason he had gone down to the plantation in the first place. Told him though the audio from the bugs was inadmissible, it sure as hell wasn't unusable.

Slowly, he brought Rhett around to the point where Rhett finally conceded that maybe the bugs were a good idea after all. Janzek, knowing how guys in the south liked their football analogies, told him it was like having a bug in the other team's locker room at halftime. Something his New England Patriots might actually do. That got Rhett smiling and nodding.

Middleton was the logical weak link. They tossed around different ways to get to him.

"His son maybe," Rhett suggested.

They decided they should talk to Chelsea Watson, even though both of them had reservations about getting her involved. Janzek felt guilty about not having gotten anywhere on her case. And about the promise he had made to Chelsea. So far, he was just another guy who made promises and was full of shit.

He looked at his watch. It was 8:30. He called Chelsea's number. She answered and didn't seem that happy to hear from him. He asked her if he and his partner could come talk to her. She agreed, reluctantly.

They met her at her sorority house on Pitt Street. It was a short meeting. She said she was sorry, but she had decided to drop the charges against Quatro. Janzek looked at Rhett, then back at Chelsea. She apologized again and said maybe she was mistaken about the whole incident.

Janzek said she wasn't mistaken but told her he understood.

As he and Rhett got into their car afterwards, Janzek said to Rhett that Middleton had probably had a little talk with Chelsea. Or maybe had gotten his son to.

Rhett nodded and said, maybe Middleton wasn't such a weak link after all.

FIFTY

NOTHING WAS GOING ANYWHERE.

Janzek felt totally dead in the water. Desperate to get traction. Anywhere he could.

He suggested he and Rhett go have a chat with Mrs. Reed, widow of George Reed. See if they couldn't persuade her to swear out a statement about the men she had seen leaving the barn.

Ten minutes later, they were on their way to her house in Summerville.

They drove past a Costco. "That's my new favorite store," Janzek said.

"Why? It's not exactly bachelor friendly," Rhett said.

"What are you talking about?"

"Well, you gotta buy in bulk. Like sixteen tubes of toothpaste or five hundred rolls of toilet paper. I mean, you might not live long enough to use up all that bumwad."

He had a point.

They went another mile or two. Janzek came up with another idea about the tapes. It might work, he thought. He wanted to tweak it a little more before he sprang it on Rhett. His last idea hadn't worked out so well.

HENRY REED'S WIDOW LIVED IN A BIG, IMPRESSIVE COLONIAL house in Summerville. What was immediately obvious, however, was that she either didn't have the money to maintain it, or just didn't care how it looked. There was a drainpipe dangling off the edge of the roof in front, paint peeling off the columns, and all of the bushes and landscaping desperately needed a haircut.

NO ONE ANSWERED WHEN THEY PRESSED THE DOORBELL. THEY tried it again. Still nothing.

They walked around back and saw movement in the kitchen, then knocked on the back door, and Mrs. Reed finally opened it.

"Hi, Mrs. Reed," Rhett said. "Me again. And this is my partner, Detective Janzek."

She nodded wearily.

"May we come in, just ask you a few questions?" Rhett asked.

She didn't look thrilled with the idea.

"Just take a few minutes, promise," Janzek said.

She stepped back from the door. "Oh, okay."

Inside, it was more of the same: A musty odor that hit you when you first walked in and an overall untidiness that cried out for a cleaning lady who was a good scrubber.

They followed her through the kitchen that had dishes stacked high in the sink and smelled of cat food.

They sat down in a sitting room that had dark curtains pulled over all three windows, not letting in a ray of light.

"We need to catch those men who killed your husband, Mrs. Reed, and really need your help," Rhett said.

She cocked her head to one side.

"So, are you saying the official version now is it wasn't a suicide?" she asked. "Cause that's what Detective Driggers and the medical examiner said it was."

Janzek had read the report. He had also gone back and looked at the stories in the *Post & Courier*. There wasn't even a hint that it was anything but a suicide.

"What do you think really happened, Mrs. Reed?" Janzek asked.

"I think my husband was very depressed and in a state of deep despair," she said, "but I don't think those two men coming out of the barn right after I heard the shot were spectators."

She said it with no trace of irony.

"So, you think those men shot your husband and made it look like he committed suicide?" Janzek asked.

"Yes, I do."

"Why'd they do it?"

"'Cause a man named Rutledge Middleton hired them to."

"Why'd he hire them?" Janzek asked.

"'Cause he'd called Henry a bunch of times. Henry told me he was an investor of his and also the lawyer for one of the largest investors. He was demanding they get their money back."

"What did your husband say?" Janzek asked.

"He told him he didn't have any money left, which was true."

"And what did Middleton say?"

"He accused Henry of having money stashed away in some Swiss bank or an offshore account somewhere, but he didn't. Then Middleton told him to sell the house or whatever he had to do so he and the big investor could at least get some of it back. This house was all we had left."

"How long before your husband's death did this occur?"

"About two weeks before."

"And your husband never paid him any money?"

"No, whatever he had the government had frozen," she said. "He did put this place on the market, but there were no bites."

"Then the two men came?" Rhett asked.

Mrs. Reed nodded. "Yes, then the two men came."

"Would you be willing to swear that you saw them leave your barn right after you heard the shotgun blast that day last April?" Rhett asked.

She looked perturbed. "I told you last time. No."

Janzek shot a look at Rhett, then back to Mrs. Reed.

"But these men killed your husband, Mrs. Reed," Janzek said.

"Yes, but would that bring him back? Or the money?"

"But, please—"

"All it would bring back is those men," she said. "You don't think I haven't thought this through? That they'd come and threaten to kill me if I testified. Or forget about threaten... *just do it.*"

She was dug in, Janzek could see. Not only that, he couldn't argue with her.

"You'd get the satisfaction of seeing your husband's killers brought to justice," Rhett said.

"Not if I was dead."

FIFTY-ONE

CARLINO WAS FINISHING UP A LONG BREAKFAST MEETING WITH Rutledge Middleton at the Yacht Club, a private club on East Bay Street, when Janzek's call came in.

Carlino had set up the meeting with Middleton because he was still concerned about the casino vote. Yes, they had the votes—in theory, at least. But Carlino still worried that several of the voters seemed capable of changing their minds.

They were at a table overlooking the wide Cooper River. Carlino started in on a diatribe about some ad hoc group that was—quietly and behind the scenes—turning people against the casino. He showed Middleton a flyer that went into exhaustive detail about Monarch Hospitality and all the class-action suits that had been brought against it.

Carlino told Middleton that he had heard about a certain book-store owner who was apparently spearheading the opposition. It was almost like she had some vendetta against Monarch, Carlino said. Then he ranted on about obsessed do-gooders and conspiracy theorists who had nothing better to do with their time.

Middleton listened patiently all the way to the end of Carlino's tirade, then informed him that the bookstore owner just happened to be none other than Nick Janzek's girlfriend, Geneva Crane. Or at least they'd seemed very cozy at a dinner party he had attended with them the night before Janzek went down to Pinckney Hall. He told Carlino she had a store on King Street called Red Truck Books.

Carlino looked out the window and thought for a moment. His first reaction was to call his brother and have him arrange a "package deal," or a "two-bagger," as Rich liked to call it.

But Carlino was still concerned that if anything happened to Janzek after the aborted hit at his plantation, the whole Charleston Police Department would come after him with everything they had. He decided he should just concentrate on the bookstore owner. He knew where Geneva Crane worked, now he just needed to find out where she lived.

Sooner or later, he'd have to do something about Janzek. But not right away.

Coincidentally, right after that, he got a call from Janzek.

Not sounding as repentant as Carlino would have liked, Janzek asked if he could stop by to see him. They set a time for later that afternoon.

It was actually Rhett's idea for Janzek to wear a wire.

Brindle said Janzek didn't have to mean it when he apologized to Carlino, he just had to say the words. Just get it over with. Otherwise, for all Brindle knew, Carlino could bring an embarrassing action against Janzek and, by extension, the whole department. A "nuisance suit" was how Brindle described it, one that would probably grab bold headlines.

Janzek, wired up, was wondering exactly what he was going to say. The point of the meeting was not the apology, but to steer the conversation around to a certain subject and then get a few good, pithy quotes. And coming up with an insincere, bullshit apology was a cheap price to pay. To begin with, the whole apology thing was kind of high school. Maybe even middle school. What exactly was he supposed to say? "I'm very sorry, Mr. Carlino, for what happened and promise it will never happen again?"

Come to think of it, that sounded pretty good.

The receptionist led him into Carlino's office. Carlino was on the phone. He said, "call you back later" to someone and quickly hung up.

Janzek sat down.

Carlino dialed up the same smile he wore down at Pinckney Hall when Justine was accusing Janzek of excessive drinking and pot smoking.

Janzek just launched right in. Did his best impression of an eighth-grader.

"I am very sorry, Mr. Carlino, for what happened, and promise it will never happen again."

Carlino gave him an icy stare. He was not amused. "You know, Janzek, you're starting to wear really thin on me."

"What do you want? I apologized to you. That's what I was told to do by the principal—I mean, chief," Janzek said. "I don't hear you apologizing for trying to kill me."

Carlino just shook his head and scowled. "If you had proof of that, you'd have pulled it out of your ass by now. Same thing goes for trying to pin the mayor's hit on me. If you had anything, you would have played that card." Carlino said. "I think we're done here, Detective."

Janzek didn't move an inch. "I just don't get it."

Carlino tapped his fingers on his desk. "Get what?"

"Your lawyer, Rutledge Middleton, the guy who supposedly wrote that whole bullshit account of what happened."

"What about him?"

"I gotta tell you, Ned, between you and me the guy seems like a total lightweight. Not in your league at all."

"I like it better when you call me Mr. Carlino."

"Yeah, but you told me to call you Ned."

"Well, now I'm telling you go back to Mr. Carlino and, while you're at it, why don't you get the fuck out of here," Carlino said. "Oh, and, by the way, don't go underestimating Middleton. He's a bulldog who, unless you back off, is gonna make you look like an overzealous prick out to bust everyone's balls. This town, 'case you haven't noticed, is still licking its wounds from the Civil War. Last thing they're gonna put up with is some pushy cop from up north coming down here and throwing his weight around."

Janzek laughed. "Last time I checked, you were from the City of Brotherly Love. That's up north, isn't it, Ned?"

"Yeah, but the difference is, I hire Charleston people to do my grunt work." Carlino paused. "Speaking of Charleston people... what's with that girlfriend of yours and her little half-assed campaign to kill the casino? I heard it's all about her bleeding heart for our Afro-American brothers and sisters. She was actually married to one? Is that really true? Guy right before you was a—"

In his earlier days, that would have been the moment when Janzek took a big, roundhouse swing.

Instead, he just smiled. "Whatever," he said, "but I still don't get you and Middleton."

"You're a goddamn broken record. What's your thing with him anyway?"

"Like I said, guy's just a total lightweight."

"Don't be surprised if he ends up taking you down."

"And don't you be surprised if he flips on you."

"There's nothing for him to flip about, he's just a lawyer." Carlino waved his hand. "Now, get the hell out of here."

Janzek got up.

"Well, thanks for everything, Ned," he said.

"You got nothing from me, pal."

That's what you think.

FIFTY-TWO

Janzek felt like a Hollywood director splicing together different scenes.

Rhett was assistant director.

Instead of film, though, their medium was tape. Tapes from the wire Janzek had been wearing in Carlino's office, as well as from the bugs that he had planted in the living room of Carlino's guesthouse.

So far, they had spliced together Carlino saying, "Anything happens, Middleton's gonna take the fall." That came mainly from bits and pieces of the conversation he just had with Carlino.

"All we need," Janzek said, "is one or two more good lines."

Rhett nodded. "I love that one about the necktie," he said. "That's a classic, we gotta use that."

Janzek liked it too. It had come from the bug under the bar at Carlino's plantation.

Carlino and his brother, Rich, were talking about the vote for the hotel-casino. Ned was clearly still anxious about it. They were going down the list of people voting on it. At the top of the list was Peter Pollack, the new mayor.

"Think he's still solid?" Rich Carlino asked.

"Oh yeah, he's a lock. That fucker flips and his whole family ends up with Sicilian neckties."

Rhett asked Janzek if he knew what a Sicilian necktie was.

Janzek said he wasn't absolutely sure, but he thought it was when a guy's throat was slit and they pulled the tongue down through the hole.

"Jesus," Rhett said, shaking his head in disgust, "how sick is that?"

Janzek nodded his agreement. "Okay, what about we take where Carlino says 'pin the mayor's hit on me' and splice it together with where he says 'flips' and then the necktie line."

"Yeah, perfect," Rhett said.

Ten minutes later, they had it. Janzek played it back. Then he turned to Rhett and raised his fist.

Rhett bumped it.

"That's Oscar-quality editing," he said.

THEY TALKED ABOUT RUNNING THEIR PLAN BY ERNIE BRINDLE, but quickly vetoed it. They were so far off the reservation that they were deep in rogue cop territory.

Janzek looked up Middleton's number and dialed it.

It went straight to voicemail. He decided this was too good to do on the phone. He grabbed his jacket and headed to Middleton's office on Broad Street.

Janzek didn't even mind waiting the half hour Middleton made him wait. It gave him more time to think about exactly what he was going to say.

Finally, Middleton came out into the reception area and walked up to him. He was wearing a supremely bored expression. "Yes, Detective," he sighed. "What is it now?"

Janzek stood up. "I think you should be sitting down for what you're about to hear."

Middleton rolled his eyes. "Christ, Janzek, you turned into a real drama queen," he said, turning back to his office.

Janzek followed him. "You might want to close the door."

Middleton sighed again, ignored the suggestion, then went around his desk and sat down.

"So, give it your best shot, Detective," he said, mocking. "Blow me away with whatever it is you got."

Janzek reached into his breast pocket, pulled out the little micro-recorder, and clicked the green button.

"Anything happens, Middleton's gonna take the fall. We pin the mayor's hit on him and make it clear if he flips, his whole family ends up with Sicilian neckties," said Carlino's voice.

Middleton listened, then halfway through started hyperventilating like he was going to have a heart attack.

After the tape stopped, Janzek spoke. "I know it's tough. Finding out you can't trust your old pal, Ned. A guy you've probably worked long and hard for. Done a lot of dirty work for. Like calling up poor old Henry Reed, for one. Threatened his life a couple of times. Just so you know, we got pictures of two guys coming out of Henry's barn right after he was killed. Yeah, *killed*—not committed suicide. Who do you think's gonna take the fall for that one? Think it would take a jury long to fill in the blanks? You called Henry, threatened his life, then two weeks later he ends up dead. Gee, I wonder."

Middleton's face went white and parched looking.

"But, I got a lot more... you being tight with Jefferson Davis, for one. Him being in the driver's seat of the car that killed the mayor. Then, next thing you know, Jefferson is dead. Even a shitty prose-cutor could finger you as the guy who ordered Jefferson's hit. Why? 'Cause you saw the evidence piling up that Jefferson did it. You panicked, thinking we were gonna bring him in and he'd roll on you. So you make a call to Rich Carlino, and lo and behold, Jefferson can't roll anymore 'cause he's got a dumdum bullet in his head."

Middleton looked nauseous and corpse-like, all in one.

"I got even more," Janzek said, standing up, "but I'm gonna leave you now. Before you start heaving into your waste basket."

Janzek left Middleton's office with a spring in his step. If he were a boxing judge, he definitely would award this round to himself.

FIFTY-THREE

GENEVA WAS THE ONLY ONE AT RED TRUCK THAT SATURDAY morning.

The two men came in and walked up to her. They were her first customers of the day. It was a little past ten.

"Hi," one of the two men said pleasantly, "just wondered if you had any books about serial killers or mass murderers?"

"Or cop killers?" the other added.

These were hardly normal requests, Geneva thought. Books about cop killers? Just flat-out creepy.

"Let me think," Geneva said gamely. "Pretty sure I have a couple copies of that book about Charles Manson—"

"*Helter Skelter*?" said the short one, who had teeth that looked filed down a quarter inch.

Geneva nodded. "Then there's another one that came out a little while ago called *My Friend Dahmer*," she said. "Like who'd ever admit he was his friend?"

The other one laughed. "Yeah, I hear you," he said. "Might want to keep that under your hat, right?"

"What else ya got?" asked sawed-off teeth.

"There's one about Ted Bundy, the guy who—"

"Yeah, we know all about Ted," he said.

"I'm not sure I have that one in stock, though," Geneva said. "Was there anything in particular... anyone who—"

"Yeah, Zodiac or the Green River Killer." Sawed-off teeth again. "Or, like I said, anything about cop killers. I always liked a good cop-killer yarn."

Geneva tried to hide her shudder.

"There was this dude," the guy went on, "can't remember his name, blew away a bunch of cops in Albuquerque."

Geneva wished a few other customers would walk in.

"Follow me," she said. "I'll show you where everything like that would be."

They followed her over to a rack near the back.

She pointed to several books. "There you go," she said. "And, it turns out, I do have that Ted Bundy one after all."

"Thank you," the taller one said.

"You're welcome," she said and left them alone in the murder and mayhem section.

A few minutes later, they came up to her desk near the front.

The short guy had one called *Serial Killers: The Method and Madness of Monsters*. He looked very excited about having something to while away his free time with.

The other guy had two books. One was called, *A Norwegian Tragedy: Anders Behring Breivik and the Massacre on Utoya*. The other book was called simply *The Manson File*. He set them down to the right of the register.

"Did you know," he said to Geneva, "that shooter at the school in Connecticut was trying to break the Norwegian guy's record? Or maybe it was the other way around."

She didn't want to make eye contact with him. "No, I didn't."

She rang up his two books, wanting them to take them and get out of there. Never come back.

He pointed at the Manson book. "Can't go wrong with good old Charlie," he said.

She really wanted them out of there. But neither one of them was handing her a credit card or cash.

"Miss Crane," the shorter one said, and she looked up. "We have a message for you." He smiled a lopsided, diabolical grin. "If the casino gets shot down, so do you."

The taller one nodded solemnly.

"What my friend is saying—case you didn't get it— is you should cease and desist in your efforts to get people to vote against the casino. We find out you're sending out any more flyers, you die. We hear you're talking negatively about the casino, you die. We see any more of those little signs of yours, you die."

"Do you get the message?" the shorter one said, leaning to within a foot of her face.

She nodded.

"Good," he said, patting her cheek.

They turned to go. Then the tall one turned back to her.

"Put these books on Nick Janzek's charge account."

TREMBLING, SHE CALLED JANZEK, HER VOICE BREAKING.

He came right over.

She had gone into her bathroom several times and scrubbed her cheek where the man had touched her. But she wasn't doing much better by the time Janzek got there.

He asked her to describe them. It didn't take much of a description for him to know who they were.

FIFTY-FOUR

Rhett was in Janzek's office.

Janzek told him about Rich Carlino and Chris Martone going to the Red Truck earlier that morning. About buying the books, charging them to him, and telling Geneva she better hope Charleston got the casino.

Neither of them spoke for a while.

"Right now, we still got nothing we can get 'em on," Janzek said finally. "They'd just deny the whole thing at Red Truck, say they went there, bought a few books for cash, then left."

"Or deny they were ever there," Rhett said. "No eyewitnesses, right?"

Janzek nodded. "Right. So, at this point, the key is still Middleton."

"What do you think he's doing?"

"My guess, he's talking to a bunch of lawyers way smarter than him and keeping his distance from Ned Carlino."

"Think he's gonna flip?"

Janzek thought for a second. "Yeah, I do."

"Beats getting a Sicilian necktie, right?"

Janzek told Ernie Brindle about Carlino's guys threatening Geneva and got the chief to authorize posting two undercovers outside of the Red Truck. He told Geneva and she wasn't thrilled. For one thing, she said she didn't believe that the men who came to her bookstore would actually do anything to her, that they just struck her as creepy men who were trying to intimidate her.

Janzek tried to set her straight, pointing out that they both had long histories of being men of action. He reminded her of his trip out to Pinckney Hall and told her about what had happened at George Reed's barn.

She changed her mind.

Then she said what she really needed was a "handsome man of action to personally protect her at her house that night."

"That would be you," she added.

He thanked her for the compliment and told her there was nothing he'd like more, but he had to work late. She asked him what late was, and he said nine or so. She said fine, come on over at nine and I'll cook you a nice late dinner.

No way he was going to turn that down.

Janzek saw Andy Cleveland and Scott Salvo outside of Geneva's house on Savage Street when he got there a little after nine. Undercover cop Cleveland was in a car across the street from her house, slumped down in his seat, playing a game on his iPhone. Salvo was trying to look like a tourist, walking up and back on the street like he was checking out architectural details on old, historic houses. Which was kind of a weird thing to be doing that time of night.

Janzek went up and knocked on the window of Cleveland's car. Cleveland rolled it down.

"Hey, I'll take over now," he said.

"Good, 'cause this is like watching paint dry."

Then Janzek walked up to Salvo. "I got it, Scott."

"'Bout time, my legs are startin' to go rubbery on me."

Janzek waved at Cleveland and Salvo as they drove off. He watched their taillight go down to the end of the street and disappear to the right before he knocked on Geneva's door.

He pushed her buzzer.

She opened the door and looked dazzling. She was dressed simply: blue jeans and a T-shirt. No bra, he couldn't help but notice.

"The next shift has arrived," he said, leaning to kiss her.

"The next shift?"

"I just relieved your armed guards out front."

"You're kidding, you had men—"

"See, you didn't even know they were there. You need 'em, Geneva. Trust me, those guys who came to the Red Truck are real bad guys."

She put up her hands.

"Okay, I trust you," she said, turning and walking into the living room. "You hungry?"

"I'm always hungry," he said.

She turned to him and put her arms around him. "Well, we're just going to postpone dinner a little," she said, leading him in the direction of her bedroom.

THE NEXT MORNING, JANZEK WAS HAVING A DREAM ABOUT showing up for a test in college that he hadn't studied for. He had had the dream before but hadn't yet figured out what it meant.

Suddenly, there was a massive explosion.

It was not a dream.

A next-door neighbor described the noise to a newspaper reporter the following day as an "ear-splitting blast." To Janzek, it was louder than that, considering he was one story above where it went off. It was a homemade bomb, ballistics later confirmed, but built by someone who had experience at bomb-making.

When it exploded, Janzek didn't even think, he just reacted. He put his arms around Geneva, who was completely naked, and, holding her like a baby, grabbed his gun and holster, which was slung over a chair near her bed. He ran into her bathroom and into the tub-shower combo. Instinct told him that if there was going to be another explosion, the inside of the shower was the safest place around. She was holding her ears and looked like she was in shock.

"You okay?" he asked, still holding her tight.

She blinked a few times.

"Oh my God, what was that?" she said, removing her hands from her ears.

They untangled.

"I don't know exactly." He didn't want to alarm her. "I'm gonna go see."

She grabbed his arm. "Please, Nick, be careful."

"Don't worry," he said, walking to the door of the bathroom in a crouch, two hands on his Sig Sauer automatic.

Janzek stuck his head out and looked into the bedroom. He smelled smoke now and—he thought— the distinctive odor of cordite.

He ran across the bedroom and stopped at the door. Gun raised, he looked out onto the hallway. Seeing nothing, he walked down it, then crept down the staircase. He got to the bottom and smelled the cordite—acrid now, thick in the air. He heard a siren, maybe five blocks away. Then he heard another one. That was fast, he thought. The second one, he was pretty sure, was a fire truck. Pistol in both hands, he slipped out of the stairway into the living room. It was a complete shambles, cloaked in smoke and dust. He scanned the room for any movement. All he saw was a graveyard of broken, shattered, and mangled furniture. Geneva's paintings, books, and TV were in a thousand pieces strewn around the room.

The sirens were a screaming cacophony now, getting closer.

Then he noticed a massive hole in the floor five feet from the front door.

A uniform cop suddenly burst into the room, gun drawn. Janzek knew him by sight. "You all right?" the cop shouted, then coughed from the thick, pungent smell.

"Yeah, I'm fine. I'm Janzek, Violent Crimes," he said, realizing all he had on were his boxers. "There's a woman upstairs—I'm gonna get her."

"Okay, be careful," the uniform said. "Any idea what it was?"

"Yeah, a bomb," Janzek said, and disappeared around the corner to the stairway.

He ran up the steps. Geneva was pulling on her blue jeans.

"Where'd you go?" she asked.

"Downstairs. Cops are here." He went over to her and put his arms around her. "It's really bad down there. Thing caused a lot of damage."

She started to cry. He felt her warm breasts on his chest and felt her trembling. He pulled her closer.

"How bad is it, Nick?"

"Pretty bad."

"Was it—did it—it had to do with the casino thing, right?"

"Yeah, pretty sure it did."

FIFTY-FIVE

The person who planted the bomb had wormed his way into the crawl space beneath Geneva's house from the outside and hid it just inside the front door.

Fully dressed now, Janzek was talking to three uniforms and two firemen in the living room when Ernie Brindle walked in. Geneva, in a daze, was wandering around the room looking at her smashed and destroyed possessions. Janzek had whispered to her that it would be better if they pretended not to know each other.

"How'd you get here so fast, Janzek?" Ernie Brindle asked. "Oh, yeah, that's right, you live just up on Queen."

"Yeah, couple of blocks away." It wasn't a lie.

"So, what exactly happened?" Brindle asked.

"Someone planted a bomb in the crawl space under the house?" Janzek said.

Brindle shook his head. "You know, Janzek, ever since you got here, weird shit's been goin' down. The mayor gets hit, guys try to turn you into a hunting accident, someone blows up a goddamn house. I mean—"

"Hang on, Ernie, the mayor got hit before I got here."

"Yeah, like five minutes before."

Brindle looked around the living room. His eyes fell on Geneva.

"That the owner?" Brindle asked.

"Yes, she's Geneva Crane. The woman I told you about, owns the Red Truck bookstore. Those two guys came to her store and threatened her because she organized a bunch of people to fight the casino."

"Oh, yeah, right?" Brindle said. "They didn't even wait to see how she responded to their threat."

"Yeah, I know," Janzek said.

Brindle started across the room toward Geneva, Janzek beside him.

Geneva turned around to face them.

Brindle smiled at her. "Hi, my name is Ernest Brindle, ma'am. I'm chief of police. I can't tell you how sorry I am about what happened here. Detective Janzek here told me about how you were threatened by two men at your bookstore. They actually threatened to kill you?"

"Yes, as a matter of fact, three times. Just in case I was a little slow on the pickup."

Geneva's sense of humor went right over Brindle's head.

"Who is *they*, Ms. Crane?"

"I assume men who work for Ned Carlino," Geneva said. "Not that they told me that."

"And you'd be able to identify these men?"

She nodded. "You bet. They looked like a couple of lizards in bad shirts."

Brindle nodded back.

"I definitely know what they look like, Chief," Janzek said, then an aside: "Those guys I told you about at Carlino's plantation. One's his brother. They fit the description Ms. Crane gave me."

Brindle nodded. "Well, thank you, Ms. Crane," he said, "we

might have some more questions. Do you mind giving Detective Janzek your phone number?"

"No, I suppose not."

She gave Janzek her number and snuck him a smile.

"Thank you very much, Ms. Crane," said Janzek.

"You're very welcome, Detective Janzek."

FIFTY-SIX

RUTLEDGE MIDDLETON DIDN'T CARE IF THE REST OF HIS FAMILY
ended up with Sicilian neckties or not. Priority number one was to
save his own ass before he took the rap in the deaths of Henry Reed,
Jefferson Davis, and the mayor. Time to cut the best deal he could.

Time to sell out Carlino before Carlino did it to him.

Middleton could see it all unfolding pretty much the way Janzek
had spelled it out in his office. First, Reed's widow testifying that he
had called her husband and, on numerous occasions, threatened him.
Who else would get the rap when a short time later Reed ended up
dead? Especially when she testified that she saw two men coming out
of her barn right after she heard the shotgun blast. It would be a very
short leap for a jury to conclude that they were men Middleton had
hired.

Then there was Jefferson Davis and Middleton's initials on the
matchbook found in Davis's car. Followed by his admission that he
met with Davis at Fuel. Hmmm...and two weeks later the mayor was
killed, and Jefferson Davis was implicated as the driver of the car.

If he was convicted of setting up Henry Reed's murders, that
alone was enough to send him away for life.

But, then add to that, McCann and Jefferson Davis.

And the fact that South Carolina still had the death penalty,

Much as Middleton hated to admit it, Janzek was right: Even a bad prosecutor would be able to come up with enough circumstantial evidence to connect him to Davis. Show how Middleton was worried that if Davis was arrested, he'd give Middleton up in a heartbeat. Therefore, Middleton had hired the two guys who killed Henry Reed to kill Jefferson Davis.

Yup, Middleton couldn't sell out fast enough.

―――――――――

Middleton's lawyer, Myron Dapp, and DA Johnny Applegate, along with Middleton, a stenographer, and Janzek, all met in a conference room off of the DA's office. Dapp, having consulted extensively with his client, had just cut a deal with Applegate.

Middleton was agreeing to cop to fifteen years for conspiracy to commit murder. Basically, the official charge was Middleton's involvement in recruiting Jefferson Davis to kill the mayor. There were a whole host of other charges too: his participation in bribing the present mayor, Peter Pollack, to vote for the casino; knowledge of the attempted homicide on Janzek down at Carlino's plantation; the Henry Reed charge—the list went on. Dapp took Middleton aside and told him he was damn lucky to get off so lightly. The implication was that it was all due to his dexterous, legal maneuvering.

But obviously, the DA was after bigger fish—that being Ned Carlino and his whole far-flung criminal network.

Middleton's biggest concern was what could happen to him in jail. He pointed out that it wouldn't be hard for Carlino to pay another inmate to kill him. A sharpened spoon, maybe, or garroting him to death with the drawstring from a laundry bag. They had their ways.

So, Middleton tried to get Dapp to make a convincing case to Applegate why it should not be divulged what institution Middleton would be remanded to when he served his time. But then Dapp pushed his luck and proposed that Middleton should go into the witness protection program and, effectively, serve no time.

Dapp should have known better. That was something that involved the feds and it didn't fly at all. Lastly, Middleton was ordered to put up a half-million-dollar bond, which he was barely able to scrape up.

After all the horse-trading and plea-bargaining was done, Janzek called up Rhett and told him what had happened.

"Hey, man, good job," Rhett said. "Not exactly by the book, but—"

"We'll take it, right?"

Rhett laughed. "Damn straight."

"So, get ready," Janzek said.

"For what?"

"What do you mean what?" Janzek said. "The real fun part's about to begin."

FIFTY-SEVEN

JANZEK AND RHETT WENT TO CARLINO'S OFFICE WITH AN arrest warrant. The charge was first-degree, premeditated murder. They had Carlino dead to rights on the murder of Mayor Jim McCann, Jefferson Davis, and Henry Reed. Middleton had spelled it all out in vivid detail, and before going to take in Carlino, Janzek and Rhett had gone back out to Mrs. Reeds' house in Summerville. They told her that they were about to arrest the two men who she had taken pictures of coming out of her barn. They assured her that the two men had no chance of getting out on bail, and would she help put them away for life? She promised that, just as soon as they were behind bars, she would.

Carlino was not in his office on State Street. His receptionist said he was down at his plantation.

Janzek and Rhett got back into their Crown Vic. Three other guys from the Violent Crime Squad were in the car right behind them and another car with four men in it had a fifteen-minute head start and were GPS-ing their way to Pinckney Hall.

"You think Carlino's got any clue?" Rhett asked.

"That we're about to put him out of business?"

"Yeah, shuttin' down that pussy ranch of his too," Rhett said as he pulled onto Route 17 headed south. "You worried Carlino's receptionist might have called him after we left?"

"No, 'cause when you were on your phone, I went back in, told her she'd be serving a long bit if she did."

THEY DROVE TWENTY MILES FURTHER.

"It's up ahead," Rhett said. "A right on Coosaw Road."

"Yeah, I remember," Janzek said.

JIMMIE DRIGGERS SAW THAT THE CHIEF WAS IN. HE SMOOTHED his hair and knocked on Brindle's door.

"Yeah, come on in."

Driggers turned the knob and walked in. Brindle was on the phone. He motioned for Driggers to sit down, then hung up a few seconds later. "What's going on, Jimmie?"

Janzek, Rhett, and Brindle had kept everything secret about Rutledge Middleton's arrest and all the related activities.

"I just wanted to say, it's been a couple days and I still got no doubt my suspect is the guy who did McCann. How 'bout I bring him in so we can wrap this sucker up?"

"You know what, Jimmie," Brindle said, putting his hands together, "yesterday I mighta said go, but we just got a confession out of that guy, Middleton."

"What?" Driggers' jaw dropped. "What are you talking about? Rutledge Middleton?"

"Yeah, well—not that he did it personally—just he was up to his ass in the whole thing," Brindle said. "He implicated that lawyer from Philly, Ned Carlino. Middleton was basically Carlino's gofer. He just copped a plea with the DA."

Holy shit, thought Driggers. Lucky *he* wasn't implicated. He would be, though. After they rounded up all the big fish.

"So, who got Middleton?" He knew the answer.

"Janzek and Rhett. They're on their way to get Carlino now. His brother and another guy are in the middle of it."

"Where they going?" Driggers asked. "Janzek and Rhett."

"Carlino's plantation down in Harpersboro."

"And where's Middleton?"

"He's out on bail. At his house probably," Brindle said. "So, your guy Cannon is an innocent man."

Driggers suddenly felt dizzy. He had to steady himself.

"Well," he said, "good for them. You need me to do anything?"

"Nah, we're good. Cleveland, Salvo, and Johnson went along with Janzek and Rhett, four other guys went ahead of them. So, we got all the manpower we need."

Driggers stood up. "Okay, then," he said, "wish it was my collar, but as long as we got 'em, that's all that counts."

"We don't have 'em yet," Brindle said. "But we will."

DRIGGERS DIALED HIS PHONE RIGHT AFTER HE WALKED OUT OF headquarters on Lockwood. Three weeks before, he had read—upside down—Ned Carlino's phone number on a pad in Middleton's office. Middleton had never even mentioned Carlino, but Driggers knew about him and had put the pieces together. He figured it wouldn't hurt to have Carlino's number. Probably a good idea being on the man's good side.

He got Carlino's voicemail. "Mr. Carlino, this is Jimmie Driggers. I been working with Rutledge Middleton and have an urgent message for you. Call me right away."

Two minutes later, Carlino called back.

"No time to explain," Driggers said, "but a squad of Charleston detectives are on their way to arrest you."

"Janzek?"

"Yeah."

"Thank you." Carlino, in his living room, hung up and scrolled down his directory of phone numbers.

He stopped at Charleston Helicopter. He dialed the number.

"Bart Lindman, Charleston Helicopter," the voice answered.

"This is Ned Carlino. How long to get to my place in Harpersboro?"

"Oh, hi Mr. Carlino, how you do—"

"How long?" Carlino shouted.

"I can be there in twenty minutes," Lindman said.

"Make it fifteen," Carlino said, "and not in the usual place on my back lawn but down at my dock. There's an open field across from it."

"I know where you mean, Mr. Carlino. I'm on my way."

Carlino punched the red button, then ran down to the guest house. He saw Martone talking with Justine in the living room but didn't see his brother.

"Go get Rich," he yelled, "we gotta get out of here. Bunch of Charleston cops on the way."

Martone slammed back his drink and got to his feet.

"Chopper's gonna pick us up down by the dock. Get Rich."

Martone ran into one of the bedrooms and burst in on Rich Carlino.

CARLINO, HIS BROTHER, AND MARTONE, EACH CARRYING hastily packed bags, ran toward a Jeep in the driveway between the main house and the guesthouse.

Carlino looked down the long driveway and saw an unmarked car coming up it with its light going but no siren.

"Come on," Carlino said, and he ran toward a stand of trees nearby.

The *whoop* of a siren sounded from the car.

Carlino and the two others ran into the trees, then through a shallow brook.

"Follow me," he said. "We're gonna circle around and go to the dock—chopper's comin' in there."

"What the fuck happened?" Rich asked.

"I don't know," Carlino said. "I just got tipped they were coming."

"Ned Carlino, stop where you are and get your hands up," came Andy Cleveland's voice from a megaphone.

Carlino swung around and saw four men a hundred yards behind them. They had guns raised.

Rich and Martone didn't hesitate. They turned and fired off long bursts with their automatics.

Carlino just ran.

One of the cops got hit. The other three fired back.

Rich and Martone turned and took off as bullets thudded into the trees around them.

"Fuck!" Martone suddenly cried out.

Carlino glanced back to see Martone go down like he'd been hit by an invisible tackler. Blood spurted from the back of his leg just below his knee.

Carlino paused and eyed his brother.

Rich nodded, then wheeled and pumped three bullets into Martone's chest.

***

JANZEK ANSWERED HIS CELL.

"Nick," Andy Cleveland said, breathing heavily, "we're near Carlino's house. He and two other guys just went into the woods. Salvo got hit, we're in pursuit."

"Alright," Janzek said, "we're close. Let's get these bastards."

Janzek clicked off and heard a *thup-thup-thup* as they drove down a back road.

Janzek looked up at the descending helicopter, a speck off in the distance. "Wonder what he's doing out in the middle of the boondocks?"

"I could hazard a guess," Rhett said.

"Yeah, me too," Janzek said, jerking the wheel hard to his left and stomping the accelerator.

He got it up to seventy as he watched the helicopter getting closer to the ground. Janzek checked his rearview mirror but didn't see the backup car behind him anymore.

―――――

CARLINO, STRUGGLING TO KEEP UP WITH HIS BROTHER, LOOKED back and didn't see anybody behind them.

"I hear the chopper," Rich said, looking back at his brother. "Got the jet ready at the airport?"

"Fuck, no, not like I had time," Carlino said. "I'll call him from the chopper, get him ready to take off as soon as we get there."

Carlino got to the edge of the field. He looked around and didn't see anyone behind him. Then he turned and saw the Bell JetRanger helicopter kicking up a thick dust storm all around it.

He looked back at his brother and smiled. "Looks like Janzek and the boys are gonna be late to the party."

They sprinted to the helicopter.

Carlino heard the wail of a siren off in the distance but knew it was too far away to get there in time to stop them.

He got to the helicopter and Rich opened the door for him.

A Sig Sauer P226, Glock 45, and a Smith & Wesson .38 greeted them from the cockpit.

Behind the Sig was Janzek.

"You're under arrest for the murder of James R. McCann, Jefferson Davis, and Henry Reed," Janzek said.

"And while we're at it," Rhett said, "the attempted murder of Nick Janzek."

FIFTY-EIGHT

Janzek and Rhett walked into the frat house. It was a
pigsty. Not in much better shape than Geneva's living room after the
bomb went off. A girl came out of one of the bedrooms wearing a
wrinkled dress.

She walked past them, not making eye contact, then went out the
front door, doing the walk of shame.

A preppie-looking kid in khakis and a blue polo shirt walked into
the living room.

"Where's Quatro Middleton's room?" Janzek asked.

"Upstairs, second one on your right," the kid said.

"Thanks."

The kid nodded and walked out.

They walked upstairs and knocked on Quatro's door.

"Who is it?"

Janzek just knocked louder.

Quatro came to the door. He was wearing boxers and a fuzzy,
hungover look. Behind him, Janzek saw decor that consisted mainly
of empty beer cans and Jack Daniel's bottles.

"Well, if it ain't the bad seed. It's good to see you again, Quatro," Janzek said. "My partner's gonna read you your rights."

"What—"

Rhett cut him off with the Miranda.

"I didn't do anything," Quatro said when Rhett was done.

"You're under arrest for the rape of Chelsea Watson," Janzek said, reaching for his handcuffs. "Hold your hands out."

"But, I—I never—"

"Tell it to the judge. We got the whole story from a very reliable source."

Janzek grabbed Quatro's wrists and put the cuffs on him.

"Who—who was that?" Quatro asked, dread in his shifty blue eyes.

"Who ratted you out, you mean?" Janzek said. "None other than dear old Dad."

———

JIMMIE DRIGGERS HAD DRIVEN PAST RUTLEDGE MIDDLETON'S house on Church Street three times now. He only saw one car in the driveway in back—Middleton's Audi. He knew Wendy Middleton drove a red BMW, and it definitely wasn't in back or on the street in front of their house. He eased over into a spot across from Middleton's house and down a few doors.

He looked down Church Street, then up. He only saw one person two blocks away, walking in the opposite direction. He reached over for his big-brimmed cap on the passenger seat. He put it on, pulled it down as low as he could, then opened the car door and got out. He walked across the street and up the path to the house, turning the knob.

The door wasn't locked, and he pushed it open.

He stepped inside and stopped, trying to see if he heard the sounds of anyone in the house.

Nothing.

He walked through the foyer into the living room, then went through the dining room into the kitchen. He grabbed a banana out of a bowl and stuck it in the pocket of his jacket.

Then he heard footsteps upstairs, then a cough.

He pulled out his Glock and starting walking toward the staircase in the living room.

He went up, taking two steps at a time, slowly and deliberately.

He heard another cough and walked toward where it came from down a long hallway.

He stopped again and listened, then walked toward a door of the bedroom at the end.

He raised his pistol with both hands. He got to the bedroom door and looked in. There was an adjoining office off of the bedroom. Rutledge Middleton was sitting in a leather chair, staring up at him.

Jimmie Driggers decided he had no final words for Rutledge Middleton. He aimed the pistol at Middleton's head.

Out of nowhere a baseball bat smashed down on his hands. His pistol went off and the bullet crashed into the thick bedroom carpet.

Ernie Brindle came into sight, dropped the baseball bat, pulled out his Smith & Wesson, and aimed it at Driggers.

"I can't fuckin' believe it," Brindle said. "When Rhett told me you were dirty, I told him he was full of shit. This hurts, man, this really hurts—after all we've been through." He paused. "Gonna hurt you way more, though. Now, put your dirty fuckin' hands on your head."

FIFTY-NINE

AFTER DEPOSITING THE CARLINO BROTHERS AND CHRIS Martone at Charleston County Detention, then Quatro Middleton a half an hour after that, Janzek had two more stops to make.

He was with Rhett, pulling into the parking lot at the station.

"I'm gonna go talk to Chelsea Watson, see if she'll testify now," Janzek said, getting out of the car.

Rhett rolled down the window.

"So, after that," he said, "what do you say we go get a couple pops, chill for a change?"

"Can't, man, gotta go check in on a friend. Later maybe," Janzek said, walking over to his car and getting in.

He turned on the ignition, pulled out of the parking lot, and headed to Chelsea Watson's house on Pitt Street.

He pulled into a spot in front of her house. He knocked and her roommate answered. Janzek identified himself, and she let him in.

Chelsea was writing a paper at a desk in the corner of the living room. She looked up at him uneasily.

"Hey, how you doing, Chelsea?"

"Okay," she said.

"I just wanted to stop by and tell you that Quatro Middleton's father confessed to what his son did to you."

"You're kidding? Why?"

"Well, it's a long story," Janzek said. "But, suffice it to say, Quatro won't be threatening you ever again. I know you just want to get the whole thing behind you, but if you testify against him, it might stop him and those other guys from ever doing something like that again."

She sighed and closed her eyes for an instant.

"I don't know, it would just—"

"I know, just bring back the whole terrible thing," Janzek said. "In the short time I've gotten to know you, I know that getting revenge isn't what you're all about."

She looked away, then came back at him with a smile.

"You know something, Detective, you're wrong," she said. "I would love to see every single one of those bastards in jail. They don't deserve to be walking around campus like nothing ever happened. One of 'em smirks at me every time I see him. Revenge... hey, bring it on."

She put her fist out. Janzek bumped it.

"Okay, then, we'll nail 'em," Janzek said. "Get 'em off campus for good. I got the perfect place for 'em. Place where I just dropped off Quatro."

Chelsea's smile was ear to ear. She probably hadn't smiled like that in a long time.

SIXTY

JANZEK HAD TOLD GENEVA WHEN HE LEFT HER EARLIER THAT morning that she should come stay at his place. Cramped as it may be, at least it was safe and... quasi-clean. She thanked him but insisted that she wanted to fix up her house. She couldn't just go away and leave it the way it was. He told her again he was concerned it wasn't safe there, but she didn't want to hear it.

She had to call her insurance company, she said, then probably have a little breakdown and a good cry. She told him a lot of her possessions were irreplaceable, passed down from generation to generation through her family. There were a lot of paintings that she loved that were destroyed. Janzek patted her softly and said he wished they had bombed his place instead.

Then later that morning, before going after Carlino, Janzek and Rhett had made a quick stop back at Geneva's house. Parked in front, Rhett said it didn't look too bad on the outside. Except the downstairs windows that were blown out and a big crack in the front door.

Janzek got out of the car and told Rhett he wouldn't be long.

When he went inside, he hugged Geneva again, and that seemed to help a little. He was about to leave when the doorbell rang.

She went to answer it. It turned out to be Dorothea Davis, Geneva's mother-in-law, who Janzek had interrogated a few days before. She was with her son, Ronnie, the man Rhett had pointed out in the bar a while back. There were five other people with them.

"Nick, you remember Dorothea," Geneva said.

"Of course. Hi, Mrs. Davis, nice to see you again," Janzek said.

"Me, too," Dorothea said.

"And this is Ronnie Crane, my brother-in-law," Geneva said, "and a few of my old friends."

She introduced the others.

Janzek shook hands with all of them.

"We heard about what happened," Dorothea said. "Figured you could use a hand."

Janzek saw Geneva brush away a tear in her eye, which this time had nothing to do with the loss of her possessions.

She took two steps toward her brother-in-law and hugged him.

"Thank you, Ronnie," she said, then turned to the others. "Thank you, all of you. Thank you so much."

Then the doorbell rang again, and Geneva went to answer it.

It was Geneva's friend, June Porcher.

June was dressed in blue jeans and a work shirt. She walked in, gave Janzek a kiss, and Geneva a long hug, then Geneva introduced her to all of the others.

"Okay," June said, rubbing her hands together. "So, what are we waiting for? Let's get the show on the road. Get this place cleaned up."

Janzek walked outside and got back into the Caprice with Rhett.

"What the hell are Ronnie Crane and his mother doing there?" Rhett asked.

"They came to help Geneva clean up the place," Janzek said. "Pretty nice."

"Who's surprised?"

It was seven p.m. when Janzek drove back down Savage Street and found a spot in front of Geneva's house. The door with a hole in it was open a crack, and he walked in. Geneva, June Porcher, Dorothea Davis, Ronnie Crane, the other two women, and three men were all in the kitchen. The women all had glasses of white wine in their hands; the men had bottles of beer.

The living room looked totally different. Instead of a dirty, dusty, gaping five-foot hole in the floor, there was a piece of brand-new plywood covering it. The shattered furniture and the smashed and torn paintings were nowhere to be seen. The whole room was empty, but it was spotless and sterilized. It had a hopeful look about it. When Janzek had left that morning, he would have given it no chance to look like it did now.

"Oh... my... God," he said to Geneva, walking into the kitchen. "Look at what you all did."

She smiled. "Thanks to my friends." Her arm swept the kitchen.

"What did you do with everything?" Janzek asked.

"We put it all in the garage. Ronnie has a friend who fixes furniture. He's got a pretty big job ahead of him."

"Don't worry, Geneva," Ronnie said. "Hubie'll make your stuff better than new."

Geneva raised her wineglass and clinked Ronnie's beer bottle.

"I hope so," Geneva said, "'cause some of that stuff's been in my family since the Irish potato famine."

Dorothea Davis laughed "Thought your people were all English bluebloods, honey."

"Yeah, by way of County Galway," Geneva said, then gestured to Janzek. "Come with me."

They went into the living room

"How about all your paintings?"

Geneva looked down and shook her head.

"I'm not so hopeful about them," she said, "but what could I do? I couldn't just throw them away."

He put his arm around her.

"What about the make-out couch?" he said. "I mean, my best moments in Charleston were spent sitting—"

"*Sitting?* I'm insulted."

He laughed and patted her shoulder.

"So, did you catch the bad guys?"

"We caught a whole bunch of bad guys," Janzek said, sliding his arm around her and walking her back toward the kitchen. "I'll tell you all about it at dinner."

He followed her into the kitchen. "Okay, everybody," he said, "you had yourselves a long day. Time to go get some dinner. I'm buying."

"All right," Ronnie said, with a fist pump. "No offense, Geneva, but that bologna sandwich didn't really do it for me."

"Yeah," Dorothea said. "And I got news for you: Yogurt's not real food."

"Or quiche," another woman said.

"So, where you taking us, Nick?" June asked.

"I'm open to suggestions," Janzek said.

Geneva's paintings reminded Janzek of a call he needed to make. He walked over to a corner of Geneva's living room and dialed his cell

A woman answered. "Ella Fitzmorris Gallery. This is Laura."

"Hi, is Ella there, please?"

"Who's calling?"

"Nick Janzek, I bought a painting there."

"Oh, sure. Just one sec, please."

Janzek waited a few moments.

"Hi, Nick, how's the painting?"

"I love it. It makes my apartment."

"I'm glad."

"So, I have a quick question... does the name Roy Jenkins mean anything to you?"

KILLING TIME IN CHARLESTON   263

Ella thought for a moment. "No, I don't think so. Is he an artist?"

"Well, yes and no. He's actually a forger. Might have moved here from Palm Beach, Florida."

"Sorry, I haven't heard of him."

"No problem. But if the name ever comes up, let me know, please. In the meantime, I'm saving up for my next painting."

"Sounds good, Nick. Come by the gallery anytime."

"Will do, thanks."

"Bye, Nick."

He had squeezed in a couple of calls to several other galleries on Broad Street and in the area, but no one had heard of Jenkins. He had also spoken to two detectives in what was called the Property Unit of the Charleston Police Department. They were the ones who would investigate suspected art forgeries, but they hadn't heard of Jenkins. Just to cover all his bases, he'd also spoken to a female detective at SLED, who he had worked with previously. SLED stood for South Carolina Law Enforcement Division and was based in the state capital, Columbia. She did what was called a SLED CATCH which was a criminal records check but came up empty when she input the name Roy Jenkins.

He dialed his cell.

"Crawford."

"Hey, Charlie, it's Nick Janzek, Charleston PD."

"Oh, hey, Nick. Thanks for getting back to me."

"You're welcome, but sorry to say I came up dry. No one around here knows the name Roy Jenkins."

"Well, I appreciate your looking into it anyway. And if anything ever does come up, please let me know."

"Sure will."

"Thanks, man," Crawford said, clicking off.

BERTHA'S KITCHEN WAS PRETTY FAR NORTH ON MEETING Street— almost in North Charleston.

Janzek had Geneva on one side and Dorothea on the other. He had just put away a bowl of the best tasting okra soup he ever had. Actually, he had never had okra soup before. Though he planned to have it again.

Now he was looking down at a plateful of fried pork chops, collards, and a big hunk of corn bread.

"This is my new favorite place," he said to Geneva. "You can have the Average *and* the Ordinary." Then to Dorothea, "Got any other recommendations?"

"I'll give you a list," she said. "Dorothea's top culinary picks."

Geneva finished a fried chicken drumstick and put it down.

"So, tell me," she said, "you got those heathens who bombed my place?"

Janzek nodded, and everyone at the table was listening now.

His cell phone rang. He didn't recognize the number and clicked it off.

"Same guys who came to your bookstore," Janzek said to Geneva.

He turned to Dorothea. "I can promise you," he said, "those men are gonna be in jail for the rest of their lives. One of them was the man who killed Jefferson."

Dorothea looked sad and exhilarated at the same time. "Why did he do it?"

"We think he wanted to make sure that if Jefferson ever got arrested, he wouldn't implicate anyone."

"Who else was involved in it?" Dorothea asked.

"Rutledge Middleton and another man named Ned Carlino. Probably never heard of him."

"No," Dorothea said, shaking her head. "Who is he?"

"A rich man who wanted to get richer," Janzek said.

His cell phone rang again. It was Rhett.

He punched the green button. "Yeah, Delvin?"

"Sorry, man, hope you're not in the middle of something. We got an assault victim at Ned Carlino's house on Sullivan's Island."

"Who is it?"

"I don't know."

"Meet you there in fifteen."

SIXTY-ONE

JANZEK PULLED UP TO NED CARLINO'S STATELY HOUSE ON Sullivan's Island. Rhett was outside waiting for him in the driveway.

"Hey," said Janzek, getting out of his car, "so what's the deal?"

Rhett waved for Janzek to follow him. "Come on," he said. "Police chief here called you, but when he couldn't get you, he called me. An assault just went down at the Carlino's pool house."

"But why's he calling us, it's way out of our jurisdiction?"

"Cause it's Carlino's house, I guess. Thought it might be relevant to our case," Rhett said, walking toward the guest house. "Told me Carlino's cleaning lady called, said she heard a bunch of screams from his pool house. She grabbed a fire poker and went down there. Got there and saw this big guy jump into a pickup, then a woman hopped into a Jag and hauled ass out of there."

"When was this?" Janzek said as they got to the pool house.

"Like a half hour ago."

Janzek saw a Sullivan's Island cop talking to a man and a woman.

"Hey," Janzek said approaching the cop, "Nick Janzek, and this is my partner, Delvin Rhett. Violent Crimes, CPD."

"Officer Perry," the cop said.

"So, what's the story?"

"Well, that woman's the cleaning lady for the house," Perry said, pointing. "She found—"

The cleaning lady came over. "I found this man"—she pointed to the man— "he was unconscious on the floor. Then he woke up and started moaning—"

Janzek looked over at the man. "Excuse me, sir," Janzek said, motioning. "Could you come over here, please."

The man walked over. He looked somewhere between dazed and in shock.

"What's your name, sir?" Janzek asked.

"Trajan. Trajan Volmer."

"And what exactly happened here?"

"I was with a woman friend, and this big bloke burst into the guest house and attacked me with absolutely no provocation," Trajan said. "He hit me with this big piece of wood."

Janzek looked at Rhett, then back at Trajan. "You mean, like a two by four or something?"

"I guess that's what you call it."

"What were you doing here?" Janzek asked. "This is Edward Carlino's house."

"Yes, I know, he's a friend," Trajan said. "He lets me use it when he's away."

Rhett chuckled. "I got news for you, your friend's gonna be away for a long, long time."

"So, he lets you *use* his house—use it for what?" Janzek asked.

"Well, ah, I just... entertain clients and crash here every once in while."

Janzek eyed Trajan. "You don't look so good. Maybe you ought to go to the emergency ward, have 'em check you out."

Trajan ran his hands through his hair. "I'll be okay."

Rhett took a step closer to Trajan. "So, this 'big bloke'... you have any idea who he was?"

Trajan shook his head. "Absolutely no clue."

"What about the girl?" Janzek asked.

Trajan's face went ashen, like he'd just seen a ghost, and he whispered, "Ah, her name is Mona."

THE END

AFTERWORD

I hope you enjoyed the first in my Charleston series, *Killing Time in Charleston*. If so, **please leave a quick review on Amazon**. Thank you!

To receive an email when the next Charleston mystery comes out, sign up for my free newsletter at **tomturnerbooks.com/news**.

What follows is the first chapter of the second book in the series, *Charleston Buzz Kill*.

Best,
Tom

CHARLESTON BUZZ KILL
(EXCERPT)

ONE

Vermelle LeGare had one of the oldest, most prominent surnames in Charleston. Fact is, the nicest street in Charleston was LeGare Street—pronounced Le-gree, as in Simon. Close seconds being Tradd and Church Streets.

Vermelle, though, was black and poor, a fifth-generation cleaning lady. Her husband, Willie, had just dropped her off at the corner of Broad and Church—a ten-minute walk to the house on Stolls Alley where Vermelle was working that day. Willie'd dropped her there because he had a big roofing job that day and didn't want to be late. Vermelle didn't bother to point out that his being on time would make her late for Mr. David.

Mr. David was David Wayne Marion, a rich, handsome, fifty-year-old man. Vermelle knew just how rich he was because his net worth had been published in an article in the *Post & Courier* when he took an ill-fated run at becoming governor. Seventy-five million, mostly in real estate, she recalled.

After he lost in his bid to become governor, Mr. David veered off in a whole different direction and—of all crazy things—ended up becoming the star of a TV reality show. He had money, looks, and success, fame was all that was left. But Vermelle had seen the show and...well, she intended to keep her opinion to herself.

She walked down Church Street and marveled, once again, at the beautiful houses on the street shaded by live oak trees with their wide, majestic canopies. Her favorite was a four-story brick Georgian with a dark mahogany door and antique-glass fanlight above it. The house had graceful pediments above the windows and a perfectly proportioned wall to its right. On the second floor was a classic piazza where she imagined the husband and wife sipped their sloe gin fizzes as soon as the clock struck five. Maybe earlier.

On the next block, she passed the garage door of an elegant Federalist-style house and chuckled to herself at the angry, red letters stenciled onto its garage: *Do not block driveway. Violators will be persecuted to the full extent of the law.*

Did that mean hanged, she wondered, or merely tarred-and-feathered? And wasn't it...*prosecuted*? White people didn't make mistakes like that...did they?

Her favorite wall in Charleston was on the next block. Its surface was dirty concrete with patches of green lichen making it look a thousand years old. The highlight of the wall was what was attached to it: the most intricately detailed wrought iron gate she had ever seen. She wondered if it had been crafted by Philip Simmons, a blacksmith by trade and a black man by birth, whose work, she had heard, had ended up in the Smithsonian Museum.

Then she passed the decrepit house with a severe lean to one side that always caught her attention. It was a stately colonial with imposing columns but was rundown and neglected. Like the owner couldn't afford to keep it up. She had heard Mr. David on the phone once making fun of a woman who was "house rich and check-book poor" and wondered if this was her place. Mr. David went on about how the woman was from an old Charleston family but had been spotted using food stamps on the down low at the local Harris Teeter food market.

Vermelle turned left on Stolls Alley and walked over the bumpy, broken-brick pavement. The roads were in far better shape up on Nunan Street—in the heart of the hood—where she lived in her two-bedroom freedman's cottage. She had observed how the well-to-do south-of-Broad-Street folks leaned toward the old, worn, distressed look. She had heard the word "quaint" used a lot but just couldn't see it.

At number 5 Stolls Alley, she rang the bell and waited.

David Marion's Greek Revival featured grey stucco over brick—the brick peeking through in several places. Vermelle had heard how, at one point in history, brick had lost favor with the rich folk, so they had simply stuccoed over it. As she fumbled for her key, she looked over at the bulky, two-inch-thick shutters with cutouts of palmetto trees and the flickering-gas lanterns that David Marion kept on at all times.

After a minute or so, she knocked and waited.

Nothing.

She knocked again.

Nothing.

Out of options, she tried the doorknob. To her surprise, it opened.

That was odd. She pushed it open and stuck her head in.

"Mr. David, it's me, Vermelle."

She walked into the hallway, the rare herring-bone heart-of-pine floor at her feet.

"Mr. David," she said again a little louder. "It's Vermelle."

She walked into the living room, recently decorated by Madeline Littleworth Mortimer herself.

"Mr. David?"

She figured he must have hurried off to shoot a scene for his dopey TV show and had forgotten to lock the house. It had happened before.

She went down the hallway to his bedroom to get the sheets, towels, and his dirty clothes, the first thing she always did.

The bedroom door was open, and she went in.

And there, sprawled atop the 1000-thread-count Egyptian-cotton sheets of his king-size bed, lay David Wayne Marion. A bullet hole in his forehead and buck naked.

First, Vermelle screamed, scaring the hell out of Mr. David's Labrador retriever napping at the side of the bed. Then she called the cops.

Finally, she fled the house and headed straight to the AME Church up on Calhoun. All she could do now was pray for the soul of poor Mr. David.

First on scene at Marion's house, at 9:10 p.m., was a Charleston Police Department rookie who was mostly clueless about murder scene protocol. But at least he knew enough not to disturb the scene, which was better than most.

Next to arrive was homicide detective Delvin Rhett, a wiry, well-dressed, twenty-eight-year-old black man. His father was a philosophy professor at The Citadel, the military college just up the road, and a strict disciplinarian who outlawed hip-hop in his house and forbid his kids to call their friends "dawg" or "niggah."

After Rhett did a cursory once-over of the crime scene, he called the uniform over. "Tape off the house, Bobby," he said. "Stay outside and don't let anybody in except the ME, the techs and my partner."

Bobby scratched the back of his head. "Your partner's the new guy, right?"

"Yeah, Nick Janzek."

Bobby nodded, then pointed down at Marion's body. "You know who this is, right?"

"'Course I do," Rhett said, "now go watch the door."

Rhett flicked his hand, and Bobby headed toward the front door of the house.

The detective took out his iPhone and started snapping pictures of Marion. He clicked off a few shots of the four blood-stained pillows, a couple more of a blue needlepoint pillow with the monogramed initials DWM on it, and several more full-lengths of Marion's body, tanned to a dark brown and in sharp contrast to the pure white sheets. Marion, for an older guy, had a nice assortment of traps, lats, delts and a quasi-six-pack. He clearly spent time in the gym and, judging by his lack of body fat, steered clear of the Golden Arches.

A few minutes later, Rhett heard the front door creak open.

"Delvin," he heard a voice say, "where y'at?"

It was his partner, Nick Janzek, a Boston transplant doing his best to talk southern.

"In here," Rhett shouted from the first-floor master.

A few seconds later, Janzek walked in. He was wearing khakis, a blue blazer, and a striped tie and looked more like a forty-year-old accidental preppie than a highly decorated homicide cop from the mean streets of Beantown.

Janzek, six-feet and a solid one hundred seventy-five pounds, had cat-like emerald green eyes and dark hair he wore on the long side. A two-inch scar ran down the left side of his face and stopped just above a sturdy chin. He came in and looked down at D-Wayne Marion's naked body.

"Guy make you feel a little inadequate?" Rhett asked.

Janzek didn't respond.

"Never seen a johnson like that on a white boy before," Rhett said.

Janzek shook his head and sighed. "Okay, Delvin, knock it off."

Janzek pulled on his plastic gloves and took in the whole scene for a few moments.

Then he noticed something and went around and crouched down at the foot of the bed.

"Whatta we got here?" Janzek said, pointing to a lump under the sheet.

"I didn't see that," Rhett said, walking closer.

Janzek untucked the sheet and covers and pulled them back.

It was a balled-up pair of women's underwear. Black and lacy. Janzek took out his phone and snapped a few shots.

"You know who this guy is, right?" Rhett asked.

Janzek shook his head and shrugged

"Seriously?" Rhett said. "You don't know?"

Janzek shook his head. "Why? Am I s'posed to?"

"Shit, man, you livin' under a rock. It's that guy, D-Wayne, from the reality show, *Charleston Buzz*."

"He a rapper...like Vanilla Ice or something?" Janzek said.

Rhett snarfed a laugh and shook his head. "Not hardly. Some white guys have nicknames like that too."

"Is that the show that's got the whole town pissed off? S'posed to make us look bad or something?"

"Us? How you figure you're *us*?" Rhett said, "you being a Yankee who got down here day before yesterday."

"Correction," Janzek said, "it's been four long months of your bullshit."

Rhett laughed. "Aight, so here's the lowdown on the guy. D-Wayne's the star of the show...was, I guess that would be. Even though he lives down in New Orleans most of the time."

"How do you know all this?"

"How do you think? I watch the show," Rhett said. "Enough to know the guy married a little cupcake half his age. Just had a kid too."

"So, if he lives in New Orleans, what's he doing here?"

"Shootin' the second season of the show. Rents this place, I think."

"And the wife?"

"Article said she lives down there, raising their kid."

Janzek rubbed his chin for a moment, then picked up the panties.

"Okay, then, if she's down there," he said, holding up the underwear, "who do you suppose these bad boys belong to?"

"Could be anyone," Rhett said. "Dude's a notorious poon hound."

ACKNOWLEDGMENTS

To a few old Charleston friends... first, Kathleen Rivers, chic, sweet and forever young. Thanks to Margaret von Werssowetz, one of Charleston's grandest grande dames, and all my best to the ever-charming, Carroll Hobbs, and real estate agent extraordinaire, Jennifer LePage .

Then, in no particular order, to Wayland and Brooke Cato, Ben and Suzette Bussey and all the gang at the Charleston Library Society.

And, as always to my incredible daughters, Serena and Georgie.

ABOUT THE AUTHOR

A native New Englander, Tom dropped out of college and ran a bar in Vermont...into the ground. Limping back to get his sheepskin, he then landed in New York where he spent time as an award-winning copywriter at several Manhattan advertising agencies. After years of post-Mad Men life, he made a radical change and got a job in commercial real estate. A few years later he ended up in Palm Beach, buying, renovating and selling houses while getting material for his novels. On the side, he wrote *Palm Beach Nasty*, its sequel, *Palm Beach Poison*, and a screenplay, *Underwater*.

While at a wedding, he fell for the charm of Charleston, South Carolina. He spent six years there and completed a yet-to-be-published series set in Charleston. A year ago, Tom headed down the road to Savannah, where he just finished a novel about lust and murder among his neighbors.

Learn more about Tom's books at:
www.tomturnerbooks.com

facebook.com/tomturner.books

ALSO BY TOM TURNER

CHARLIE CRAWFORD PALM BEACH MYSTERIES

Palm Beach Nasty

Palm Beach Poison

Palm Beach Deadly

Palm Beach Bones

Palm Beach Pretenders

Palm Beach Predator

Palm Beach Broke

Palm Beach Bedlam

NICK JANZEK CHARLESTON MYSTERIES

Killing Time in Charleston

Charleston Buzz Kill

STANDALONES

Broken House

For a current list of all available titles, please visit
tomturnerbooks.com/books.

Made in the USA
Middletown, DE
24 December 2019